THE NUMB3RS MAN

a novel by
CARROLL RAY, JR

To Graham &
Jenny
From Carrol Ray

TATE PUBLISHING, LLC

ISBN: 1-5988629-9-5

DEDICATION

This book is dedicated to my wife, Joyce, for whom it became a labor of love and source of frustration, often on the same day.

Also
In loving memory of my Dad, Carroll, Sr., (1907–2004) who graced several Texas pulpits in his time. The word games we played during his last months encouraged me in my pursuit of just the right word. To Mom whose burning desire was that I would be published someday. She never gave up. She is a warrior.

And
To Valinda, Steven, and Marci . . . hold tight to your dreams.

CHAPTER ONE

"Taylor, this may be your big day. You'd better climb out of the sack."

Cyndi's voice interrupted his slumber like a clumsy gate-crasher. Taylor had been elected to entertain three Japanese vendors the night before, and they had made the rounds on Greenville Avenue until two in the morning.

"Are you going to get up?" Cyndi repeated, "or shall I call the wolf and tell him you're too hung over?"

The wolf was Taylor's nickname for G. Preston Wilson, chairman of Western Datacorp, and Cyndi never had quite understood why Taylor picked that particular epithet. Old G. Preston seemed like a good sort to her, but then she only saw him at company functions, where he was always charming.

Taylor and Cyndi Davis were classic achievers, products of the eighties, children of greed. After he earned his MBA from Wharton Taylor had entered the management training program at Western Datacorp and within a year caught the attention of the

chairman himself with a study on third world investment opportunities. One of the outside directors had
seen a copy and mentioned it personally at a board
meeting. By the end of Taylor's first year, he was
firmly established on the fast track at Western Data.

Cyndi met Taylor during his first year at Western. She had graduated from SMU two years earlier
and was working as a public relations specialist at
First National Bank in Dallas. A mutual friend introduced them at a United Fund reception where they
discovered they were both transplanted New Eng-
landers.

Taylor grew up in Boston, the son of a promi-
nent attorney, and Cyndi was from Rhode Island
where her father owned a fashionable department
store in Providence. She had developed a flair for
public relations in her father's store, learning how to
attract and please customers. Working for her father
had only fueled Cyndi's ambition to make it on her
own. Her decision to attend SMU had been a dec-
laration of independence from her father, and First
National had given her a chance to prove she could
make it.

Taylor and Cyndi's goals were a perfect match:
financial independence, nice things, exotic vaca-
tions–the things money can buy rather than building
net worth for its own sake. Neither had any interest
in parenting. They viewed children as interruptions
to career planning.

In due time, a wedding at Lovers Lane United
Methodist had been followed by a short honeymoon

in Acapulco, a condo on Turtle Creek, and a tennis membership at Preston Trails Country Club.

During the years that followed their marriage, Taylor had been promoted to controller at Western and Cyndi had advanced to public relations director at First National. Now Taylor was about to be named chief financial officer. Charlie Sullivan had died suddenly, and although the position normally would have gone to his assistant, G. Preston had delayed naming a replacement. He sent signals throughout the company that he was looking at a wide range of candidates.

That was all the encouragement Taylor needed. He and Cyndi began working their network of friends, making certain that G. Preston would hear from more than one source that Taylor Davis was perfect for the position. Some of Cyndi's contacts on the Arts Council had proven especially helpful.

The wolf had called Taylor in for a talk the previous Tuesday. Although he didn't actually offer him the position, it was pretty clear that Taylor had a lock on it. This was the day the grapevine had predicted the announcement would be made.

Cyndi took the croissants out of the microwave and placed two bowls of granola on the table as Taylor shuffled into the kitchen.

"My head is splitting," he groaned. "Is the coffee ready?"

"Ready and waiting, master. Would you like for mommy to pour you a cup?"

Taylor normally admired Cyndi's biting sarcasm, but he was in no mood to be her target this particular morning. "Stop kidding. I think I'm going to die."

"What a shame," she said. "Just when you're about to grab the gold ring."

"Cut it out," he pleaded. "It's not written in concrete that I'll get Charlie's job."

Cyndi was confident, if he wasn't. "According to my sources, you're a cinch. Who else could it be?"

"Number one, I'm only thirty-five," he reminded her. "Nobody under forty has ever been named to that position before. Number two, I haven't arrived at my present spot without stepping on a few toes. We can't assume that all the input on me has been positive. And number three, the last three CFOs have been Harvard B-school men. You know how the wolf feels about his alma mater."

Cyndi was undaunted. "You'll get it, sweetheart. After that report you did on third world investments, you were unstoppable. Western has made a fortune off that report."

"Well, maybe so," Taylor agreed. "How shall we celebrate if I do get it?"

"How about a quick trip to Aspen?"

Taylor liked that idea, turning it over in his mind as he spread butter and raspberry jam on a croissant. "It would have to be a weekender . . . wouldn't look very good if I started my new position with a holiday."

"Come to think of it, I don't know how I would

get away either," Cyndi replied. "My schedule the next two months is impossible. Since American Airlines announced their move to Dallas, every bank in town has been wining and dining their officers. We've got luncheons scheduled all next week."

"What about trading the Prelude for a new BMW?"

"Now you're talking!" Cyndi exclaimed. She'd been wanting to trade up for several months, ever since Blair Robertson got her new one.

Taylor was pleased with himself. He enjoyed the feeling that power to grant wishes bestowed on the grantor. "All right, it's settled then. If old G. Preston comes through, we'll stop by Overseas Motors tonight and see if they're in a mood to deal."

"Can we afford a Beamer?" Cyndi asked, thinking about their present budget.

"I think so. The CFO is a member of the Executive Committee, and they get loans at three per cent."

Cyndi seem surprised. "Three percent? That doesn't seem fair when everybody else is paying ten plus."

"What's fair got to do with it?" he responded. "It's a perk, sweetheart. Your husband is going to be entitled to quite a few new privileges. Company car, stock options, salary continuation at retirement, company jet when available, and first class cabin when it's not. Just a few of the finer things in life."

"Which means I get to drive the BMW," she grinned.

"You got it."

Cyndi was excited, as pleased with Taylor's promotion as if it had been her own. She poured another cup of coffee and finished her cereal while Taylor busied himself with the financial page of the *Times Herald* After a few minutes, Cyndi broke the silence.

"I bet your father will be proud of you."

Taylor looked up from the paper and thought for a moment before he replied. "Not very likely. He never has forgiven me for choosing finance instead of law.

"Why didn't you go that route?" she asked.

"It takes too long. I couldn't have done it without joining the firm, and they're so hidebound with their traditions, it takes fifteen years to make partner."

"I guess you're right," Cyndi said thoughtfully. "Still . . . a partnership in Rollins, Davis, Cabot, & Smythe isn't exactly chopped liver."

"I know," Taylor replied. "But I couldn't wait that long. Why should I?"

Cyndi couldn't think of a good answer to Taylor's question. His meteoric rise at Western had obviously justified his decision. She had been attracted by Taylor's aristocratic bearing and handsome build at first, but after they started dating, it was his calculated approach to life that appealed to her, matching her own instincts in ways she didn't quite understand.

While loading the dishwasher, Cyndi had a

flash of inspiration. "You don't suppose the new CFO could afford a half-time maid, do you?"

"Maid?" Taylor asked incredulously. "Why do we need a maid?"

"For the house work, you jerk. If you spent as much time helping out as you do reading financial reports, you'd know how much there is to do."

"Okay, okay," he agreed. "Don't give me one of your shared responsibilities lectures. You liberated women are all alike. Why, my mother . . ."

Cyndi playfully threw a dish towel at him. "Don't tell me about your mother. She didn't have to keep house after slaving over a career all day."

Taylor threw it back at her. "Okay, career woman, you win. If I get the appointment, it'll be a BMW and a part-time maid for Mrs. Davis."

Cyndi rushed over, plopped down in Taylor's lap, and smothered him in kisses. "What a man. I knew you'd see it my way."

Taylor spread his hands in mock surrender. "Okay, okay, enough already. Now, let's get moving or there may not be a promotion."

Later at the office, Taylor was studying the joint venture report and was disturbed by the Latin-American section. As a result of his paper on third world investment opportunities, Western had entered into several joint ventures with Latin-American governments, and the computer assembly operation in Costa Rica was in trouble. Originally, the Costa Rican government had allowed Western to repatriate its share of the profits, but when the new regime came into power, they reneged on the deal and insisted that all profits remain in Costa Rica. Taylor was beginning to wonder if his report might backfire on him.

Jenny's voice crackled over the intercom. "Mr. Davis, there's a call for you on line four."

He picked up the phone and answered, "Taylor Davis."

"Taylor, this is Mr. Wilson. Can you come up to my office for a few minutes?"

"Yes sir. I'll be right up."

This has to be it, he thought. *G. Preston wouldn't call me in to tell me I haven't been promoted.* Taylor felt a rush of adrenaline. He took a shoebrush out of a file cabinet and gave his shoes a quick brush, then put on his coat, straightened his tie, and headed for the elevator. As he walked through the outer office, Jenny looked up and added, "Good luck, Taylor."

The eighteenth floor had been dubbed "the power tower" by lower-ranking executives at Western. The entire floor contained only five offices and the board room; G. Preston's office occupied the entire northwest corner. It had a view toward the Trinity River on the west and Las Colinas in the north. From his office you could watch a steady stream of commercial and private jets taking off and landing at Love Field, or check the traffic on Stemmons and the north tollway.

The other offices on the eighteenth floor belonged to the top four officers at Western. Sullivan's office was vacant pending selection of his replacement, and Taylor hesitated for a moment when he walked past what he hoped would be his future office. *This is it,* he mused. *This is what it's all about. I've worked hard for this, and I deserve it.*

Mr. Wilson's secretary directed Taylor to a chair in the reception area and asked if she could bring him a cup of coffee.

"Yes, thank you."

"Mr. Wilson will be with you in a moment. He's on long distance."

"I don't mind waiting," he replied, trying his best not to look like an eighth-grader waiting nervously in the parlor for his first date.

G. Preston's secretary effected an I-know-something-you-don't-know smirk, and he wondered if she already knew the verdict. Probably did. Secretaries on the eighteenth floor were legendary sources of information. He had barely finished his coffee when the chairman's voice came over the intercom, directing her to bring Taylor in.

"Good morning, Taylor." He smiled pleasantly. "How are you?"

"Fine, sir. And you?"

"Good, good. Things are looking up. I was just talking to one of my friends at the Fed, and he thinks the discount rate is headed south."

"That's good news," Taylor responded hesitantly, wondering what to expect next.

"Yes, it certainly is. Which brings me to the reason I asked you to come up. I've got some good news for you, young man. You've made quite an impression on several members of the board, not to mention our executive committee, and we've decided to offer you Sullivan's spot. What do you think of that?"

Taylor tried to look surprised. "Sir, I'm honored. I never dreamed I'd be in the running for CFO."

G. Preston cleared his throat, trying to appear thoughtful. "I'll admit you're a little young for such a heavy responsibility, but we think you're the man. How about it?"

"I accept, of course."

"Good. It's settled then. We've cleared Sullivan's office, and I'd like you to move in on Monday. We had to leave his office vacant for a decent period, of course. It would look bad if we moved someone in too soon after his death. Poor old Charlie. Three more years, and he would've been eligible for a pension. Too bad."

Taylor shifted nervously, not knowing what the wolf expected in response.

"You know, Taylor," he continued, "Charlie could have done a lot for Western. He was extremely talented."

G. Preston made it sound like Charles Sullivan had let the company down in some way, and Taylor was confused. Rather than take a chance, he remained silent with a puzzled look on his face.

The chairman paused a moment, then looked Taylor squarely in the eye. "Charlie was a brilliant financial man. If only he hadn't been so inflexible. Such a stickler."

The wolf was sending Taylor a signal, and he

needed to pick up on it. There would be no honeymoon in this position. G. Preston was already putting him through some kind of test, and Taylor desperately wanted to pass it.

"I know what you mean," Taylor replied hopefully. "Sullivan was definitely from the old school."

G. Preston acknowledged Taylor's comment with a knowing look. "Yes, he was. Times have changed, Taylor. There used to be an unwritten code of ethics in our business. No more. With deregulation, it's every man for himself . . . a lot more gray areas now. Not so many blacks and whites. Are you following me?"

Taylor was tracking with him now. The wolf was trying to let him know that the new CFO was expected to be more "creative" in his approach to accounting and reporting matters. *That old devil,* he thought. *He's laying down a precondition.*

"I understand completely," Taylor said enthusiastically. "Western has to do more than merely react to conditions in this environment. We have to find new ways to gain an advantage on the competition."

G. Preston looked pleased. "Exactly. I knew you would understand. I predict a long and successful career for you, young man. Welcome to the eighteenth floor."

Taylor floated back to the fifth floor on a cloud of euphoria. When he stepped off the elevator, the entire department had been decorated with balloons and streamers, and a banner stretched across one end of the room said, "Congratulations!" Taylor gave the thumbs up sign, and the room exploded in applause. Jenny appeared with two bottles of champagne and some paper cups, and an impromptu celebration replaced the morning coffee break.

After the champagne was gone and everybody returned to work, Taylor called Cyndi at the bank.

"This is Cyndi Davis."

"And this is Taylor Davis, the new chief financial officer at Western Datacorp," he reported proudly.

Cindi was ecstatic. "Taylor, this is fantastic. I told you it was a done deal."

"I know," he said. "I should've placed more confidence in that fantastic network of yours. What do you say we meet at *Overseas Motors* around six-thirty?"

"Whoooeeeeee," she squealed. "Let's do it."

CHAPTER TWO

Taylor moved his things into Sullivan's office on Saturday, and Monday morning his first order of business was the matter of his secretary. Not wishing to bother the chairman with such a trivial matter, he broached the subject with Fred Hartwell, the executive vice president.

Everybody assumed Fred was next in line for the chairmanship, since the executive v.p. had traditionally been viewed as chairman-in-waiting. Fred was a street-fighter, a tough veteran of turf battles, a man who had earned his spot by climbing slowly but relentlessly up the ladder of succession. He had been foreman, factory manager, group manager, manufacturing vice president, and finally made it to the eighteenth floor. Taylor didn't think of him as competition since Fred was in his early sixties. At the rate G. Preston was going, if Fred made it to the chairmanship, it would only be as caretaker for a few years.

Taylor didn't know if it was okay to walk into Fred's office unannounced, so he played it safe and rang his secretary. "This is Taylor Davis. Is Mr. Hartwell in?"

"Yes, Mr. Davis. I'll put you through."

"Hello," Fred drawled in his west Texas accent. Fred sounded like he chewed on the middle of a word before he let it out, like a cow chewing her cud.

"Fred, this is Taylor Davis. I was wondering if you could see me for a minute."

"Of course, come right over," Fred said cheerily. "Next time, just ring me direct. We don't stand on formality up here."

That was a relief. Fred had welcomed him as a full-fledged member of the club. Taylor knew better than to take his role for granted, however. There were bound to be unwritten rules for behavior in the power tower, especially for new members, and he would need to be on his toes. He walked into Fred's office, and Fred motioned him to the couch in the sitting area. *That's a good sign,* Taylor thought. *These guys only use the sitting area in their offices when they want a visitor to feel like an equal.*

"Welcome to the eighteenth floor," Fred said, offering Taylor a congratulatory handshake. "We're pleased to have you on the team."

"Thanks Fred," Taylor responded, feeling a bit more relaxed. "I was shocked when Mr. Wilson offered me the position. I hope I can make a contribution."

"You will. No doubt about it. Now, what can I do for you?"

Taylor had figured Fred as a bottom line man like himself–straight to the point. "It's a somewhat delicate matter," he said, "and I was hoping you could give me some guidance."

"I'll do my best," Fred responded, puzzled that Taylor had more on his mind than social courtesy.

"It's about my secretary," Taylor said. "Jenny has been like a right arm to me in my old position, and . . ."

Fred interrupted him in mid-sentence, happy to demonstrate his power for the new kid on the block. "Don't give it a second thought. You're entitled to bring your secretary with you."

"But what about Mrs. Tidwell?" Taylor asked with mock concern. Elaine Tidwell had been Charlie Sullivan's secretary, having moved to the eighteenth floor with him when he was appointed CFO. She was an older woman, and Taylor wondered what would happen to her.

"We'll find another spot for her," Fred assured him.

Taylor was embarrassed. "Should I have a talk with her?"

"No, leave it to me," Fred said. "I'll take care of it."

That was a relief. Taylor had thought he might have to break the news to her. Even though Fred said she would be transferred to another position, Taylor knew they would put her out to pasture. She had made it to the top of the bank's secretarial subculture, and now she would be demoted to the status of female drone, just one of them again.

Elaine had arrived and was going through the

Monday morning routine by the time Taylor got back to his office. "Good morning, Mr. Davis. Congratulations on your appointment. Is there anything I can do for you?"

Yeah. Don't look like a lamb being led to the slaughter, Taylor thought to himself. "Thank you, Elaine. I can't think of anything at the moment. Unless . . ."

"Yes sir?" Elaine said hopefully.

"Perhaps you could give me a briefing on Mr. Sullivan's weekly schedule, regular meetings, that sort of thing."

"Of course."

The most important meeting of the week was the executive committee, which met every Monday morning to review activity reports. Taylor wanted to be at his best, so he asked Elaine to bring in the file of reports for the prior six months. Returning with the file, she said, "I'll be away from my desk a few minutes. Mr. Harwell asked me to come to his office."

That's fine, Elaine." *Good grief,* Taylor thought. *Fred sure didn't waste any time.*

When Taylor went to the men's room a half hour later, he noticed that Elaine had been crying. Obviously, Fred had already axed her. Not that she wouldn't have expected it, but then hope always holds out for a miracle. *Too bad,* Taylor thought. *She's really a nice sort.*

The executive committee convened in the board room precisely at eleven. Taylor had been there for meetings before, but there always seemed to be twenty or thirty people present. To hold a meeting in these august surroundings with only five executives plus G. Preston's secretary was intoxicating–the sheer statement it made, the symbolism. The future of Western Datacorp and its thousands of employees and shareholders would be determined by the decisions made by this small group.

The board room was located at the southwest corner of the eighteenth floor. The floor-to-ceiling windows there afforded a magnificent view of downtown Dallas on the south and Reunion Tower on the west. The furnishings were elegant. The carpet had been custom-designed with the company's logo cleverly worked into the border, and a Chagall graced the wall above a room-length credenza. The Russian-born artist wouldn't have dreamed that one of his creations would witness discussions of microchips, yield rates, earnings-per-share, and international investments.

A small conference room connected the board room to G. Preston's office, and he entered through that door precisely at eleven and took his place at the head of the huge mahogany table. Miss Roberts sat just behind and to his right. Kathryn Roberts had been G. Preston's secretary for twenty years, and always affected a no-nonsense, businesslike attitude. The chairman called her "Roberts."

Taylor waited momentarily before he selected a chair, correctly assuming that there would be a protocol for seating. There was. Fred Hartwell took the position directly to the right of the chairman, and the other two senior vice presidents filled in to Fred's right and the chairman's left. Taylor then took the second seat to G. Preston's left.

The executive committee was comprised of the chairman, executive vice president, two senior vice presidents, and chief financial officer. Taylor knew the two senior VPs only by sight.

Ryan Phillips was in his mid-fifties, a rotund, balding man who had long since lost the war of calories. He was a pleasant man, always smiling and taking notice of the people around him. The story was that he and G. Preston had started in the office machines business together, and the chairman had always made sure that Ryan followed him up the ladder. He didn't appear to be a towering intellect, and Taylor wondered how he had made it this far.

Forbes Barrett was a New Englander like himself, and Taylor had pegged him as his primary competition since he was only ten years older. Forbes had graduated first in his class at West Point, served a tour of duty in the Army as an intelligence officer assigned to the CIA, and joined Western after his discharge. The fact that Forbes's uncle was on Western board had no doubt helped smooth his journey to the eighteenth floor.

It was rumored that Forbes's IQ was in the genius range, but Taylor figured he could overcome any disadvantage in raw intelligence with cleverness. If there was a single attribute that personified Taylor Davis, it was cleverness. He had an uncanny ability to size up a situation and understand the dynamics underlying the surface complexities. Taylor was also a shrewd judge of people and seldom wrong about their motives.

G. Preston called the meeting to order. "I think we ought to start out by welcoming Taylor Davis to our group. I'm sure we all want to do everything we can to make him feel at home. Shall we start with the executive report?"

Fred passed copies around the table and waited momentarily while each man scanned the summary attached to the five-page report. Taylor was familiar with this report, since he had been on the distribution list as controller, but there was an extra sheet attached that he'd never seen. It was titled "Consultants," stamped "Exec-comm Only," and it listed several firms and individuals with whom Western had consulting agreements. Taylor was surprised not only by the size of the amounts paid during the previous quarter, but by some of the names on the list. Most were based in Washington, and he recognized one of them as Senator Harding's old law firm. Harding was chairman of the Senate Commerce Committee, and rumored to be one of the most powerful men in Washington.

Taylor was curious about the list. "Fred, who are these consultants?" he asked.

"They advise us on governmen matters," Fred responded testily, obviously considering Taylor's question out of order.

Taylor was flushed and embarrassed. He had been in his new position for three hours and had already blundered. It was obvious that the company had retained various lobbyists and referred to them as consultants.

Taylor wasn't naïve. He knew Washington was full of people who peddled influence and favors to companies who needed approvals from various regulatory agencies, but he hadn't thought of his own company being involved in that game.

He tried to recover from his blunder. "I see. Very sensible," he offered. Taylor cursed silently. *You idiot! Now you're passing judgment on a practice you just learned about.* Fearing he would make matters worse by explaining, Taylor tried to escape by fiercely concentrating on the rest of the report.

Ryan Phillips broke the silence. "This Costa Rican venture is becoming a real irritant. Does anybody know what's going on there?"

"They claim it's a misunderstanding," Forbes interjected.

G. Preston frowned, a clear sign that he was displeased and looking for someone to blame for his discomfort. "What kind of misunderstanding?" he snapped.

Forbes tried to explain. "When the deal was finalized, we were told that profits were exempt from prohibitions against repatriating funds to the United States, and now the minister of commerce is claiming otherwise."

The chairman had zero patience with explanations. "How are we supposed to get our profit?" he demanded. "In bananas? Fred, what are we doing about this?"

Fred kept his cool, in spite of G. Preston's obvious anger. "We've talked to one of our consultants," he replied. "He's trying to set up a meeting with Senator Harding. I should hear from him this week."

"Call him today," G. Preston barked. "Tell him to remind the good senator that he owes us."

"Let's move on to the next item," the chairman said impatiently. "Forbes, you have a report for us on the competition?"

"That's right, Mr. Wilson." Forbes took several copies of the report from his briefcase and handed them around the table. It showed current unit sales for computers and peripherals by Western Data's ten largest competitors, including new corporate customers signed during the previous month. Taylor was amazed that Forbes had this information. Except for published reports of total sales required by the SEC, most of this data was private. *Where do they get these numbers?* Taylor wondered.

Forbes summarized the report for the group. "The most significant item on the report is a new contract for minicomputer systems between Unicomp and Republic Bank. Republic has been our customer for nearly twenty years, and we've had no indication they were unhappy. We need to get on this. Taylor, don't you have a contact at Republic?"

Forbes had just handed him a chance to get back in the flow of the meeting, and Taylor was determined not to blow it. "As a matter of fact," he offered, "I play tennis with their senior trust officer every Thursday night. I'll talk to him about it."

"Call him today," G. Preston said angrily. A competitor had hustled one of his best customers, and he was in no mood to stand idly by and watch it happen.

"Yes sir," Taylor said. "I'll see if he's available for lunch."

The balance of the meeting was consumed with a discussion of the economy, its effect on the computer industry, and the current wave of takeovers.

Takeover frenzy had gripped Wall Street, and companies were being gobbled up right and left. Investment banking firms had formed unholy alliances with arbitrageurs, and they were like buzzards lined up on a barbed wire fence, waiting for potential victims to stumble. Three major corporations had been led reluctantly to the altar during the previous year, with the SEC performing the marriage vows. Even though Western had a strong capital base, they were by no means immune. If the Japanese continued to muscle their way into the U.S. market, and if the Costa Rican situation wasn't resolved, they could very well find themselves the target of a takeover effort. Fred turned the discussion in a new direction.

"If worse comes to worse, at least we finally got the board to approve a decent severance package for senior officers."

"You mean our golden parachutes?" Ryan asked.

"That's precisely what I mean," Fred responded.

"At least if we're acquired, we'd have the satisfaction of knowing that funding our packages would be the new owner's first responsibility."

G. Preston said, "They don't care about that. It comes out of the shareholder's hide anyway. Is there anything else?"

That was his signal that the meeting was over, so they gathered up copies of the reports and returned to their offices. Taylor stopped Forbes in the reception area and asked him about the competition analysis report.

"I was curious about the source of those numbers," he said. "Like the unit sales."

"We get that from the HK Digest," Forbes said.

Taylor had never heard of it. "The HK Digest?"

"Henry Keating. You've never heard of him?"

Forbes enjoyed this little game. He had a piece of important information that Taylor knew nothing about, and it gave him a temporary advantage. It put him in the position of patron with Taylor as the supplicant. Taylor had no choice but to go along. "I don't think I have. What does he do?" Taylor asked.

Forbes was happy to explain. "Henry publishes a weekly insider's report on the computer industry. We have no idea where he gets his information, but we have to assume it's accurate because he's reported our own numbers correctly. Obviously, he has well-placed sources who feed him information. How he rewards them is anybody's guess."

"I see," Taylor said. "Any idea who the mole is at Western?"

"Impossible to tell. There are too many people who have access to the data."

"Thanks, Forbes. I guess I've got a lot to learn."

"It's a different scene up here," Forbes said condescendingly. "I'm sure you'll get the hang of it."

"I sure hope so," Taylor said wistfully.

CHAPTER THREE

Taylor did get the hang of it. By the end of his third month on the eighteenth floor, he had mastered the human dynamics in the group and was beginning to find ways to make his own mark. One of his better ideas was to change the way the company funded its pension obligations.

It was a simple matter of exchanging stock of Western's wholly owned subsidiaries for long-term notes, then funding the annual pension obligation with notes rather than cash. This questionable practice had to be approved by the investment committee, but that was no hurdle since the committee consisted of G. Preston, two company officers, and a representative from the bank that handled the fund. The banker wasn't likely to question it since the bank earned a nice fee from administering the pension trust.

The new funding scheme improved Western's earnings-per-share and cash flow, but it also weakened the pension fund's investment portfolio. Before the change, the fund's investments were concentrated in blue chip stocks and government bonds, and now future payments to retirees would be dependent upon the success or failure of Western's own subsidiaries. Taylor wasn't thinking about the pensioners; he was only concerned about making a name for himself.

Taylor had always been a pragmatist, more interested in what works than the right or wrong of a situation. Fairness or justice were not concepts that entered into his deliberations. He simply never thought in those terms. His parents weren't religious people, and the only time he had ever been inside a church was for a wedding or funeral.

He was forced to think about the moral dimension of business decisions, however, when Elizabeth Sullivan came to see him.

Charlie Sullivan was in his early fifties when he died, and Taylor expected Elizabeth to look like a widow. He was surprised by her youthful good looks when Jenny ushered her into his office.

Taylor offered his hand. "How are you, Mrs. Sullivan?"

"I'm fine, thank you," she responded quietly. "Please call me Elizabeth."

"I'm sorry I didn't make it to the funeral," Taylor lied. "I was out of the city on business." He had missed Charlie's funeral because of a tennis game at Preston Trails.

"I understand," she replied gracefully. "I appreciate your willingness to see me today."

Taylor had no idea why she had asked to see him, and it made him uncomfortable to meet her in Charlie's old office. "What can I do for you, Elizabeth?" he asked cautiously.

"You're probably wondering why I look so much younger than Charlie," she said. "We met at Dallas City College. I was in the accounting class he taught on Tuesday evenings. One thing led to another, and before I knew it we were married. After our children came along, I settled down to homemaking and never thought about having to earn a living some day."

Why is she telling me this? Taylor wondered. "How old are your children?" he asked, trying to appear interested.

"Thirteen and eleven."

"Just entering the expensive years," he sympathized. "Braces and all that."

Elizabeth lowered her eyes, her expression changing noticeably. "Actually, that's why I came to see you. I thought perhaps you could help."

"I'll do what I can," Taylor offered.

"Charlie was great at protecting Western's assets, but I'm afraid he wasn't so good with his own investments. He handled all our finances, and after his death I discovered that I was responsible for several notes on oil deals he was in. Most of his life insurance went to pay off those loans. I suppose there may be some income from the wells some day, but it's so far in the future it doesn't do us much good now."

"I'm sorry to hear that," Taylor said. "Some of my friends got stuck with similar deals."

"I'll have to go to work, of course, and I doubt

that I can expect much more than clerical wages. Unless . . ."

Elizabeth's voice trailed off. Obviously, she was about to get to the point and was reluctant to involve Taylor in her dilemma. Taylor shifted nervously in his chair.

"Unless what?" Taylor asked.

"Elaine took me to lunch the day I came up to clear out Charlie's things, and she told me there was a possibility that we might be eligible for pension benefits after all."

Taylor remembered G. Preston's remark about Charlie being three years away from his pension. Obviously he had meant the wage continuation plan for senior vice presidents and members of the executive committee, since they became eligible for salary continuation at age fifty-five. If they retired any time after that, they received full salary for ten more years.

Puzzled by her comment, Taylor encouraged Elizabeth to continue.

"Elaine told me the salary continuation plan has a disability provision that begins at age fifty. I checked it with the personnel department, and they said it requires action by the board. If the board declares a senior officer disabled between age fifty and fifty-five, then he becomes eligible for salary continuation, and in the event of death, the family receives his salary. Since Charlie was unable to work for six months after his heart attack and before his death, it seems to me the board could properly declare him disabled. That's why I asked to see you. I was wondering if you would be willing to speak with Mr. Wilson about it."

"I wasn't aware of that provision," Taylor said, wondering why she had picked him for this chore. *Why doesn't she ask the wolf directly?* he thought.

Elizabeth continued, almost as if she had read Taylor's mind. "You may be wondering why I don't speak to Mr. Wilson myself. It's hard to explain, really. It's just that I don't want it to look like I'm asking for something I didn't earn. I thought if it came from a fellow officer it might carry more weight."

In other words, you want me to ask for something you didn't earn, he thought. "I don't know if I can help," Taylor said. "But I'll be happy to try."

Elizabeth visibly relaxed. "Thank you, Mr. Davis. This has been such a burden on my mind."

"I understand," he responded. "I'll be in touch as soon as I've had a chance to speak to Mr. Wilson."

Taylor walked her to the elevator, said goodbye, and on the way back to his office, he stopped by Jenny's desk. "Jenny, bring me a copy of the salary continuation plan."

When Taylor read the plan, he came to the same conclusion. Charlie would have been entitled to disabled status. He wondered if it had simply been overlooked and decided it would look good if he brought it to G. Preston's attention, but that was a gross miscalculation. When he went to speak to the chairman, he walked into a firestorm.

"Come in, Taylor. What's on your mind?"

"It's about Mrs. Sullivan," Taylor said tentatively. "She came to me with a problem, and I told her I would speak with you about it."

"Oh yes. Elizabeth, I believe. How's she doing?"

"She seems okay," Taylor said.

G. Preston leaned back in his chair and lit a cigar from his private stock of Havanas. Western's manager in Costa Rica kept the wolf supplied with the famous cigars, which had been banned in the U.S., and he loved to make a show of retrieving one from the massive box on his desk. After a couple of long drags, he said pensively, "Good looking woman. Quite a bit younger than Charlie. I was surprised the first time I met her."

"I was too," Taylor responded. "It didn't fit Sullivan's image, did it?"

"No, not really. Now what's this about a problem?"

The wolf was impatient, and Taylor knew he'd better get to the point. "Charlie's secretary told her about the disability provision in the salary continuation plan, and Elizabeth asked if it shouldn't apply to Charlie."

G. Preston was agitated. "Why should it apply to Charlie? He's dead."

"As I understand it," Taylor continued, "if the board declares an officer disabled between the age of fifty and fifty-five, then salary continuation goes into effect and in the event of death, it goes to his beneficiary. Since Charlie was off work for six months before his death, Elizabeth is wondering if he wouldn't be eligible for the disability provision."

"Do you realize what that would cost?" the chairman demanded, his voice rising in volume.

"No sir. I only saw Elizabeth this morning, and I haven't thought about the specifics of her proposal."

"Two million dollars. Sullivan's salary and bonus was around two hundred thousand. Multiply that by ten and you're talking about a lot of money."

"I understand that," Taylor pleaded, "but wouldn't the company purchase an annuity to fund the payments? I don't have my calculator handy, but surely the cost of a ten year annuity would be less than half the face value." Taylor wasn't pleading for Elizabeth. He was trying to recover from his own blunder.

"It's out of the question," G. Preston growled. "It would set a bad precedent, and besides, I don't see why Sullivan should get special treatment. It's just tough luck he died before fifty-five."

Taylor was astonished. *Tough luck?* he thought. *Is that all he can say about a member of his executive committee?*

The wolf continued his diatribe. "It was no secret that Sullivan and I didn't see eye-to–eye on a lot of things, but I put up with it because he was a brilliant financial man. When he publicly opposed me in a board meeting last year, though, I had to banish him from the inner council. I can tolerate a lot of things, Taylor, but never disloyalty. Everybody knew he was in Siberia after that, and if I made an exception on this pension thing, it would send the wrong signal to the troops."

"I see," Taylor said sheepishly. "I wasn't aware of the implications."

"It doesn't matter. It was noble of you to listen to Elizabeth's story, but you'll have to tell her it's impossible. Just tell her the board has a policy against making exceptions in personnel matters."

"Yes sir. I'm sure she'll understand."

Taylor knew she wouldn't understand at all. Or perhaps she would. She was bound to know about the conflict between Charlie and G. Preston, and she knew the score. Charlie Sullivan could have done a thousand good things during his career, but it only takes one screw-up with the power structure to fall out of favor. Too bad. Taylor liked Elizabeth, and he wasn't looking forward to dumping this news on her.

His concern for Elizabeth was short-lived, however. Leaving the chairman's office, his thought turned to his own career. He understood the law of the jungle. Kill or be killed. After all, he hadn't made it to his present position by practicing the golden rule. His allegiance had been to G. Preston's version: "He who has the gold makes the rules." Taylor was angry with himself for taking Elizabeth's petition to the chairman in the first place.

Driving home that night, Taylor was stuck on North Central for the umpteenth time, and he used the opportunity to do some serious thinking. Obviously, the eighteenth floor wasn't a place for tea parties and polite conversation. It was governed by unwritten rules and subtle shifts in power, like a play with no script where the actors make up their parts as they go along, each trying to capture center stage. And Taylor desperately wanted top billing someday; the good life, starring Taylor Davis.

But there would be a price to pay. The path to success had toll booths at regular intervals. Charlie Sullivan had refused to pay at the booth of blind loyalty, and now his family would suffer as a result. Taylor wondered what the next toll booth would require of him. Whatever it was, he was ready to pay.

CHAPTER FOUR

If there had never been a public relations director, somebody would have invented the position for Cyndi Taylor. She was a natural. She loved the glittering parties, the cultural events sponsored by the bank, and the contacts with trendy people. The biggest event on Cyndi's calendar was the annual "Night With The Stars," a benefit sponsored by the Arts Council for the performing arts in Dallas. If you could get a ticket to "Night With The Stars," you were guaranteed a chance to see and be seen with the movers and shakers in Dallas.

As a founding patron, First National was allotted fifty tickets, and even though they cost the bank $500 each, there was such a demand for seats, it was considered money well spent. Forty went to the bank's top executives to give away to their biggest customers, and the remaining ten went to Cyndi to distribute at her discretion, a perk that made her a must-know person in Dallas. During the weeks leading up to the big event, her telephone was jammed with calls from people who hoped to break into the next level of Dallas society.

Cyndi had landed a choice assignment on the stars committee this year, the group which made local arrangements for the performers. She made sure that their demands were met as nearly as possible, and things had gone well until she got around to Ron Blakely, Candy Holland's agent.

Candy was a media phenomenon. She was a struggling actress when she landed a job as the "answer girl" on a television game show. Her job was to walk across the set with a billboard that showed the correct answer to the audience. Her trademark was a different gown every night, sometimes sexy, sometimes dazzling, sometimes extravagant, and sometimes outlandish.

Nobody in the industry understood why, but Candy had become a star. She was a regular in *People* magazine, often appeared as a guest on talk shows, and had recently produced a best-selling exercise video. She wasn't a stunning beauty, at least not by Hollywood standards, and most people thought she was an air-head. It was strange, almost as if the American people had decided to exalt banality. A well-known news commentator had decried the phenomenon by announcing that America had been "Candy-ized," his way of protesting the public's taste.

Nevertheless, the Arts Council had invited Candy to appear on the program and she had accepted. Cyndi's immediate problem was making contact with her agent. She had called and left messages for two weeks before Ron finally returned her call.

When she picked up the telephone, she heard a high-pitched, syrupy voice. "Hi Cyndi, this is Ron Blakely in Beverly Hills. How goes it in Big D?"

"Ron . . . I'm so glad to hear from you," Cyndi lied, surprised that he had called direct. "I'm chairing the stars committee for "Night With The Stars" in Dallas, and I wanted to thank you for Candy's willingness to appear on our program."

"We're always glad to appear for a good cause," he chirped. "What did you say the charity was?"

"It's the Arts Council in Dallas," Cyndi said, irritated by his condescending attitude.

"Of course," Ron said. "What can we do for you, sweetheart?"

"My committee is taking care of arrangements," Cyndi explained, "and I was calling to see if you have any special preferences, you know, hotels and so forth."

"How kind," he responded. "As a matter of fact, there are some minor details. Just one moment."

Ron left Cyndi on hold for nearly twenty minutes, aggravating her irritation. If she hadn't had so much trouble getting through to him in the first place, she would have hung up on him. It was bad enough to be put on hold, but a receptionist with a raspy voice kept coming on the line saying, "Are you still there, dear?"

Finally, he returned. "Sorry, dear. I'm just loaded with calls this morning. Johnny Carson was calling about Candy's appearance next week, and Revlon wants to do a perfume deal. You know how it is."

No, I don't know how it is, you jerk, she thought. "It's quite all right, Ron. I know you're busy."

"Super-duper," he said. "We just love the Fairmount, and if you can give us the penthouse for Candy and a couple of suites for the staff, that would be lovely. We'll need a limo, of course, and please arrange for it to be on standby, since you never know when we might have an urge to go somewhere. I understand you're sending the bank's Lear jet to pick us up."

"That's correct," Cyndi replied.

"Oh that's fab, dear. And please arrange for Trader Vic's to cater room service for us. Candy just loves Chinese."

It's Polynesian, not Chinese, you idiot. "Trader Vic's?" Cyndi said, trying to sound cheerful. "No problem. They'll probably figure a way to get some publicity out of it."

"Good, good. There are a few other things, but you won't have any difficulty with them. Must run now, dear, I'm doing lunch with the Revlon people."

"Thanks for returning my call, Ron. Goodbye."

Cyndi hung up the phone and exploded with laughter. She had seen and heard caricatures of Hollywood types, but this was the first time she had dealt with one, and it gave her a chance to regale her staff with an imitation of dear sweet Ron and his editorial "we."

Later that afternoon, an appointment with the

ad agency ran overtime and put Cyndi behind schedule. She and Taylor were due to play tennis at the club, and it was obvious that she wouldn't make it, so she called him from her car phone.

"Mr. Davis's office."

"Jenny, is Taylor available?" Cyndi asked.

"Yes," Jenny replied, "but he's on the telephone right now. Would you like to leave a message?"

"No, I'm stuck in traffic on Stemmons. Will you tell him I'm on hold, please?"

"Of course. Just one moment."

After a short wait, Taylor came on the line. "Hi, sweetheart. What's up?"

"Stuck on Stemmons again. I swear, Taylor. Dallas is almost as bad as Boston or New York."

"Really," Taylor said. "Don't tell me you called just to gripe about the traffic."

"No. I'm way behind, and I'm not going to make our tennis date."

"Are you sure?" he pleaded.

"Positive. I've still got to dictate the weekly report, and I have to get started on my stars committee work."

Taylor had forgotten about Cyndi's assignment. "Stars committee?"

"You know . . ."Night With The Stars." I'm chairing the committee that makes arrangements for the performers. You won't believe the conversation I had with Candy Holland's agent today."

"Candy Holland? Is she on the program this year?"

"The very one," Cyndi replied.

Taylor was amused by the thought of Candy as a performer. "What's she going to do, walk across the stage announcing each act on a billboard?"

"I have no idea," Cyndi said. "Maybe she'll appear in a different gown between each act."

"Hmmmm," Taylor responded. "I hope she wears that blue low-cut job."

"Well, it won't do you any good. You'll be too busy entertaining the bank's guests with me."

"How about getting me backstage?" Taylor asked playfully. "I'd love to see what she looks like close up."

"You men are all alike," Cyndi said. "If it looks good, grab it. Never mind about depth or intelligence."

"Booooo. . . . sounds like sour grapes," Taylor teased.

Cyndi laughed. "I'm sorry about the tennis game," she said. "Why don't you go on without me?"

"Can't you come later? I hate having to work up a game. I always get some klutz who thinks tennis is only a way to meet people."

"Sorry," she said. "I've got an appointment with Dr. Russell at five, and since there's no way I can finish before then, I'll have to work tonight."

Taylor was puzzled. "Your gynecologist? Why are you seeing him?"

"It's just a routine checkup."

"All right, I'll see you later tonight," Taylor

said. "You know, babe, I'm not so sure the good life is all it's cracked up to be. When you get there, you don't have time to enjoy it."

Cyndi said, "Yeah, well, it beats the alternative."

She placed the phone in its cradle and maneuvered the BMW into the express lane. She hadn't told Taylor the whole truth about her appointment. Cyndi had missed her period, and since she was on the pill, she was worried that something might be wrong. She had seen the doctor the previous week, and now she was going for the results, harboring fears of a tumor or worse.

The digital clock on the instrument panel told her she might as well go straight to Dr. Russell's office in north Dallas, so she made a U-turn, took Carpenter over to Central and headed north. North Central was a disaster. At least with her car phone, she was able to knock off a few calls while creeping northward in the bumper-to-bumper traffic.

It bothered Cyndi when the nurse directed her into Dr. Russell's office instead of one of the examination rooms. Offices were for serious talk. *He's going to tell me I've got a tumor,* she thought. She tried to relax with a magazine, but the words were just dark objects against a white background. When the doctor finally came in, he was smiling.

"Hello, Cyndi, how are you feeling?"

"I'm feeling fine," she answered tentatively. "Is there any reason I shouldn't?"

Dr. Russell smiled. "On the contrary, I have

very good news for you."

Cyndi visibly relaxed. "Good news?"

"There's nothing wrong with your ovaries or uterus. In fact, they appear to be quite normal and healthy. You missed your period for a very good reason. You're pregnant."

"Pregnant?" she shouted. "That's impossible!" Cyndi hadn't considered this possibility. How could she be pregnant? She was on the pill.

"It's not at all impossible," the doctor responded, surprised by her reaction.

"But I'm on the pill," she protested.

"Oh, I didn't realize," he said. "I just assumed that you and Taylor had decided to start your family."

"No way. This is a complete surprise. Are you absolutely sure?" she pleaded.

"There's no mistake. You're about six weeks by my calculations."

Cyndi couldn't believe it. The doctor told her it was rare, but there were cases of women conceiving while taking the birth control pill.

She found his explanation little comfort. "What am I going to do? This is terrible."

Cyndi began to weep. Dr. Russell, looking decidedly uncomfortable, handed her a tissue. "I'm sorry it was such a shock, Cyndi. As I said, I just assumed that you would be glad to hear the news."

"Far from it," she replied. "This was definitely not in my career plan."

"It's not the worst thing that could happen,"

he offered. "Millions of women have babies and live normal lives. Even career women."

"Maybe so," she said, "but I'm not one of them. Isn't there something I can do?"

"You mean terminate the pregnancy?"

That's a nice euphemism for abortion, Cyndi thought. "Well, yes, that's what I was thinking."

"I'm afraid I can't help you with that," he said disapprovingly. "I would advise against it."

"Why?"

"Abortion was never intended to be a method of birth control, Cyndi. I realize it may have come to that, but there are too many unknowns."

"What do you mean?" she said, puzzled by his obvious disapproval.

"Psychological reactions. There aren't any definitive studies on the subject, but there are indications that unnecessary abortions can cause long-term psychological dysfunction."

Cyndi hated it when doctors used medical terms to describe something with the potential to change a person's life forever. It was so impersonal . . . so clinical. "What do you mean by dysfunction?" she asked.

"Abnormal psychological profile. Neuroses. That sort of thing."

Cyndi felt like Dr. Russell was lecturing her. "I see. Well, there are plenty of other causes of neuroses in our crazy society, including unwanted babies."

"It's your decision, of course," he said defensively. "If you insist on considering termination, ask my nurse for the Women's Clinic brochure on your way out. They may be able to help you."

Cyndi's mind was churning as she left Dr. Russell's office. *Pregnant. It's impossible. Maybe he's wrong. Of course, he's not wrong. What am I going to do? My career is over. I don't want to be a mother, for god's sake. I need a drink.*

Since she was headed south on the tollway, Cyndi got off at the LBJ exit and pulled into the Galleria. There was a bar at the Weston that was a popular watering hole for Taylor and Cyndi's crowd. She automatically headed that direction, hoping to find solace for her predicament.

Armando's was a laid-back place known for its hot hors d'oeuvres, eclectic design, and lively conversation at happy hour. Locals shunned the place after eight, since the late-night crowd consisted entirely of business types hoping to find some action in the hotel bar, but during happy hour it was their domain.

After exchanging quips with Armando, Cyndi spotted Blair Robertson, a tennis friend from Preston Trails who had recently been divorced from Kip Robertson, a north Dallas real estate developer. When Blair spotted Cyndi, she left her groups and came over to talk.

"Cyndi, what are you doing here alone?"

"Hi, Blair. I was headed back to the office and decided to stop off for a minute."

"Where's Taylor?"

"Playing tennis," Cyndi said absent-mindedly.

Blair looked surprised. "Alone? What's with

you two?"

Cyndi was still upset by Dr. Russell's news, and Blair had automatically assumed it had to do with Taylor. "It's not that, Blair," she said. "I was supposed to meet him at the club, but I had to beg off. I'm buried with work and if I don't work a couple of nights, I'll never catch up."

"I'll never understand you career women," Blair said. "It's always work, work, work. Come on, let me buy you a drink."

Blair led Cyndi to a corner table and signaled for the waitress. She ordered a wine cooler and turned to Cyndi. "What'll it be Ms. Career Lady?"

"Vodka martini."

"Martini? My goodness, we are having a drink. What's wrong, dear?"

"I just got some bad news, Blair."

"Oh dear. And I thought the golden couple was immune to that sort of thing. What is it, lost an important client or something?"

Cyndi looked up from her drink, reluctant to share her news with Blair, but desperately wanting someone to care. "It's a lot worse than that," she said.

"One of your investments went belly-up?" Blair asked frivolously.

"Stop it, Blair. This is no laughing matter."

"I'm sorry, Cyndi. What is it? You can tell me."

Cyndi blurted out, "I'm pregnant."

"Pregnant? That's all?"

"That's all?" Cyndi said, her voice quivering. "Blair, this is serious. It could end my career."

Blair looked relieved, as if she had expected something earth-shatteringly serious. "Well, get rid of it, silly."

"You mean abortion?"

"Of course," Blair said. "What's the big deal? Don't tell me you've never had one."

Cyndi was insulted that Blair would make such an assumption. "No, as a matter of fact. I've been on the pill since I was fifteen and I've never even thought about it."

"Cyndi, grow up," Blair responded indignantly. "Nowadays, abortion is like having your teeth cleaned almost. In and out in an hour."

"You sound like you're speaking from experience," Cyndi said.

"That's because I've had two, myself. Daddy paid for the first one when I was a sophomore at Haockaday, and Kip and I got a little careless in Aspen one time and I had the second one as a result. I'm telling you . . . it's no big deal."

"But didn't you feel something?" Cyndi asked. "I mean . . . it's your baby after all."

"You sound like one of those fundamentalist pro-lifers, dear. It's not a baby, it's only tissue. It's like having a mole or something taken off."

"I guess you're right," Cyndi replied.

"Of course, I'm right. Now, tell me. What do I have to do to get a ticket to 'Night With The Stars'?"

"Blair, you're incorrigible. You know those tickets are like gold."

"Can't hurt to ask," Blair said. "Kip has tickets, but he's not about to share. You'd think he would for old time's sake, at least. Oh well, such is life."

Cyndi looked at her watch. "Thanks, Blair. I've enjoyed it, but I have to earn my keep. I'll see you around, okay?"

"Sure," Blair said, "any time."

CHAPTER FIVE

A week went by before Cyndi told Taylor about her problem. It was their anniversary, and Taylor had taken her to The Mansion for dinner.

"Cyndi, what is wrong with you? You've been moping around for a week."

"I'm sorry, sweetheart. I haven't been very good company, have I?"

"More like the walking dead. What's the deal?"

"I'm pregnant."

Taylor's mouth fell open and his hand dropped to the table with a thud, spilling a portion of veal marsala on the starched linen tablecloth.

"Pregnant?" he gulped. "Are you sure?"

"There's no mistake, " Cyndi assured him. "Dr. Russell confirmed it last week."

Taylor was stunned. "How could you be pregnant? You're on the pill!"

Cyndi sighed. "Dr. Russell said it's extremely rare, but there are cases of women on the pill getting pregnant. I guess I'm in the rare category."

"This is a heckuva way to celebrate," Taylor said, upset by Cyndi's revelation. "What are you going to do?"

"What am I going to do?" she replied, emphasizing the personal pronoun. "This is your problem too, Taylor."

"I know that," he pleaded. "I just meant . . . have you thought about it? You've had a little more time to consider the implications."

"Implications?" she replied, puzzled by his choice of words.

"You know . . . your career, the cost of raising a child, our plans for the future."

The "implications," as Taylor put it, were all Cyndi had thought about during the previous week. She had weighed all the pros and cons, considered every angle, and debated every issue, hoping the decision would somehow go away. It hadn't gone away. Her stomach had reminded her every morning that her little problem was alive and well. She crossed her knife and fork on her plate, leaving the steak half-finished. A single tear coursed down her cheek as she said "Taylor, I'm considering an abortion."

"Well, that's one of the options we have to consider," he said, trying to be analytical yet sympathetic. Taylor's habit of placing everything in life on a decision grid sometimes irritated Cyndi.

"Dr. Russell's office gave me a brochure for the Women's Clinic, but I haven't had the nerve to go see them."

"Why not?" he asked.

"Taylor, this is a human life we're talking about. I don't want a baby any more than you do, but I never thought I would have to decide how I feel about abortion in such a personal way."

"It's not like it's a person, Cyndi. It's only a fetus."

"Only a fetus?" Cyndi said, her voice rising. "What is a fetus, Taylor?"

"It's just tissue," he argued, lowering his voice to a whisper. "Nobody thinks of a fetus as human until birth."

"I beg to differ with you, sweetheart. You've had your head buried too long in *Barron's* and the *Wall Street Journal*. Medical technology has gone way beyond that notion. Preemies born at six months have survived and gone on to live normal lives."

Taylor was uneasy defending a position he hadn't really thought through. He was simply repeating things he'd read or heard. "Yeah, but you're talking about a live birth."

"What's the difference?" Cyndi asked. "Is it subhuman immediately before birth, and then somehow miraculously becomes human five minutes later?"

"You sound like one of those pro-lifers."

"Sorry," she said. "It's just that I haven't been very objective about this. It ceases to be academic when it's your own baby. Pardon me . . . when it's your own fetus."

"I know," he sympathized. "Have you thought about your career? I seriously doubt that the bank would hold your job for you."

"Not if Paul has anything to do with it," she said. "He's been itching to see me stumble anyway."

"Your assistant? I thought you liked him."

"He's all right, but he wouldn't hesitate one minute to take advantage of my situation."

"The law of the jungle," Taylor mumbled, then abruptly brought up another issue. "What about our trip to Europe?"

"I've thought about that," Cyndi responded. "I don't see how we could do it if I have the baby."

"No, I guess not. Diapers and bottle warmers don't mix very well with tours on the Rhine." Taylor wiped his mouth with the starched napkin, thinking carefully about his response. "Cyndi, I have to be honest with you. Doing the parent bit at this stage of my life wasn't in my plans, nor yours either. Seems to me that abortion is the most reasonable option we have."

"Why don't we call it termination," she pleaded. "Abortion sounds so . . ."

"Criminal?" he added, anticipating her question.

"Yes. Criminal. I hate the sound of it."

"All right, then," Taylor said. "Have you talked to anyone else about this?"

"I ran into Blair at Armando's, and she said it's no big deal. She's had two."

Taylor had a smirk on his face. "Blair would say that, wouldn't she?"

"What do you mean by that?"

"Nothing," he replied. "It's just that Blair isn't someone you would expect to call mommy."

Taylor sensed that Cyndi was waiting for him to make the decision. "Why don't you check out the Women's Clinic and see what they have to say. Then we'll decide. Okay?"

"Okay," she mumbled.

"Good," he signed. "Now let's lighten up a little. This is our anniversary. How about dessert?"

The Womens' Clinic was much too business-like for Cyndi. She had expected to be treated like a patient, someone under the care of a physician. Instead, she felt like she was signing up for social security or making an application for a driver's license. It was an assembly line. There were about a dozen women going through the process, and it was "fill this out and take it over there," then "wait in that cubicle for the nurse's examination," then another interview, and finally a briefing on financial arrangements.

Cyndi left the clinic with the following information: during the first trimester, the decision to abort was solely with the woman and her doctor, and it didn't have to be her gynecologist. The physician who owned and operated the clinic, hardly a disinterested party, was legally qualified to certify her decision. During the second trimester, it was still her decision, but the state regulated the procedures. Whenever she was ready, an appointment would be made, she would be in and out in a couple of hours. The cost was $300. She could even use Mastercard or American Express.

There was one moment in the interview that Cyndi couldn't get out of her mind. When she asked what happened to the fetus, she had been told, "It's disposed of."

Is that all she was carrying in her womb, an "it"? How was "it" disposed of? Carried off in the daily garbage? Sold to some research group? These and other questions haunted Cyndi for several days after her visit to the clinic. She couldn't sleep without help, and the number of pills it took to finally knock her out left her groggy and muddle-headed the next day.

Taylor was vaguely aware of her anxiety, but they hadn't really talked about it since that night at The Mansion. He had assumed that she was only waiting to find the most opportune time. Cyndi wanted to talk about it, to let him know she was struggling, but they were both so busy it seemed there never was time. Finally, he brought it up one morning three weeks later. The BMW was in the shop, and they were driving to work together.

"Cyndi, when are you going to have it done?"

"Have what done?" she said absent-mindedly.

"The abortion." Taylor remembered their discussion at The Mansion and quickly changed his terminology. "I mean . . . terminate the pregnancy."

"I don't know," she sighed. "I can't seem to make up my mind."

"I thought we'd already decided," he pleaded. "Haven't we?"

"Taylor, have you thought about the fact that the 'we' you just mentioned includes a third party?"

"You mean the fetus?"

"I mean the baby," she said. "Our baby. Doesn't it seem ironic to you that he doesn't get to vote?"

"Cyndi, we've been through this already. It's not really a baby yet."

"Suppose it is?" she said. "What if we were convinced that it is a real human being? Wouldn't we be taking a life?"

Taylor was uncomfortable. He wasn't used to debating the right and wrong of issues, only the most efficient way to do something. "That's a value judgment," he argued. "Who can say what's right? What standard do we have other than the Supreme Court of the land? We can't set ourselves up as God."

"That's funny," Cyndi countered. "Seems to me that's precisely what we are doing."

"What do you mean?"

"Setting ourselves up as God. We conceived this person in my belly, even though we didn't mean to, and now we're deciding to sentence it to death. Isn't that what gods do?"

Taylor paused a moment, carefully choosing his words. "I don't know about the religious aspect. I look at this as a choice between conflicting values. The pro-lifers talk about the rights of the unborn. Maybe there is such a thing, but you also have rights over your own body. You can't have it both ways, so you have to choose. Who is in a better position to make that choice than you? I have to make decisions between conflicting rights all the time. What's good for the shareholders may be bad for employees, and what the government wants may not be the best thing for the shareholders."

Cyndi looked down at the tissue she had been folding and unfolding in her lap. "Maybe we could have it both ways," she said wistfully.

"What do you mean?"

"I could have the baby and then we could put it up for adoption."

"That's absurd," Taylor replied. "Married people don't put babies up for adoption. At least, not people in our economic situation."

"Why not?" she asked defiantly.

"Because . . . it would look ridiculous."

Cyndi didn't ask why, because she knew the answer. It would look patently selfish. But what they were thinking about was not only selfish, it was cruel. She turned her head to the side and concentrated on the next lane of traffic. Her stomach felt heavy, as if her breakfast had congealed and increased in weight. She wanted to cry, something Cyndi rarely did. As early as she could remember, her father had taught her to be tough and self-controlled, and she had inherited his toughminded approach to problems. But this wasn't just a problem to be analyzed; it was a life growing just beneath her heart. Cyndi was feeling something she had never felt before: femaleness, a profound femininity, a maternal instinct. She searched her purse for another tissue as Taylor broke the silence.

"Sweetheart, don't you think you better do it pretty soon? Hasn't it been nearly ten weeks?"

"Yes," she agreed. "I'll call the clinic this week."

Cyndi paused a moment, then tried out a new thought. "Taylor, a minute ago you said something about the religious aspect. What would think about me talking to a minister?"

"A minister? We don't know any ministers. Who would you talk to?"

"I don't know," she said. "How does a person pick a minister? I could ask around, I guess. I just thought it might help me put it in a broader perspective."

"If that's what you want."

Later at the office, Cyndi opened the yellow pages and turned to "churches," expecting to find twenty or thirty listings. Instead, there was a bewildering variety of denominations, groups within denominations, churches with odd-sounding names, and several spiritualists. She picked one at random and dialed the number.

"Good morning, St. Matthew's."

Cyndi hesitated, then asked, "May I speak with the minister, please?"

"Who may I say is calling?"

This sounds like one of my business calls, she thought. "This is Cyndi Davis."

"May I ask why you're calling, Ms. Davis?"

This is ridiculous. Who do these people think they are? Oh, well, I might as well plunge ahead.

"I'm faced with what could be a moral decision, and I wanted to seek a minister's counsel."

"Are you a member of St. Matthew's?"

Cyndi could feel anger rising within her. "No, I'm not a member of any church right now."

"I'm afraid our counseling services are only available to members," the voice said.

Cyndi was furious. "Oh, I see. Well, I wouldn't think any of your members would ever need counseling, you all sound so good."

"I beg your pardon?"

"Never mind."

Cyndi slammed the telephone down and burst out crying. This had been building up for three months, and she let it all out. Anger, resentment, fear, disappointment–every emotion she'd bottled up came rushing out. After a few minutes, she gained control of herself and tried to sort out her feelings. Anger was the preeminent emotion. She was angry that fate had handed her this decision in the first place, angry that she had to choose between a life and a lifestyle. That's what it was. She loved her lifestyle, and now she had to choose to terminate a life in order to protect it. It wasn't fair.

She was trying to concentrate on a new publicity brochure when Sharon Dillow dropped by. They had met in the executive dining room, and since there weren't that many women entitled to have lunch there, they sometimes ate together. There was something about Sharon that appealed to Cyndi in a way she didn't quite understand. She was a capable executive, one of the bank's trust officers, and she was ambitious but not in the usual way. She seemed to be a caring, open person, always interested in what Cyndi was doing. She never dominated the conversation with her own interests. It was refreshing.

"Hi, Sharon," she said. "How are you?"

"Great. What about you? Is something wrong?"

"Not especially," Cyndi replied, surprised by Sharon's question. "Why do you ask?"

"I don't mean to pry, Cyndi, but your mascara is streaked. It's pretty obvious you've been crying."

"Is it that obvious?" Cyndi reached for a tissue and took a small mirror from the top drawer of her desk. She debated with herself for a moment and then decided to confide in Sharon. "Sharon, this is personal. I wouldn't want it all over the bank."

"Okay," Sharon said.

Cyndi told her about the phone call and the receptionists at St. Matthew's.

"No wonder you're upset," Sharon said. "Sounds like the people at St. Matthew's need to take another look at the gospels."

"What do you mean?" Cyndi asked, puzzled by Sharon's statement.

"I don't remember Jesus turning anybody away because they weren't a member of the club."

Cyndi was confused by Sharon's reference to Jesus, wondering why she had equated the experience with St. Matthew's with the Bible. "Do you really believe all that stuff?" she asked.

"What stuff?"

"You know . . . stories in the Bible."

Sharon took a deep breath. "Cyndi, you might as well know that I'm a Christian, and yes, I do believe the Bible is true."

Cyndi didn't know what to do with this information. She had always thought of herself as a Christian in the sense that she wasn't a murderer or thief, and generally believed that people should behave in a way that promoted the well-being of society, but the word Christian had so many meanings; she had never used it as a label for her own beliefs. Sharon seemed to be using it in a different way.

"I wish it had a clear-cut answer for my situation," Cyndi said wistfully.

Sharon leaned forward, as if she was reaching for someone in distress. "I don't know about your situation, Cyndi, but I'm certain that you could find help in the Bible. Maybe not a specific answer, but at least a principle that would help."

"All right," Cyndi said, putting her to the test. "I have a decision to make that has to do with conflicting rights. If I go one way, someone will be hurt. If I go the other, another person suffers. What should I do? I've asked a couple of people for advice, and their answers didn't really help. How would you approach it?"

"That's a tough one," Sharon replied. "I don't have a specific answer, but I'll tell you what the Bible says. There's a psalm that says something like this: 'Blessed is the person who does not walk in the counsel of the ungodly, but delights in the law of the Lord and meditates on it day and night. He will be like a tree planted by water which yields its fruit in season, its leaf does not wither, and in whatever he does, he prospers.'"

Cyndi was astounded by the ease with which Sharon pulled that out of her memory. She's never heard anyone quote from the Bible like that. "Are you saying I should meditate?"

"Not just meditate," Sharon responded, "but meditate or think about what God's Word says. Do you have a Bible?"

"Sure," Cyndi lied. *We must have one somewhere*, she thought.

Sharon continued. "Basically what this psalm is saying is that you will not be blessed if you accept the advice of people who don't respect God's opinion. That's essentially what it means by the ungodly. Instead, you will get an answer if you seek God's viewpoint, and the way to do that is by reading the Bible. Does that make sense?"

"I guess so." Cyndi was thinking about her conversation with Blair Robertson.

"Please let me know if I can help," Sharon said. "I'll be praying that God will give you a solution."

"Thanks, Sharon. I need all the help I can get."

The days that followed were a nightmare. The weeks had relentlessly marched toward her self-imposed deadline of two months, and she had procrastinated beyond the deadline. One Friday morning around three a.m., she made up her mind. She called the clinic the next day and made an appointment for the following Tuesday, then told Taylor about it during lunch.

"Sweetheart, I think you're doing the right thing," he said. "We're just not cut out to be parents."

"Will you go with me?" she asked.

"Of course. Wait a minute . . . I'll be in Washington all next week."

"Washington? What for?"

Taylor had forgotten about his trip with G. Preston. "Our lobbyist has arranged a meeting with Senator Harding, chairman of the commerce committee."

Cyndi couldn't hide her disappointment. "What's it about? Can't it wait?"

"The joint venture in Costa Rica." Taylor tried to make it sound hugely important. "If we don't get some help down there, we might as well write it off. The way things stand now, we've put up all the investment, and the Costa Rican government is reaping all the profits."

"Do you absolutely have to go?" Cyndi pleaded.

"Yeah. I can't miss this one. It's just the wolf and me, and it'll be a super chance to show what I can do in the big leagues."

"I was hoping you could be with me," she said.

"I'm sorry, sweetheart. It can't be helped. Can't

you put it off another week?"

"No way," she said firmly. "Another week, and I'd have to do it in the hospital, and that would be too hard to explain to everybody. I've gone too long as it is. I've got to get this thing resolved before it drives me crazy."

Taylor tried to recover some ground. "I'll call Tuesday night and check on you."

"Don't worry about me," Cyndi said, trying to sound strong. "I'll be fine."

The waiting room at the Women's Clinic was crowded. Cyndi had made an appointment for noon, hoping to be back in her office by two at the latest, but they were behind schedule. She was the oldest woman there. Several of the "patients" were mid-teenagers, and non of them appeared to be much beyond twenty. Cyndi played a little game while she waited. She studied each face, asking "why are you here?" Then she made up a story to fit each of the players in the game.

"Ms. Davis?"

This is it. There's no second chance. I've got to do it. There's no other way, she whispered. She left the waiting room and was directed to a cubicle and given a hospital gown.

The nurse said, "Take off your clothes and put on this gown."

Cyndi did as she was told and waited in the cubicle for further directions. She could hear voices and shuffling noises in the other cubicles. Finally, a nurse led her to a brightly lit room where she was placed on an examination table.

The nurse read from a clipboard. "Your name is Cyndi Davis?"

"That's right."

"And you have signed this release of your own free will, and without coercion from anyone?"

"Yes, that's correct," Cyndi replied.

"All right, Ms. Davis, this won't take long. I'm going to take your blood pressure and give you a mild tranquilizer, then the doctor will examine you and perform the procedure. He'll give you a local anesthetic, and you may feel a slight stinging sensation. After the cervix is dilated, the uterus will be cleared with a vacuum aspirator."

"What exactly does that mean?" Cyndi asked.

"It's a suction device that removes the contents of the uterus."

Contents of the uterus? Is that all my baby is?
"How long will it take?" she asked.

The nurse was irritated by Cyndi's questions. "The procedure will be over in twenty minutes or so," she snapped. "Just try to relax."

The doctor never spoke directly to Cyndi. After her cervix was dilated and the local anesthetic administered, he inserted a tube into her womb and then attached it to the suction machine. Without any warning, he activated the aspirator. Cyndi felt a sharp pain and an incredible internal vibration. It felt like she was being attacked by a monstrous vacuum cleaner. She gripped the edge of the table with both hands, closed her eyes, and bit her lower lip to take her mind off the inhuman thing that was being done to her insides. A grotesque vision appeared on the screen of her mind. A heartless machine was sucking a tiny, perfectly formed fetus out of her womb; grasping, pulling, stretching the baby into an unrecognizable shape; consigning it to its innards with the rest of that day's victims.

Oh, God, she thought. *What have I done?* Cyndi started to weep—not only for her baby, but for all the others too. The terrible vibration finally stopped and the doctor withdrew the tube. He turned off the aspirator, but the whirring noise continued for a few moments, winding down just like a vacuum cleaner.

"All right, nurse," the doctor barked. "Let's get a move on. We've got a full day."

The nurse took Cyndi's feet out of the stirrups and helped her sit up. "Are you all right, dear?"

"I think so," Cyndi responded weakly.

"Put your clothes on and then we'll give you some juice. You can rest in the waiting room until you're ready to leave."

In the waiting room, Cyndi wrote a check for the fee and then took a seat near the back of the room. She tried to look at a magazine but couldn't concentrate, so she closed her eyes and tried to relax. She was about to doze off when the receptionist's voice jarred her awake.

"Oh no. They're here again," she shouted.

Cyndi opened her eyes and looked over toward the receptionist's area, but she had left her desk and was looking out the front window. She returned to her desk, dialed someone on the telephone, and said, "They're here again. Do you want me to call the police?"

Cyndi walked over to the window and was terrified by what she saw. There were about a dozen people walking back and forth in front of the clinic with signs that said "Abortion is Murder," "Adoption, Not Abortion," and "Don't Play God." She turned toward the receptionist with a bewildered look.

"How do I get out of here?" she pleaded.

"Don't worry. The police will be here soon."

"But I can't wait that long." Cyndi could see herself on the evening news, followed by a reporter as she fled from the scene of her crime.

"You can leave by the back door, if you wish."

"Thank God," Cyndi said.

The receptionist took her to the back of the clinic and unlocked the door. Cyndi walked around the block and slipped unnoticed into her car, which was parked in the area on the east side of the clinic. But as she backed away from the curb, the demonstrators spotted her and rushed toward her with their signs, shouting and screaming. Cyndi burst into tears, jammed her foot on the accelerator, and sped away from the clinic. She drove around for nearly an hour, sobbing, and tried to get herself together so she could return to the office. She finally gave up. She called her secretary and told her she would be out for the rest of the day, then headed the BMW toward home.

As soon as she got home, Cyndi took a couple of sleeping pills and climbed into bed. Mercifully, the pills did their work and she slept until nearly six when the telephone woke her up. It was Taylor calling from Washington.

"Hi, sweetheart. How are you?"

"Taylor, is that you?" she mumbled into the telephone.

"Of course, it's me. How many other men call you sweetheart?"

The sleeping pills had given her a splitting headache. "I'm sorry, Taylor. I just woke up."

"How'd it go? Are you feeling okay?"

"It was terrible," she replied, the memory of her ordeal registering clearly in her mind. "Horrible. I don't ever want to go through anything like it again. Ever."

Taylor tried his best to sound cheerful. "I'm sorry, sweetheart. Are you feeling okay now?"

"I'm not in any pain, if that's what you mean. A little sore, I guess. It's not the pain, it's the mental part."

Taylor didn't know what to say. He'd never been very good at consoling people. He was used to being with winners, people who were on top of things. "Yeah, I understand. But it's over now, isn't it?"

There was a hint of sadness in Cyndi's voice. "I'm not pregnant anymore, if that's what you mean."

"Boy, that's a relief. When I get home, we'll

find some way to celebrate."

"Sure . . . okay."

Taylor was uncomfortable talking about the abortion, so he changed the subject. "Cyndi, you should've seen me today. I was brilliant in our meeting at the State Department. The wolf was so impressed, he took me to Charmaine's for dinner."

"That's nice."

"That's nice? Sweetheart, the wolf didn't invite Forbes along on this trip. He invited me. Don't you realize what that means?"

"I'm sorry, Taylor. I'm still a little groggy from two sleeping pills. Let's talk about it when you get home."

"Okay," he replied. "You take care of yourself. I'll be home Friday afternoon."

"Please hurry. I miss you."

"I miss you, too. Bye, sweetheart."

Cyndi hung up the telephone and leaned back on her pillow, reflecting on her decision. *It was the best thing to do,* she argued with herself. *I'm not mother material, for God's sake, and I certainly can't see Taylor as the doting father. It was the best thing.*

She reached for the remote control and turned on the portable television. Candy Holland was prancing across the stage wearing a gold lame' cocktail dress. The screen faded to a commercial. A beautiful nymphet dressed in a filmy gown was running barefoot on a deserted beach, chased by a handsome man who was also barefoot and shirtless. The scene was played in slow-motion, and a husky female voice-over said, "Obsession. Scent of the stars. Drive your man wild with Obsession."

Cyndi clicked the selector through all the channels, finally settling on the Tuesday night movie, but she never quite got the gist of it. Her mind kept playing the same words over and over.

It was the best thing to do. It was the best thing. It was the best thing to do. I know it was.

CHAPTER SIX

G. Preston had picked the perfect time to visit Washington. Congress was in session, cherry blossoms were in bloom, and the city resonated with sights and sounds that identify a seat of power. Movers and shakers were about. The influential and the influenced and the sellers of influence were hawking their wares and maneuvering for position. Taylor felt powerful just being there.

He had tried for three mornings straight to beat the wolf down to breakfast, but no matter how early he went to the coffee shop, G. Preston would be halfway through his second cup of coffee. It was a game he played with his subordinates.

"Good morning, sir," Taylor said. "Did you sleep well?"

"Like a baby. I've already ordered."

The chairman was occupied with the *Washington Post,* so Taylor signaled for the waitress and directed his attention to the menu.

"Coffee, sir?" the waitress asked cheerily.

"Yes, please. And I'll have the Washingtonian

with a blueberry muffin on the side."

G. Preston was frowning at the paper. "I don't like the looks of this."

Taylor looked up from the menu. "What's that, sir?"

"A Japanese trade delegation met with the secretary of commerce yesterday, and it was led by Ohta-san."

"The chairman of Nippon Electrical?"

G. Preston looked up from the paper and peered at Taylor over the top of his reading glasses. "My old nemesis," he said. "The trade journal has been speculating that Nippon is about to introduce a monster memory chip in the range of ten megabytes."

Taylor let out a low whistle. "Ten megabytes on one chip?"

"That's what they're saying."

"That's impossible," Taylor replied. "Hasn't the limit been two megabytes up to now?"

"Yep," the chairman said. "But ten years ago nobody dreamed we'd be carrying computers around in our briefcases, either."

Taylor understood the implications of the rumor, should it prove to be true. "Ten meg," he said. "That's an incredible leap forward."

"You are right, young man. We managed to get an embargo on memory chips larger than one meg a couple of years ago over the administration's objections, and I would bet next quarter's dividend that Ohta-san's visit with the secretary had to do with lifting the embargo. If I'm right, then it's a cinch the speculation about their monster chip is on target."

"What can we do about it?" Taylor asked, fascinated by the talk of world-powers competition.

"The administration can't lift the embargo without Congress, so we'll have to find some way to hold their feet to the fire. Any legislation affecting trade restrictions has to go through Senator Harding's committee first. Since we're meeting with him on the Costa Rican matter today, maybe we'll get an opportunity to bring it up."

"Will the senator be there?" Taylor asked. "I thought we were meeting with his staff."

"He'll make a courtesy appearance at the beginning of the meeting and then hand us over to his people. Or at least, that's the usual procedure. Today, however, I just may have a reason for the good senator to remain a little longer."

The chairman had the look in his eyes that Taylor had often seen in meetings. While his aides were mired in the minutiae of present difficulties and complexities, G. Preston was mentally racing into the future, working out a solution that only he could understand before the fact.

"What kind of man is Senator Harding?" Taylor asked.

"Pure politician. Shrewd lawyer. Been in the Senate since the fifties, and always goes to the highest bidder. I wouldn't trust him if he was my own flesh and blood. We had an iron-clad deal with him a couple of years ago, and he sold us out at the last minute."

"Sounds like a politician," Taylor added.

G. Preston continued his story. "We were selling motherboards to the Hungarians, and the CIA found out about it and raised hell. The Defense Department sued us in federal court. We had network people all over us for a week."

Taylor hadn't heard this part of the Western legend, and he was fascinated. "Is it against the law to sell computers to Hungary?" he asked.

"It's a matter of interpretation. At that time, there was a prohibition against selling thirty-two bit computers to the Eastern Bloc, but we weren't selling computers. We were selling motherboards with a thirty-two bit chip."

That's a convenient rationalization, Taylor thought. "How did Senator Harding get involved?"

"We hired his old firm to defend us. Technically, he severed ties with the firm when he was elected senator, but everybody knew it was a farce. Our understanding was that he would pressure the pentagon to drop the lawsuit in exchange for something they wanted from his committee. At the last minute, though, he double-crossed us and we had to go along or face more bad publicity while the case was tried."

"What kind of deal was it?" Taylor asked.

"We paid a two million dollar fine and agreed to stop selling to the Hungarians. In return, they dropped the action. Some deal. Our attorneys were certain we'd win the case, but we couldn't afford the publicity."

"Do you think the senator will remember it?"

G. Preston took a cigar out of his inside coat pocket and lit it. He was formulating a plan in his mind. "I'll make sure he does," he coughed.

"How?" Taylor asked, wondering what he had in mind. He marveled at the innovative ideas the chairman came up with sometimes.

G. Preston smiled. "The senator's son-in-law works for Equity Securities."

"They're bidding on our new issue," Taylor said.

"That's right. And as you know, the underwriter keeps a bunch of options for its own account. If the stock takes off, they pick up easy money by exercising their options."

Now Taylor understood. Western had already decided to give the underwriting to Equity, but the deal hadn't been finalized. Obviously, G. Preston was figuring on using this fact as leverage with the senator. Taylor admired the chairman's understanding of the power game. Business was really just a giant game of Monopoly. Every player knows the objective is to wipe out the other players and end up owning the board, but you have to play the hand you have, maximizing your own position at the expense of the others. And yet, you have to deal with those very players to get what you want. It required skill and cunning, and the wolf certainly lived up to his nickname in that respect.

They finished breakfast and agreed to meet in the lobby at nine. Miss Roberts had arranged for a limousine to take them to the meeting and wait for them there. Jim Bridges, the company pilot, was standing by at National Airport for the return to Dallas. At the Senate Office Building they were met in the lobby by Patricia Olson, Senator Harding's press secretary.

"Good morning, gentlemen," she said. "Did you have a good trip over from Dallas?"

"We arrived last Monday, Miss . . ."

"Just call me Pat. I'm the senator's press secretary."

"All right, Pat. May name is G. Preston Wilson, and this is my numbers man, Taylor Davis."

"I'm happy to meet you both," she replied. "Have you been able to take in any of the sights this week?"

G. Preston had little patience with small talk, and Taylor could see he was irritated. "No ma'am," he said. "We've been trying to negotiate our way through the bureaucratic maze all week."

"I know what you mean," she sympathized. "The government can be impossible at times."

Pat led them toward the elevators after they cleared building security. They not only had to pass through a metal detector, but were required to answer a series of questions about their business in the building. Then Pat had to produce pre-approved passes.

Senator Harding had a choice corner suite on the fifteenth floor. There was a reception area, a conference room, a bullpen for research assistants, four private offices for senior aids, and the senator's spacious office, which afforded a magnificent view of the capitol. They were shown to the conference room and offered coffee from a sterling silver carafe adorned with the state seal of Kentucky, the senator's home state. Clay Huddleston, the senator's chief aide, joined them. After a round of introductions and small talk about Kentucky, Texas, and the weather, he invited them to take a seat.

"Senator Harding had to run over to the capitol for a vote on the Kemper bill, but he'll join us later. In the meantime, why don't we go ahead with our meeting? How can we help you?"

G. Preston knew the senator's staff had been thoroughly briefed by their lobbyist, and he was irritated by Clay's patronizing attitude.

"Hasn't Alec briefed you on our problem in Costa Rica?" he grumbled.

"Oh yes, the joint venture. He did spend some time with us a couple of weeks ago. It's a matter of repatriating funds from the venture, if I remember correctly."

Taylor sensed the chairman's frustration at having to deal with the second-in-command, so he picked up the conversation, signaling that they knew they were dealing with the senator's stand-in. G. Preston's comments would be reserved for the senator.

"Clay," Taylor said, "we met with some people at the State Department on Tuesday, and they told us the senator has a lot of clout in this matter. Our problem is really quite simple. We made a deal with the previous government, and now the new regime refuses to abide by its terms. What's the point of setting up a venture off-shore if we can't get our profits out of the country?"

"I understand your problem," Clay replied. "Yours isn't the first complaint about the new government in Costa Rica, if that's any consolation."

A commotion in the outer hall indicated that Senator Harding had returned, and the dynamics changed dramatically when he entered the conference room. Prescott Harding was an imposing figure; a tall handsome man who could have been cast in the role of senior senator from the great state of Kentucky, if he hadn't been elected to the office. He was Daniel Boone in a three-piece suit. Clay stood up when the senator walked into the room, and Taylor and G. Preston followed suit in deference to the senator's office.

"Sorry I'm late, gentlemen," he said breathlessly. "The whip needed my vote on the Kemper matter, it seems."

"We've only just arrived, Senator," Taylor lied.

"Good. I hate to be kept waiting. Shall we get down to business?"

Taylor briefed the senator on the Costa Rican matter, thoroughly reviewing the history of Western's joint venture with the Costa Rican government and their problems with the new regime. Clay took notes while the senator listened intently without comment. When Taylor concluded his review, G. Preston took over.

"There's a principle involved, Senator, but our main concern is the bottom line. We've invested fifty million in that deal, and it's sitting down there dead in the water. The people at the State Department told us you may be able to help."

Senator Harding leaned forward in his chair. "This is a tough one, I'm afraid. According to the CIA, the new Presidente has ties to the Sandinistas, and they're in no hurry to help Uncle Sam, as you know. We've also had reports that the Sendero Luminoso is operating in Costa Rica. The situation is very confused at the moment."

"Sendero what?" G. Preston interrupted. "What's that?"

"It's a Maoist guerrilla group that originated in Peru," Senator Harding explained. "In English the name means "the shining path." They've taken over the drug trade in Peru and are using their drug profits to finance the movement."

"What's that got to do with computers?" G. Preston was impatient with this talk of international diplomacy and intrigue.

"It has everything to do with your venture," the senator explained. "The Sendero Luminoso present themselves as a populist movement, enlisting the peasants with promises of economic reforms. The worse the economy, the more they enlist."

The senator continued. "It's an old story. Marx, Lenin, Castro. They all came to power with promises of economic reform and when they got control, they ignored the people and trashed the economy. Look at the Soviets. After seventy years of communism, their economy is a basket case."

"I still don't see what that has to do with our computer assembly plant," Taylor said, trying to steer the conversation back to Western's problem.

"The regime in Costa Rica has to offset the Luminoso's propaganda with its own so-called reforms, including the first step toward nationalizing industry."

"Which is?" the chairman asked, also trying to nudge the senator to his point.

"Which is prohibiting the repatriation of profits by foreign investors."

"Of course," G. Preston responded angrily. "Keep the money at home, even if it doesn't belong to you."

Taylor said, "Senator, this is all very interesting, but we were told you might be able to help us."

Senator Harding paused. "I don't know. There is a remote possibility . . ."

"We need any help you can give us," Taylor said. Begging was beneath G. Preston's dignity, so Taylor took the position in his stead.

The senator had an idea. "The minister of finance in the new regime is Ramon Pedrano, an old schoolmate of mine. We were at Princeton together. Perhaps I could give you a letter of introduction."

"You're suggesting a personal visit with the minister of finance?" the chairman asked.

"Yes. I don't think you can count on our government for any real help at this stage."

"Thank you, Senator," Taylor said. "We appreciate your advice and assistance."

"Always glad to be of service. By the way, I hear from my son-in-law that Western is about to issue some new stock."

Taylor was surprised by the senator's veiled hint that a quid pro quo was expected for the letter of introduction. *That sly dog,* he thought. *He's asking for a bribe.* Before Taylor could respond, G. Preston intervened.

"Your information is correct, Senator. Taylor, you and Clay call for the limo, and I'll say our good-byes to the senator."

That was a clear signal for Taylor and Clay to leave the two principals alone. What passed between G. Preston and the senator would be known only to the two of them. The SEC had strict rules about divulging information during the period leading up to a stock offering, but Taylor knew that G. Preston and the senator wouldn't be talking about the weather. Nobody expected the granting of a favor without compensation of some sort. The wheels of commerce were greased by the principle of the deal. It was a principle as old as Eve and the serpent.

G. Preston called Jim Bridges from the limo telephone, and by the time they arrived at National Airport, he had already filed a flight plan for Dallas, ordered box lunches from Hobbs Catering, and refueled the Sabreliner. He was in a cheerful mood as they boarded the plane. Taylor figured it had to do with his private talk with the senator.

They were fifth in line on the runway, and Taylor and G. Preston had already finished one drink by the time they were cleared for takeoff. Taylor enjoyed watching the pilots during takeoff. The awesome power that surged through the craft as Jim pushed the throttle forward never failed to give him a rush of adrenaline. During the climb, they could see the Potomac, Capitol Hill, and the Washington monument fading away beneath them. *Incredible*, Taylor thought. *This is the only way to go.*

G. Preston devoured his box lunch of fried chicken and potato salad, reviewed the afternoon edition of the Washington Post, which Jim had placed on board, and then turned to Taylor just as he was about to doze off.

"Well, Taylor. Looks like you'll be going to Costa Rica. How's your Spanish?"

"I had little bit in high school and college," he replied. "I guess I could get by."

"Good. We'll plan for you to visit Senor Pedrano after we get that letter from the senator. Who knows? The minister of finance may be interested in our new stock issue also."

Taylor smiled at the chairman. *That old rascal. He's trying to catch two fish with the same bait,* he thought. "I wouldn't be at all surprised, sir."

The senator was alone in his office, thinking about his meeting with Taylor and G. Preston. At first he had dismissed it as a simple opportunity to give and receive a favor, to make a deal. But now he was mulling over another possibility.

The administration had been looking for a way to pressure the new regime in Costa Rica to back away from the Sandanistas, but they had no evidence that there was a connection. The Democratic majority in Congress had refused to impose sanctions without proof. Senator Harding knew that the secretary of state planned to retire in a year, and he was rumored to be on the president's short list for the appointment. If he could do the administration a substantial favor in the Costa Rican matter, it might tip the balance in his favor. He picked up the phone and called Bill Powers, director of the CIA. After being shuttled through several secretaries, he heard the director's voice on the line. "This is Bill Powers, Senator. How are you?"

"Fine, couldn't be better," he replied. "What's your afternoon like, Bill?"

"Nothing I couldn't get out of for you, Senator."

Senator Harding knew the director wouldn't refuse his offer unless there was an emergency. "Good," he said. "How about a little handball over here in the senate gym?"

"I didn't know you played handball, Senator."

"Not seriously, Bill. Just a way to loosen up the old joints."

Bill Powers knew this wasn't a social call, and he was curious about the senator's real purpose. "I could stand a little recreation," he replied. "What time?"

"Four o'clock sound okay? I've got a Commerce Committee meeting at two, but we should be through by then."

"I'll see you at four," Bill said.

Bill Powers was amazed at the senator's stamina. They had played two sets of five games, and the senator had nearly run him off the court. Obviously, his age hadn't affected his physical condition.

"Thanks for the workout, Bill. How about a sauna?"

"Anything sitting down would be great. You're quite an athlete, Senator."

"There's still some life in the old body," he said. "You just have to keep it in shape."

They were alone in the sauna, stark naked except for the towel each man carried. Bill knew the senator hadn't invited him over just for handball, and he figured he had arranged to talk in the sauna to guard against hidden microphones or recorders.

The senator leaned against the wall and stretched his feet across the length of the redwood bench. "Bill, I have some information you may find useful."

Here it comes, Bill thought. *I was right about the sauna.*

"What kind of information?" he asked, feigning surprise that the senator had some business to discuss.

Harding plunged into his scheme. "I'm sure you're familiar with the situation in Central America. The Soviets and the Cubans have been doing their best to install puppet regimes down there for thirty years, and with some success, I might add. Now one of our strongest allies down there is on the verge of caving in, but we can't get Congress to see the problem."

"You're talking about Costa Rica?" Bill replied.

"Right," the senator said. "You fellows at CIA know that the new presidente is cozy with the Sandanistas, but we can't get the Democrats to believe it. And then there's the Sendero Luminoso. Hardly anybody in Congress even knows about them."

"How do you know about them?" the director asked warily, surprised at the senator's knowledge about a highly classified matter.

"I have my sources," Senator Harding said matter-of-factly. "And I know they could be a serious threat if they get a foothold in Costa Rica."

The director was still unsure what he was leading up to. "You seem to be well informed on the situation, Senator."

"I try to be," he replied modestly. "I have an idea that I think would be a big help to the administration."

"I'm sure the president would welcome any constructive suggestions."

Senator Harding looked the director square in the eye, not wanting him to make any mistake about his proposal. "This is not for the president's ears, Bill. At least not the details."

Here it comes, Bill thought. "Of course."

"What we need is some way to get the press on this thing, some dramatic development that would stay on the front page of the *Post* for a week, or *Nightline* for several nights."

The director was genuinely in the dark, with no idea what the senator might have in mind. "I don't understand," he said.

"I'm talking about an expose," the senator whispered, then raised his voice for effect. "Some way to prove to the American people that the communists are about to take over Costa Rica, our one true ally in Central America. Something that would force the new presidente to show his true colors."

"Go on," Bill prodded. "How do you propose to accomplish this?"

"Would I be correct in assuming that you have infiltrated the Sendero Luminoso?"

"Senator, you know that's classified information."

"Come on, Bill," the senator said. "Thanks to the Hatfield Commission, you guys don't have any secrets left . . . not that I agreed with the public airing of your dirty linen, mind you."

The director could only agree with the senator's assessment. The Hatfield Commission had gutted the CIA and exposed most of its methodology to the public. The KGB was delighted with the revelations. "Suppose we do have agents inside the Luminoso," he said. "And I'm not saying we do. What's your idea?"

"A kidnapping," Senator Harding replied, his

brow deeply furrowed, a mannerism he had developed during his senatorial campaigns. It made him look serious and thoughtful–some even said presidential.

He continued with his hypothesis. "The PLO never could gain a hearing with the American people because of the kidnappings in the Middle East. Even hijackings don't cause the outcry that a kidnapping does. People identify with the hostages because the press keeps it in front of them. As long as there is a hostage, the press will keep it alive."

"Agreed," Bill said. "But what's that got to do with Costa Rica?"

"If the Luminoso were to take an American hostage, the press would jump all over it. It would prove they're operating in Costa Rica, and the presidente would be forced to line up on one side or the other. If he wavered, then Congress would have to act, and the administration would be free to carry out its policy."

"Sounds reasonable," Bill replied, thoughtfully examining the senator's scenario.

Senator Harding played his trump card. "I happen to know that the CFO of Western Datacorp will be in Costa Rica in the near future. They've got a joint venture down there, and they're having some trouble with the new regime. Western has a high profile in the business press, and if he were taken hostage by the Luminoso, it would be a front page story."

The director was shocked by the senator's suggestion, but he tried not to show it. "I see what you mean," he said. "It could be useful to the administration's goals in the region."

"Very useful," Senator Harding said, emphasizing the adjective. "The minister of finance is an old classmate of mine, and I'm sure he would be anxious to help us any way he could. Especially if it advanced his own political ambitions."

The director laid it out. "Senator, are you suggesting that we arrange a kidnapping?"

"That's your department, Bill. I'm not interested in methods, only the final outcome.""

"Yes, of course," the director replied. "Your information might be useful to our people in the region. I'll make a few inquiries and get back to you. When did you say this person will be in Costa Rica?"

"That's up to me. I offered to give him a letter of introduction, so I can arrange it at our convenience."

"Okay," Bill said. "I'll get back to you tomorrow."

"Good," the senator replied. "And this conversation never took place, Bill."

"Of course not."

G. Preston was in an expansive mood. "Well, Taylor, I think we've earned our keep this week, especially if the senator's friend is disposed to help us. And if I know anything about that culture, he'll be ready to deal."

"I hope so," Taylor said. "We need the cash flow."

"Right you are," the chairman agreed. "By the way, I want you to call the people at Equity and tell them I've decided to give them the underwriting."

Taylor understood this instruction as a signal that the wolf had made a deal with Senator Harding. "Okay," he responded. "I'm sure they'll be pleased."

The Sabreliner began its descent to Love Field, and Taylor's thoughts turned to Cyndi. *I hope she's over it by now,* he thought. *I wonder if it was a boy.*

CHAPTER SEVEN

"Garfield, is that you?"

Savannah Wilson always called G. Preston by his first name. Instead of going to the office, he had driven straight home from Love Field, and since he rarely got home before eight, she was surprised to hear him opening the front door of their elegant home in Highland Park.

"Yes, it's me. I thought I'd surprise you and come home early."

Savannah was in the library, browsing through a magazine and nursing a scotch and water. She was a Southern girl, born in Atlanta to parents who considered themselves southern gentry, and they had named her after one of the South's proudest cities.

G. Preston was surprised to find her with a drink at this hour. "It's a little early for a scotch, isn't it?"

"What do you mean early?" she snapped. "How many drinks did you have on the plane?"

"That's different," he replied.

"Excuse me," she said, "but I fail to see the

difference. You men think business and liquor go together, but somehow it's not okay for us to unwind from domestic chores."

"All right, all right. Don't start with that women's lib nonsense. Besides, what domestic chores are you talking about, supervising Laura?" Laura Davenport had been the Wilson's housemaid and cook for nearly fifteen years.

The scotch had emboldened Savannah, and she retorted testily, "My, my, we are in a mood, aren't we? What's the matter, Garfield? Didn't you get what you wanted from that senator?"

"Sorry," he said, not wishing to provoke an argument. "I'm just tired. We spent the entire week being shuffled from one bureaucrat to the other. I tell you, I don't know what this country's coming to."

He poured himself a drink, took off his shoes, and shouted for the maid.

"Laura!"

"Garfield, must you shout at her like that?"

Laura came into the library, wiping flour from her hands. "Yessir, Mr. Garfield?"

G. Preston didn't like his first name, but Laura had picked it up from Savannah and used it too long and often to change now. "I'm starved. What's for supper?"

"Beef pot pie, Mr. Garfield. With fresh vegetables."

"Sounds good," he replied. "Hurry it up, will you? I've had a hard week."

Laura had her own independent streak, an attitude that was encouraged by Savannah when it came to dealing with G. Preston. "You know supper's always at eight-thirty, Mr. Garfield," she said jauntily.

"Well, can't we break the sacred rule just this once?" he pleaded.

Laura looked at Savannah for guidance. "It's okay, Laura. It won't hurt to have supper a little early tonight. Just tell us when it's ready."

"Yes, ma'am."

G. Preston picked up his drink and the afternoon Times-Herald and headed for his study. "I'm going to make a few calls. Tell Laura to call me when supper's ready."

"Suit yourshelf," she slurred.

He took a close look at Savannah. She had always taken more than one drink at social functions, and had even been tipsy a time or two on the way home from cocktail parties, but he had never thought about her drinking alone at home. She always had a couple of glasses of wine with supper, but he couldn't remember her drinking after supper. But then he wouldn't really know, because Savannah always retired to her own bedroom right after the evening meal, and he usually worked in his study until the ten o'clock news.

Where did she get those lines under her eyes? he wondered. *She looks old. Why haven't I ever noticed that before?* Her hands were old and wrinkled and unsteady.

"Savvy, are you all right?" He hadn't used his

pet name for her in months, and it startled her.

"Of course, I'm all right. Why?"

"You just don't seem yourself. I thought maybe you weren't feeling well."

"I'm perfectly fine, thank you."

Once in his study, G. Preston sat down at the antique desk and began to work through the memory dialer, starting with Roberts. She was still at the office faithfully manning her battle station in his absence.

"Mr. Wilson's office."

"Roberts, this is Mr. Wilson. What's going on there?"

"Mr. Wilson, are you back in Dallas?" She was surprised that he had gone straight home from Love Field.

"Yep. We got in about five, and I decided to come on home. Anything important I ought to know about?"

"The usual stack of calls," she said. "I've handled most of them, but there are one or two you might want to know about."

"All right. I'm listening."

"The attorney from Equity Securities called twice. He didn't state his business, but I'm sure it's about the underwriting."

"Well, he can relax. I told Taylor to call Monday and give them the green light."

Roberts continued reading from her telephone log. "You have a couple of telexes from Costa Rica. Apparently the meeting our people had with the minister of com-merce produced very little. They said it was a bust, whatever that means."

"Not surprised," he replied. "We may have a new card to play down there. What
else?"

"Elizabeth Sullivan called to make an appointment. She wouldn't say what it was about, so I told her I'd check your schedule and get back to her."

"Tell her it's impossible," he sighed. "Tell her you'll call if anything opens up."

Roberts made a notation, then continued. "Mr. Hartwell would like to see you first thing Monday. Something about this quarter's earnings."

"All right, pencil him in for eight. Wait a minute. Is he still there?"

"I think so," she replied. "Do you want me to transfer you?"

"As soon as we're through. Anything else?"

"Nothing that won't wait until Monday. I'll put you through to Mr. Hartwell."

G. Preston heard the familiar clicking and buzzing sounds made by the internal communication system, followed by Fred Hartwell's familiar voice. "Fred, what's this about the earnings report?" he demanded.

"It looks like we could have a hiccup in this quarter's earnings, G.P." Fred and Ryan were the only officers at Western who used his initials instead of the more formal "Mr. Wilson."

"What are you talking about?" the chairman shouted. "I've been telling the analysts we'd have a gain in the low to mid-teens."

"I know," Fred said. "That's why we've got to move on this thing quick. Since Taylor was in Washington with you, I asked Phil to give me a briefing yesterday, and if he's correct, we could be looking at a down-tick."

There were a lot of things G. Preston didn't like, and a surprise in the numbers was at the top of his list. "That's impossible," he growled. "How could we have a down-tick on the kind of sales we've been pushing out the door?"

Fred drew a long breath. "Phil said there's a problem with inventory valuation. Since we discontinued the SX-780, the outside accountants want us to write down the parts inventory. They say we don't have any choice under accounting rules."

"Big deal," G. Preston replied. "How many parts could we possibly have in inventory for the seven-eighty? We started the phase-out for that model six months ago."

"That's what I thought too, but somebody forgot to tell merchandising we were going to discontinue it, and they bought a two year supply of motherboards, hedging against a runup in the Japanese yen."

G. Preston was fuming. "Those idiots! Don't they know that's treasury's job? Who's responsible for this screw-up?"

"Merchandising blames R&D," Fred replied sheepishly, "and they blame Merchandising. I haven't had time to get to the bottom of it yet, but my hunch is that Bud Farley failed to get it on R&D's status report in time."

The wolf was only interested in placing blame at this point. He could look for a solution later. "Find out who's to blame and show him the front door. This is terrible. Here we are about to bring out a stock issue, and we have a lousy earnings report."

"I know," Fred said. "The timing couldn't be worse."

"You and Taylor be in my office first thing Monday morning. We may have to do some creative accounting."

"Right," Fred replied.

The next hour was consumed with calls to various executives at Western. He always called after six on Friday to see who was still at his desk. It was one of his games, and they played it with a straight face, each in turn acting as if he was staying late to clear up some important matter, when the truth was they were all waiting for his call. If you wanted to advance to a higher level at Western Datacorp, you not only had to be technically competent, you had to be at your desk when the wolf called. Otherwise your name went into his prodigious memory with an asterisk, which meant "lacking in commitment." Long hours and hard work had gotten him to the top, and he wasn't going to let his subordinates slide by without paying their own dues.

Laura stuck her head in his study and said, "Mr. Garfield, supper's ready."

On the few occasions that G. Preston and Savannah ate together at home, she insisted that they eat in the formal dining room. He didn't like it, but he humored her.

The aroma from Laura's beef pot pie filled the dining room, and he tore into it the minute she served his plate. Savannah was disgusted by his crude table manners. "Garfield, must you act like you're in a boarding house?"

"Wadayamean?" His mouth was stuffed and Savannah could barely understand him. She turned away in disgust.

After a long silence, she poured herself a second glass of wine and brought up a painful subject, one that G. Preston would just as soon banish forever.

"Richie called today," she said.

He stopped chewing and looked up, astonished that she had mentioned that name in his presence. Richard Wilson was their only child, a grown man of forty.

"Let me guess," he said sarcastically. "He wants to make a payment on his loan?"

G. Preston had long since given up on his son, and he hadn't attempted to hide the sarcasm in his voice. Richard had shown no interest in sports or girls growing up, or in his father's business ventures. He always wanted to be an artist, a musician, and he had spent eight years and nearly a hundred thousand dollars of his father's money bouncing from one college to the next. For the last fourteen years, he had lived in New York with a group of artists in Greenwich Village, subsisting on a succession of loans from his parents.

"He wanted to wish me a happy birthday," Savannah said sadly.

"Oh. I was hoping he had called to announce he was engaged to marry one of the Rockefellers. Did you say birthday?"

"Yes, Garfield. Yesterday was my birthday."

He had forgotten it again. "Of course, it was. I meant to get you something," he lied, "but we were tied up with the senator. Why don't we celebrate tomorrow night at the Mansion.?"

"That would be nice," she said. "By the way, Richie said he's been invited to study with the guitarist from the Philharmonic, a man who studied with Segovia."

G. Preston frowned. "How much will that cost?"

"He didn't say, but I told him it sounds like a wonderful opportunity."

"Savannah, you know how I feel about Richard's so-called career. I should have cut him off years ago and forced him to make it in the real world."

G. Preston hadn't spoken directly to his son in years. Savannah was the go-between, forever caught in the middle, relaying and interpreting messages back and forth. "Your problem is you have no appreciation for the arts," she said. "All you think about is your precious business."

"It's my precious business that keeps our precious artist afloat," he responded, his voice rising. "If you hadn't spoiled him with music lessons and tutors, he might have turned out to be a real man. Look at him now, useless to society."

Savannah placed both hands palm down on the table, her signal that she'd had quite enough. "Oh it's all my fault, is it?" she cried. "If you had been around at all, he might have wanted to be like his father, but how could he when he didn't even know you? On the rare occasions when you were home, you treated him like a stranger, an interruption in your precious business day."

She took her napkin and wiped the tears from her eyes. She stood up, threw the napkin down on the dining room table, and stormed up to her room. "Tell Laura I don't want to be disturbed."

"Savannah, please," he shouted.

It was no use. They had played this scene so many times they were on autopilot, going through motions they both detested but were powerless to prevent. He finished his dessert, directed Laura to make a fresh pot of coffee, and headed for his study to read a stack of reports that Roberts had sent out that morning. Savannah locked her bedroom door, crawled into bed with a fifth of vodka, and drank herself into unconsciousness.

In his study and alone, G. Preston was unable to concentrate on the rows of numbers and tightly-crafted arguments and positions his executives had put forward in their memos and reports. He couldn't get his mind off family matters.

Where did I go wrong with Richie? Why couldn't he see what I was teaching him? Maybe I should have spent more time with him when he was young. Might've offset Savannah's music and art lessons.

"Spilled milk," he muttered under his breath, then turned his attention to a report on the inventory reduction plan.

Taylor had called Cyndi from Love Field, arranged to meet her at Armando's, and then driven to the office to check in. He had planned to take her out to dinner, but their reunion at Armando's turned out to be less than joyful.

He was at the bar with some friends when Cyndi arrived. He left them to greet her, but when he tried to kiss her she pulled away. They found a booth in the corner and ordered drinks.

"How was Washington?" she asked, trying to appear interested.

"It was okay," Taylor replied. "How've you been?"

"I'm okay, I guess. It's been some week," she said, obviously referring to the abortion.

Taylor tried to effect the right response. *Sympathy? Understanding?* He wondered. *But how could he understand? He was a male. Why did modern women insist that men display female instincts like tenderness and vulnerability in order to be true partners with them?*

He tried to sound sympathetic. "Sweetheart, it must have been awful. I'm so sorry I couldn't be with you. Are you feeling okay now?"

"I think so," she said. "I haven't been able

to sleep without help all week, but physically I'm okay."

Tears welled up in her eyes, and she started to weep. Taylor was embarrassed. "What's the matter, sweetheart?"

"I guess it's the aftermath," she sobbed. "I keep having these horrible flashbacks."

"What do you mean?" Taylor asked. "What kind of flashbacks?"

"Taylor, you can't believe how awful it was. They come at your insides with this giant vacuum cleaner, and you can almost feel the baby being sucked out. It was terrible, and I keep thinking about him or her being terrorized by that awful machine."

Taylor was startled. He hadn't thought about the abortion in any kind of detail. It had simply been a transaction, a solution to a problem. "I'm truly sorry, sweetheart. You've had a traumatic experience, but you'll get over it. Thousands of women have been through it, and they live perfectly normal lives after-ward."

"I know," she said. "I'm sorry I've been such a baby about it."

"Why don't we split and go somewhere special for dinner?" he offered, trying to change the subject.

Cyndi wiped the remaining tears from her cheeks. "I don't think I'd be very good company tonight. Can't we just call out for some pizza?"

"Okay, whatever you say." Taylor signaled for the bill, and they headed toward the exit. None of their friends said anything, but one could tell by their expressions they knew something was wrong.

Later at the apartment, Taylor busied himself with some financial reports while Cyndi looked through a stack of trade journals. "I may be taking a trip to Costa Rica," he said abruptly.

Cyndi was surprised. "Costa Rica? Whatever for?"

"The wolf thinks I may be able to convince the finance minister to let us take our profits out of the country."

"That sounds like an interesting challenge," she said.

"Indeed," Taylor replied. "The only problem is it puts me on the spot. If I succeed, I'm a hero, but if I fail I get to be the goat."

"You won't fail," Cyndi said. "You've got the law of the pyramid working for you."

"The law of the pyramid?" he replied, puzzled at her use of terms.

"Sure," Cyndi said. "The higher up the pyramid you get, the more people there are below to blame your failures on."

Taylor smiled. "Thanks," he said. "I'll try to remember that."

CHAPTER EIGHT

Taylor and Fred were waiting in G. Preston's outer office when he arrived a little before eight-thirty on Monday morning. Fred had briefed Taylor on the problem Saturday, and Taylor had spent the rest of the day tracking down the specifics and preparing for this meeting.

The wolf motioned for them to follow him into his spacious office, buzzed Roberts for coffee, and sat down behind the massive desk. He was in no mood for preliminary chit-chat. "Mr. Davis, can you tell us what the hell is going on with the March numbers?"

Taylor cringed. *Uh oh, it's Mr. Davis when there's bad news, is it? I'd better calm him down.* "Mr. Wilson, I spent all day Saturday going over the numbers with Phil, and the whole thing revolves around the seven-eighty. We've got fifteen million in motherboards, and since that model has been discontinued, the outside auditors want us to write them down to scrap value."

G. Preston never had liked outside auditors. They were leeches, sucking your blood with exorbitant fees and then issuing meaningless opinions worded in a way that relieved them of any responsibility for subsequent surprises. He didn't even pretend to mask his contempt for their opinion.

"Mr. Davis, I would remind you that this company's financial records don't belong to the auditors, they belong to us," he said in measured tones.

"I realized that, sir," Taylor countered. "But according to accounting principles, we have to provide for any potential loss as soon as we know its magnitude."

Fred interrupted, mercifully coming to Taylor's defense. "He's right, G.P. We've got to figure some way to give the auditors an out. We can't just ignore them"

"Why do we have to figure it out?" the wolf demanded. "That's what we pay them for, isn't it?"

Taylor picked up the ball. "Perhaps there is a way we can at least put the problem off for a while."

"All right, Taylor. What is it?" the chairman asked.

Good. At least he's calling me Taylor again. "Sir, the key fact is that the seven-eighty was discontinued in February. What if we planned to use those motherboards in a new model? Then we wouldn't have to write them down at all."

G. Preston wasn't impressed. "A new model? Taylor, the seven-eighty's architecture is history. Obsolete. We'd have to sell it to Eskimos and hope they never read the trade journals."

Fred stared at Taylor, signaling that he was on

his own, but Taylor was undaunted. "I didn't say we had to actually do it. I only said if we were planning to do it, then we wouldn't have to take the hit in the March quarter. We could wait until June or September when the numbers will be stronger, and then announce that we had changed our minds because of market conditions."

G. Preston and Fred were silent, considering the implications of Taylor's plan. Fred watched the wolf, waiting for a clue to his reaction before he ventured an opinion. Taylor took a deep breath and offered his clincher.

"We've got the stock issue coming out in late May or early June. If we report a down-tick in earnings at this stage, it will kill the new issue. After the stock comes out and we've got our money in the bank, then we can say we changed our mind and take the hit in the September quarter."

G. Preston turned to Fred. "What do you think, Fred?"

Fred squirmed in his seat. Without a clue to the chairman's thinking, he would have to guess which way he was leaning. "I think Taylor may have something, G. P.," he offered weakly.

Taylor knew what Fred was up to. *What a wienie,* he thought. *He says I may have something. Then again, I may not. Right, Fred?*

The wolf turned to Taylor and smiled. "Just how do we accomplish this sleight-of-hand, Mr. Numbers Man?" That was a good sign. Taylor had liked it when the wolf introduced him to Senator

Harding's aide as "my numbers man," the possessive pronoun being the critical feature. "My" numbers man, he had said. It made him feel important.

"Simple," Taylor said. "We just prepare a back-dated memo from you to Bud Farley directing him to draw up a plan for using the seven-eighty mother-board in a new model."

"Fine," the chairman responded. "But the memo should come from Fred, not me."

Taylor could hardly keep a straight face. *Serves Fred right,* he thought. The wolf was going to hang Fred's tail over the cliff on this one, and if anything went wrong, he'd have to be the front man. Taylor was smugly proud of himself. He got credit for the idea, but he wouldn't share in the risk. Since he had nothing to do with operations, there was no reason for him to sign the memo, and if it hit the fan some-time down the road, it would be Fred's word against his. . . . and the chairman's!

Fred was looking for company, in case some-thing went wrong. "Shouldn't I bring Bud into this?"

The wolf didn't want anybody else to know about their plan.

"Just tell him as soon as you heard about the problem, you were surprised since you had written a memo about the new model back in February. Taylor, you send a copy to the auditors and get them off their high horses."

"Yes, sir," Taylor responded. "Fred, if you will make a couple of extras for me, I'll get with Phil as soon as possible and straighten him out."

"I'll bring it over later this morning," Fred said sourly. The episode had temporarily positioned Fred as Taylor's inferior, and he didn't like it. He didn't like it at all.

"Well, then. Let's get to work, shall we?" With that, G. Preston pronounced the meeting finished, and Taylor and Fred went back to their offices. Jenny always took note of Taylor's mood when he returned from a meeting with the wolf, and she noticed that he was whistling.

"You seem rather cheerful this morning," she said.

"Jenny, my girl, this is going to be a great day. Any calls?"

"Senator Harding's office. They wanted you to return the call as soon as possible."

Taylor took the phone slip and headed straight for his desk. He placed the call himself, and after a long wait Senator Harding came on the line. "Good morning, Taylor. How's the weather in Dallas?"

"Sunny and warm, Senator. How about D. C.?"

"Muggy," he replied. "I hate Washington this time of the year. The humidity is awful, up in the nineties most of the time. Makes me wonder why I ever left Kentucky."

"I know what you mean," Taylor said. "Dallas gets that way sometimes. What's on your mind, Senator?"

"I talked to Ramon Pedrano, and he agreed to

meet with you on the joint venture problem, but it has to be the third week in May. Can you make that schedule?"

Taylor opened his desktop diary and flipped through the pages. "I don't see why not, Senator. I've got a couple of things penciled in that week, but nothing I can't reschedule."

"Good," he replied cheerily. "I asked Ramon to make reservations for you at the Cariari in San Jose. Do you play golf?"

"No sir," Taylor replied. "Tennis is my game."

"The Cariari is on the grounds of the Cariari Country Club, and hotel guests have use of all their facilities. I thought you would enjoy staying there."

"Sounds terrific," Taylor responded, wondering why the senator had personally made the arrangements. "Maybe I can work in a few vacation days. Thanks."

"Clay will fax your travel documents this afternoon. Let him know as soon as you finalize your plans so we can have someone from the embassy meet your plane."

Someone from the embassy to meet him? Taylor was beginning to like the sound of this. "Thank you, Senator. I appreciate your help, and I'll brief Mr. Wilson on the plans. I know he'll be pleased."

"Excellent," the senator replied. "By the way, Clay will include the letter of introduction with the other material.""

"Thanks again, Senator." Taylor hung up the phone and buzzed his secretary. "Jenny, I want you to reschedule everything on my calendar the third week in May. I'll be in Costa Rica that week."

Jenny gave him a knowing look as she made some notes. "Costa Rica, huh? Sounds like you're going to be suffering in the tropics for good old Western?"

"Don't be smart, young lady." He grinned. "This is a very high-level deal. If I pull this off, it could mean big bucks for the company."

Jenny smiled. "Of course, it will. But would I be correct in thinking that you just might have time to visit one of their fabulous beaches?"

Taylor abandoned his "strictly business" pose and smiled. "Well, there may be a few scarce moments for some well-deserved relaxation. By the way, call the travel agent and get them started on reservations, and ask them to send over anything they have on the Cariari country Club in San Jose. Better telex senor what's-his-name that I'm coming."

Jenny said, "Senor who?"

"Western's manager in Costa Rica."

After Jenny returned to her desk, Taylor called Cyndi. She sounded tired. "This is Cyndi Davis."

"Hi, sweetheart, how's it going?"

"It's a typical Monday," she moaned. "What's happening at your place?"

"Well, as a matter of fact, I may have an interesting proposition for you. Picture yourself on the beach, soaking up the sun, sipping a fruit punch, beach boys attending to your every whim."

Cyndi said, "Sounds like you're reading a brochure from Cancun."

"Not Cancun, my dear. The Cariari Country Club in San Jose, Costa Rica. I'm going down the third week in May, and I thought you might like to join me for a few days."

"Taylor, it sounds delicious, but that's 'Night With The Stars' week. There's no way I can miss that."

He had hoped some time away might take her mind off the abortion. He was ready for her to be the old Cyndi again. "I forgot about that," he said. "Maybe I should scout it out first, then if it's really special we can go back sometime."

"That would be great, Taylor. I'm truly sorry."

"No problem," he said, masking his disappointment. "You sound a little down. Are you okay?"

"I'm fine," she lied. "Why?"

"You just don't sound like yourself. I'm worried about you."

That did it. First, there was silence. Then Taylor heard the unmistakable sound of crying. He clumsily tried to recover from his blunder. "Sweetheart, I'm sorry. I didn't mean to make you cry."

"I'm sorry too, Taylor. I can't seem to get it out of my mind. I keep thinking about that scene at the Women's Clinic, and it's driving me crazy."

"What scene?"

"I keep seeing those pro-life crazies with their signs calling me a murderer."

There was more silence while Taylor tried to think of something to say. "Cyndi, you've got to snap out of this. It's over and done with, and there's no way you can go back and do it over. Put it behind you."

Male logic, she thought. "Snap out of it? Put it behind me? One, two, three, just like one of your business memos, with positions neatly laid out and persuasively argued. But I'm the one who carried a child in my womb. I was connected to it, feeding it with my own life . . . and then I . . . killed it. Oh God, what have I done?" she cried.

Taylor waited helplessly on the other end of the line. Finally, she whispered, "I'm sorry, Taylor," and hung up.

Taylor held the receiver to his ear with Southwestern Bell's familiar dial tone his only company. The abortion was beginning to intrude on his life like a guest who stays too long, and he was ready for their lives to return to normal.

Cyndi was standing at the window of her fifth floor office, gazing north toward Love Field, and trying to sort through her feelings. *Taylor's right,* she admitted to herself. *I really do have to snap out of this. I can't let my feelings get in the way of my career. Not now, when I'm just beginning to roll.* Cyndi walked back to her desk, checked the bank's internal directory, and dialed Sharon Dillow's number.

"Sharon, this is Cyndi Davis. I was wondering if we could have lunch today."

"Sure," Sharon replied, surprised by Cyndi's call. "Just say where and when."

Cyndi didn't want to meet in the bank. "Let's

go out somewhere. What about the coffee shop at the Adolphus?"

"All right," Sharon replied. "Do you want to meet there, or shall I drop by your office?"

Ever since Sharon told Cyndi she was a Christian, Cyndi had more or less steered clear of her, not wishing to cause unnecessary talk around the bank. "Let's meet at the Adolphus," she said.

"It's a date, then. Twelve o'clock okay?" Sharon asked.

"Twelve will be fine. I'll see you there." Cyndi hung up the phone. *I'm not going to tell her about the abortion,* she thought. *Why am I doing this? Because I need someone who understands what I'm feeling, that's why.*

The Adolphus was crowded with business types, dealmakers in search of a deal, investors pursued by budding entrepreneurs, and brokers of various types touting their latest offerings.

The hotel had recently redecorated the downstairs coffee shop. The new French-country look irritated some of the old-timers, but it suited the increasing numbers of female executives just fine. They felt more comfortable in bright, airy surroundings with soft pastels and fresh flowers on every table. Gone was the dark paneling, ubiquitous cigar smoke, and vulgar conversations. Good riddance, as far as they were concerned.

Conversation was difficult at first. Cyndi was wary of Sharon. She was so different than Cyndi's friends, less interested in trendy things, more open, more at ease. They talked business mostly. Then Cyndi put out a feeler.

"Sharon, can I ask you a silly question?"

Sharon returned her coffee cup to its saucer and momentarily studied Cyndi's expression. "Sure," she said. "I don't mind silly questions. I've got some myself."

"Do you ever find yourself crying for no reason?"

Sharon grinned. "Of course. Once a month, just like clockwork."

Cyndi smiled. "I don't mean that, silly. I mean, do you ever feel that events are controlling your life instead of the other way around?"

"What kind of events?" Sharon asked, trying to get on Cyndi's wavelength.

Cyndi was cautious. "Things that happen. Things you hadn't counted on or figured into your goals and plans."

"I guess I know what you mean," Sharon said. "I'm sure there have been times when I felt that other people were controlling events that affected my life. Is that what you mean?"

"Sort of," Cyndi answered. "How did you handle it?"

"Well, I have a situation right now that probably qualifies. My dad has lived alone since Mom died, and last week he almost burned his house down. Luckily, it happened during the day and the fire department was able to contain most of the damage to the kitchen."

"What happened?" Cyndi asked, intrigued by Sharon's story.

"He left a skillet full of grease on the stove and it caught fire."

"That sounds scary," Cyndi said, "but I don't understand what that has to do with my question."

Sharon explained. "It's forcing us to decide whether or not to put Dad in a nursing home. We all knew this was coming sooner or later, and now it's here."

"You know what nursing homes are like," Sharon replied. "Even the best ones are awful, and Dad is absolutely against it. My sister has three kids of her own to raise, and she can't possibly take him in. And there's no way I could fit him into my apartment. Even if I could, who would look after him while I'm working?"

Cyndi tried to visualize herself in Sharon's predicament and forgot about her own problem for the moment. "What are you going to do?" she asked.

"I don't know, to be honest. Right now I'm just trying to deal with the guilt feelings."

Cyndi was startled by the mention of guilt, and she immediately felt a bond with Sharon. The abortion itself hadn't been all that bad, but the guilt feelings that remained were threatening to bring her down, draining her energy and leaving her with an empty feeling, a vacuum at the center of her being.

Sharon brightened momentarily. "If it weren't for my prayer group, I'd be in real trouble."

Uh oh. Here comes the religious thing, Cyndi

thought, but for some reason, she was compelled to pursue it. "Prayer group? Do you mean people at your church?"

"No," Sharon replied. "I meet with a small group of people every Friday morning before work. We've been meeting for a couple of years now and honestly, I don't know what I'd do without their support."

Cyndi was curious. "What sort of people?"

"Different types—a couple of executives, three secretaries, a teller. Oh, and the data processing manager."

They didn't sound like a bunch of fanatics. Cyndi pursued the question. "What do you do?"

"We meet in the third floor conference room for donuts and coffee and talk about our week. Then we have a time of prayer for individual needs or concerns that have come up during the discussion. Sometimes Jim reads a portion of scripture and we discuss it for a few minutes before we pray."

"Jim?" Cyndi asked. "Do I know him?"

"Jim Peterson, one of the senior VPs."

Cyndi was surprised. Jim Peterson was a heavyweight. Some people figured he was third in line for president of the bank. "Oh sure, I know Jim. I didn't realize he was into religion." Cyndi paused, embarrassed. "I'm sorry, I didn't mean it like that."

"That's okay," Sharon said. "I know what you mean. Anyhow, as I was saying, the group has been praying about my problem for a couple of weeks now, and it really has helped me to stay calm even though I still don't know what I'm going to do."

They were silent for a moment, but it was a shared silence, not at all awkward. Then Sharon turned the conversation back to Cyndi's original question. "Cyndi, why did you ask that question?"

Cyndi dropped her voice. "Oh, I'm going through a thing myself right now. I had to make a decision recently that hurt someone else, even though I think I was right. But now I've got these guilt feelings, and I can't seem to get myself together. I start crying at the oddest moments. I've never done that before."

Sharon didn't probe for details, but she knew Cyndi was reaching out to her, desperately wanting someone to understand. "Cyndi, has anybody ever told you the difference between true guilt and false guilt?"

"No, I don't think so," Cyndi responded, puzzled by the question. "I thought guilt had to do with cultural conditioning. Is there a difference?"

"Yes, there is," Sharon said. "True guilt comes from breaking God's laws and principles, and false guilt comes from Satan."

Cyndi was startled. "Satan? Don't tell me you believe that nonsense."

"I believe the Bible," Sharon continued, "and the Bible says there is a cosmic battle being waged for the souls of men and women. God is on one side offering redemption and wholeness, and Satan is on the other side offering temporary pleasure or power, but delivering only pain and misery."

Cyndi leaned back in her chair, her body language signaling that she was rejecting what she'd just heard. "Sharon, you sound like one of those hellfire and damnation preachers."

"I'm sorry," Sharon replied. "I didn't mean to come across that way. Let's start over. I don't know what your decision was, and I don't know why you continue to feel guilty about it, but I do know that God knows and he cares. He loves you, Cyndi, and he wants you to experience life at its best. For whatever it's worth, I care too, and I'll be praying that God will give you an answer."

Cyndi was thinking about something Sharon had said earlier, that true guilt comes from breaking God's law—like murder. She sat quietly, folding and unfolding her napkin.

"Cyndi, did you hear what I said?"

"Yes. And I appreciate your prayers, Sharon." Cyndi looked at her watch. "Oops, I've got to run. Got a meeting at one-thirty."

On their way back to the bank, the conversation was businesslike and stilted, but something Sharon said had touched Cyndi deeply. At the elevator, Cyndi's eyes were moist, not yet tearful, but clearly on the brink. Sharon reached out and took her hand as she said goodbye. "Cyndi, God does care. I want you to believe that."

"Thanks, Sharon. Our talk meant a lot to me. Let's get together again."

"I'd love to. Just call me."

CHAPTER NINE

The four-hour flight from Houston had been bumpy, and Taylor was feeling queasy when the Pan Am jet touched down in San Jose. He stepped out of the first class section onto the staircase. The oppressive humidity surrounded him and made his wool blazer feel like a saddle blanket. He loosened his tie and followed the crowd to the customs and baggage area.

Customs was a joke. The uniformed soldier in the booth didn't even ask for his passport, merely waving him through when Taylor offered it. Outside customs, he was met by a young woman holding a home-made sign with his name on it. When he made eye contact she said, "Are you Taylor Davis?"

" That's me," he said. "You must be from the embassy." Taylor was surprised. He hadn't expected a woman, and certainly not one this young and good-looking. She was in her late twenties and she was tall, perhaps five-nine or ten, with long dark hair and a deep tan.

"My name is Janet Dempsey," she smiled.

"I'm the ambassador's executive assistant. Welcome to Costa Rica, Mr. Davis."

"Thanks," Taylor said. "It's really good of you to meet me."

"No bother. Besides . . . when Senator Harding's office called, I was curious to see what kind of businessman rated the VIP treatment. We don't get too many calls from senators down here."

Taylor was embarrassed. "Sorry. I hope it's not too much trouble."

"Don't apologize," she said. "I was just kidding." Janet grinned mischievously. "I volunteered for the job, actually. It's been a little boring at the office this week, and I was glad for a break in the routine."

Taylor was delighted. He had expected a stuffy diplomat, and Janet definitely didn't fit that mold. On the way to the hotel, she was full of questions about Western Datacorp, the joint venture, and the reason for his trip. In the middle of his explanation, she asked a totally unexpected question.

"Are you married?"

Good grief, Taylor thought. *This girl is really up front.* "Yes, I am. Why do you ask?"

"Oh, it's a silly game," she replied. "I have this theory that eighty-nine percent of the eligible men in the world are already taken, and I keep elaborate statistics on my computer to test the theory. So far, I've interviewed three thousand some odd, and it's running slightly over ninety per cent. The demographics of the eligible ten per cent are really frightening.

Would you believe that half of the eligible group have IQs in the lowest quartile.?"

Taylor laughed. "You're putting me on."

"No, I'm not," she said in mock sincerity. "And the other half are all broke." She grinned mischievously again, and then broke out laughing. Her eyes sparkled when she laughed.

"You haven't told me how you got into diplomatic work?" he asked her.

"Daddy always wanted to be an ambassador," she replied. "He made a fortune in Southern California real estate and raised a ton of money over the years for the Republi-can party. I think he assumed he would be rewarded with an ambassadorship, but somehow it never happened. The Nixon people promised him Ireland during the seventy-two campaign, but in the end it went to a fatter cat than Dad."

"Isn't that always the way?" Taylor responded.

"I suppose I'm trying to live his dream," Janet said. "I studied public affairs at UCLA, and when the State Department interviewed on campus, I signed up. I never dreamed I would end up in taco city, though.

Taylor said, "You make it sound pretty crummy."

"Not really. I enjoy matching wits with cockroaches the size of small cats. When you kill one of those suckers, you feel like you've really done something." This time, Taylor laughed uproariously. Janet was not only charming, she was genuinely funny.

"Here we are," she said, steering the Ford LTD into the grounds of the Cariari Hotel & Country Club. Taylor was impressed. It reminded him of something he had seen in an old Bogart movie. Janet followed him inside, made sure he was registered, then suggested they meet later for dinner.

"I'm supposed to give you the standard embassy briefing on the local protocol," she said. "We might as well combine it with a meal on the taxpayers."

Taylor was curious. Was she making a move on him? "Sounds great," he responded. "Where shall we go?"

"The hotel dining room is one of the best places in San Jose. Why don't I meet you here at eight?"

"You've got a deal, except dinner's on me," he replied. "I've got an expense account too, you know."

"If you insist. See you at eight." With that, she turned and headed back to the car. Taylor watched her until she disappeared through the huge revolving doors and then followed the bellboy to his room.

The embassy had reserved a cabana that opened onto the pool and contained a living room, wet bar, and bedroom with bath. Taylor unpacked his things, changed into swimming trunks and stepped out to the pool for a swim. *This is what it's all about,* he mused. *Cramming for exams at Wharton, clawing my way through the competition at Western, working weekends, it's all paying off. And who knows what this evening holds?*

When they met in the lobby at eight, Taylor

was dazzled by Janet's appearance. She was wearing a gorgeous cocktail dress that took a breath-taking plunge in the back, exposing her deep tan to the small of her back. If he had harbored any doubts about her intentions earlier, they were history now. This girl was definitely trying to impress him.

"Good evening, Miss Dempsey," he smiled. "You look terrific, if I may say so, and I do. Did the taxpayers foot the bill for that dress?" Taylor was feeling giddy. He hadn't been out on a date in so long, he'd forgotten how awkward it felt.

"Thank you," she said. "No, I'm afraid the budget doesn't include uniforms. This one's a gift from Daddy, actually. He doesn't know it yet, but he will when he gets the Visa this month."

"Good for Dad. He's got terrific taste."

Janet took Taylor's arm, and they made their way to the hotel dining room, where they were shown to a table in the corner. The dining room was decorated in subtle Latin-American themes, with a combination of paintings and statuary. Most of the countries of Central America were represented in one form or the other.

"Would you care for a drink, senor?" the waiter asked in impeccable English.

"I think I'll have something with rum since we're in the tropics. What do you recommend, Janet?"

"A good choice," she said. "Bring us two melo-sos."

"Very good, madam."

Taylor was bewitched by this woman. "What, may I ask, is a meloso?"

She smiled. "It's rum with honey and lime."

Taylor grimaced. "Sounds awful."

"I know, but it's quite good. Trust me."

"I'm completely in your hands," he grinned. Taylor watched for a reaction to his remark, but saw nothing discernible.

During the meal, Taylor was a tiny bit disappointed to discover that Janet really had come to give him a briefing on protocol for the meeting with Senor Pedrano. An appointment had been arranged for the following afternoon, and she wanted to make sure he understood the Costa Rican way of doing business.

'It's very important to defer to the minister," she was saying. "Position and power mean everything in the Latin culture, and he won't listen to your proposal unless you show the respect due his office."

"So how is that so different from the States?" Taylor countered.

"Yeah, well . . . I guess you're right. Just don't come on like the big Yankee trader who thinks he can buy the natives with a few trinkets. They are very proud of their accomplishments down here, and you won't get past first base if you talk down to them."

"Right. Do I curtsy, or bow and scrape?" Taylor asked, poking fun at her official advice.

Janet frowned, and then realized he was trying to make a joke. "Okay, I guess I am laying it on a little thick. Do you need directions to the Ministry of Finance?"

"No, thanks," he said. "I'm meeting with our people tomorrow morning and I'm sure they'll have transportation lined up."

After dessert and coffee, Taylor suggested a walk through the hotel grounds. "I haven't seen all of the grounds . . . have you?" He still couldn't read her. Did she have romance in mind, or not?

They strolled out by the pool, through the gardens, and over to the first tee of the golf course. It was a brilliant night, with no clouds and millions of stars. Janet was self-assured and showed no sign of nerves. She talked about her job, about the country, and about her interest in archaeology.

"I've been on several digs in the Meseta Central," she said. "Professor Wilmuth has uncovered evidence of pre-Aztec civilization in Costa Rica."

"Professor who?" Taylor had no interest in talking about old rocks, or old people either. This was a night made for the young.

"John Wilmuth. I took his class at UCLA, and I've been on five or six digs with his students."

"Oh, I see. Sounds like an interesting man. I hear Costa Rica has some terrific beaches," Taylor said, trying to change the subject.

"The best," she replied. "Would you like to visit my favorite while you're here?"

"By all means," Taylor responded. "When?"

"I'll call you tomorrow. You should know more about your schedule after your meeting."

"Thanks, Janet. That would be a treat."

They were walking back toward the hotel when

Taylor spotted his cabana off to the left. "Hey, that's my suite over there. Care for a nightcap?"

Janet turned toward him, and Taylor fully expected her to make a move. Everything had pointed toward it. "To be honest," she said. "I'm exhausted. It's been a lovely evening but I'll take a rain check, if you don't mind."

He felt like a punctured balloon. How could he have misread her intentions? Where did he go wrong? Just when he felt he had made a horrible miscalculation, Janet reached over, placed both hands on the back of his neck, and kissed him full on the mouth. It wasn't a goodnight kiss, either. It was sensual, a kiss that contained a thousand meanings, and he was free to choose which. She pulled away and looked at him with that maddeningly mischievous grin.

"So . . . do I get a rain check?" she said.

"Uh . . . sure. I mean . . . absolutely."

"Okay," she said. "Thanks for tonight. I'll call you tomorrow." She turned and walked toward the hotel entrance, leaving Taylor standing there mesmerized.

Taylor spent the morning with the joint venture's executive staff, and then the managing director drove him to the Finance Ministry for his appointment with Ramon Pedrano. He showed Senator Harding's letter of introduction to the first floor receptionist, and she escorted him up three flights of stairs and down a long corridor to the minister's office. Ramon Pedrano was waiting for him.

"Welcome to Costa Rica, Mr. Davis. I trust

you had a pleasant flight?"

"Yes, thank you," Taylor replied. Pedrano was a small man, but clearly in charge. An aide sat nearby holding a fat portfolio, presumably stuffed with correspondence concerning Western's joint venture.

"I was so glad to hear from my old friend, Prescott," Pedrano said. "I have many fond memories of my years at Princeton."

What now? Taylor wondered. *Do I pick up the ball, or do I wait for him? Is this where I bow and scrape?* "Princeton has a fine reputation, minister."

"What can we do for you, Mr. Davis?"

Might as well plunge right in, Taylor thought. "Senor Pedrano, when we formed our joint venture, the agreement called for repatriation of funds after a two year period. That time has come and gone, and we have not been able to get the approvals necessary to transfer our share of the profits to the States. It has been two additional years now, and as I'm sure you understand, we will not be able to maximize production in your country unless we are allowed to realize a positive cash flow from the venture."

"Yes, I do understand," Pedrano replied. "I also studied finance at Princeton, but you must also realize that things have changed in our country. The presidente inherited a very bad economic situation, with much poverty and runaway inflation. His austerity plan requires the maximum use of capital within our borders."

Taylor could care less about poverty or inflation in Costa Rica. He was thinking about the wolf.

"I understand, sir, but you must see our point of view also. The joint venture is providing hundreds of jobs for your people."

Senor Pedrano turned to his aide and said something in rapid-fire Spanish, waving him from the room. Then he turned to Taylor and very deliberately and calmly stated his case. "There is a way I may be able to help you, Mr. Davis. It will require the sum of twenty thousand dollars."

Taylor was stunned by Pedrano's blatant demand for a bribe. "I'm sorry, senor. I don't think I understand . . ."

"Come, come, Mr. Davis. Surely you realize that the wheels of commerce need to be greased from time to time."

Taylor remembered someone in Dallas using the expression "grease money" in connection with transactions in South America, but he was still surprised by the minister's straightforward demand. He would have to get G. Preston's approval first. "Senor Pedrano, I will need to make the arrangements. What do you require?"

"It's very simple," he said. "Twenty thousand dollars in cash delivered to me by tomorrow noon, and we will make an exception for Western Datacorp due to special circumstances."

There was no pretense, no masquerade. *And why not?* Taylor asked himself. *It's just their way of doing business. If twenty grand will solve our problem, it's a small* price *to pay.* "Senor Pedrano, you are very kind to help. I will make the arrangements and return with the fee tomorrow morning."

As soon as Taylor returned to the hotel, he placed a call to Dallas and after a short wait, Roberts came on the line. "Miss Roberts, this is Taylor Davis calling from San Jose. I need to speak with Mr. Wilson, please."

"He's in a meeting, Mr. Davis. Is it important?"

"Very important. I need his decision on a matter of urgency."

"Very well," she said, irritated by Taylor's insistence that she break into the meeting. "Perhaps I can interrupt him."

The wolf hated to be disturbed in the middle of a meeting, and he was obviously annoyed. "What's going on down there, Taylor? Have you got those people straightened out yet?"

Taylor had no way of knowing who might be in the room with the wolf, and he assumed that he was on the speaker-phone. He needed to play this correctly. "Sir, I think we have a solution in sight, but it's going to require an additional investment of twenty thousand dollars."

The wolf knew exactly what Taylor meant. "Twenty thousand, huh? Are you sure that will do the trick?"

"Yes sir," Taylor replied. "I have Senor Pedrano's personal assurance."

There was slight pause. "All right, Taylor. What do you need?"

"I need twenty thousand wired to the Banco

Nacional this afternoon with instructions to disburse the funds to me in U.S. dollars tomorrow morning."

"That soon," G. Preston said. "The minister doesn't mess around, does he?"

"No sir," Taylor replied.

"All right, I'll take care of it. Don't bother our people there with the details of the transaction . . . understand?"

"Right. I'll handle it personally."

Taylor hung up the phone feeling rather proud of himself. He'd been in Costa Rica two days, and the problem was solved. He called the Banco Nacional to alert them to the transaction, and they treated it as a routine request. The gringo would be in tomorrow morning to pick up twenty thousand in cash wired to him from Dallas—no big deal.

With business taken care of for the day, Taylor put on his swimming trunks and headed out to the pool to escape from the stifling humidity. After swimming several laps in the Olympic-size pool, he plopped down in a chaise lounge to read the new Tom Clancy spy thriller, but he was interrupted when one of the pool attendants called him over to the telephone. It was Janet.

"Sounds like you're really slaving over some hot business deals this afternoon." She sounded cheerful, playful. Her voice evoked feelings that both puzzled and excited him.

"Listen," he said, "I've got business taken care of for the day. What about you?"

"Just thought I'd see if you were serious about

visiting one of our fabulous beaches," she said mysteriously.

"Are you kidding?" Taylor grinned. "Just say where and when."

"Actually, I thought we'd make a day of it. Some friends of mine have a great beach house at Jaco Beach. How about it?"

"Sounds super," he replied. "I've got a slight problem, however. I need to take care of some business at the bank tomorrow morning, and I won't be free until nearly noon."

There was a slight pause. Then Janet suggested an alternative. "It'll take us about four hours to drive over there from San Jose. Why don't we leave after lunch and spend the night? I'm sure my friends won't mind. As a matter of fact, swimming at Jaco Beach is best done by moonlight, I'm told."

Taylor couldn't believe his ears. This gorgeous woman was inviting him to spend the night. "You've got a deal," he agreed. "It sounds romantic, swimming by moon-light."

Ignoring his implication, she said, "I'll pick you up at the hotel at one. Just throw a few things in an overnight bag. We'll be back in San Jose by noon Wednesday."

Taylor didn't see why he should wait a whole day to see her. "How about dinner tonight?"

"Sorry, I'm tied up. I'll see you tomorrow."

"Okay, tomorrow at one."

There was no hassle at the bank. The bank manager ushered him into his private office where twenty thousand dollars was counted out, Taylor signed a receipt, and that was it. Securing the cash in his briefcase, Taylor took a taxi to the minister's office and calmly handed over the money to Senor Pedrano. It was just like buying a ticket for the train.

Senor Pedrano grinned as he quickly verified the amount. "It is a pleasure doing business with you, Mr. Davis."

"Likewise, I'm sure." Taylor was thinking about guarantees. "Excuse me, Senor Pedrano, but what kind of assurances can you give me?"

"Mr. Davis, you have my word as a gentleman."

I deserved that, Taylor thought. *I'm handing over a cash bribe to a corrupt official, and I ask him for a guarantee. He must think I'm incredibly naïve.* "I'm sorry, Senor. Of course, you are right. Thank you again for your help."

Taylor closed his briefcase, shook hands with Senor Pedrano, and went downstairs to call a taxi. Even though the whole transaction had been very businesslike, he couldn't help feeling a twinge of guilt, like he'd been part of something dirty. On the way back to the hotel, he put it out of his mind and focused on the evening ahead.

Janet skillfully maneuvered the LTD through the buses and loaded cattle trucks competing for space on the narrow road leading out of San Jose, and within an hour they were climbing the mountain highway to Puntarenas. She seemed preoccupied.

"Is something wrong?" Taylor asked.

She was surprised, unaware that it had been obvious. "No, nothing's wrong. Why do you ask?"

"You seem preoccupied, so deep in thought."

"I'm sorry," she said. "It's this poor excuse for a highway. I never have liked driving in the mountains, and I guess I was concentrating a little too hard."

"Would you like for me to drive?" he offered.

She laughed. "Are you kidding? I don't trust my own driving in these mountains, much less a novice."

Driving slowly through one of the mountain villages, Janet pulled over and motioned to an old stoop-shouldered man guiding a burro loaded down with firewood.

"Senor, donde esta Alto Rios?"

"Este aldea es Alto Rios," he replied.

Janet waved. "Gracias, senor."

"What was that all about?" Taylor asked, puzzled by her behavior.

"I've heard there's an old dig near Alto Rios," she explained. "I thought this was it, but I wasn't sure."

"Oh . . . old rocks again," he smiled.

She frowned at him, and then they both laughed. Her eyes sparkled when she laughed, and Taylor felt good. About three miles past Alto Rios, they drove around a delivery van parked by the side of the road. Three men were looking under the hood, and Janet flashed her headlights twice as they drove slowly past.

"Why did you flash your lights like that?" Taylor asked.

"The idiots were parked half-way out in the road. I just wanted to make sure they knew I was coming around."

A little farther on, Janet turned into a roadside café and gas station. "I forgot to ask about the key," she explained. "Wait here and I'll see if they have a phone."

"What key?" Taylor replied, puzzled by her behavior. What are you talking about?"

"The key to the beach house. I forgot to ask where they stash the key."

"I'll come with you," Taylor said. "I could use a cup of coffee."

Janet seemed agitated. "No, you stay here with the car. Give these people ten minutes and they'll not only clean out our gear, they'll strip the car as well. I'll bring you a coffee."

As soon as Janet disappeared inside the café, the three men in the delivery van pulled up behind the LTD. One of them got out and walked around to the passenger side, and when Taylor turned toward the open window, he was staring at the business end of a steel blue forty-five.

"Come with me, Yankee," he growled.

There was no time to think; no time to calculate. Taylor instinctively opened the door and stepped out. The man jammed the pistol into his ribs and walked him to the back of the van. The door was pushed open, and Taylor hesitated momentarily.

"Get in, gringo, or you die right here."

Faced with no other choice, Taylor climbed into the back of the van. His mind was reeling. *Is this a joke Janet arranged? Am I being kidnapped? Who are these people?* As the driver headed the van out onto the mountain road, Taylor's mouth was gagged, a makeshift blindfold placed over his eyes, and his hands were secured behind his back with strips of leather.

Janet came out of the café, turned the car around, and headed back toward San Jose.

CHAPTER TEN

They were heading west in the direction of Putarenas, but not in a particular hurry. Taylor was paralyzed with fear, desperately trying to make sense out of his predicament. Surely Janet hadn't arranged this as a joke. It didn't make any sense.

He tried to sort through the options. *A case of mistaken identity? A random kidnapping? A terrorist group? A horrible nightmare? It wasn't a nightmare, at least not the kind you wake up from. It had to be one of the other choices. Janet! She would have returned to the car and missed him within minutes. As soon as she suspected foul play, she'd call the police, or militia, or whatever they had in these mountains, and it would only be a matter of time before they were followed.*

After a little over an hour, they left the highway and were traveling slowly over a twisting, bumpy road. *Probably a dirt road,* he thought. *So many chugholes.*

The van turned into a lane and drove about two miles to an abandoned farmhouse where Taylor was confined to a back room. One of the men removed the blindfold and gag, ordered him to lie down on an old metal bed, and then tied his hands to either side of the bed frame.

"Where are we?" he demanded. "What are you going to do with me? There must be some mistake."

"Silencio!" the man barked.

Taylor was angry. "I am a U.S. citizen, and I demand to know why you are holding me against my will."

The man whirled around and slapped Taylor across the mouth with the back of his hand. "Silencio! Usted es mi preso." Taylor had no idea what he meant, but there was no mistaking his mood. This was no practical joke, and it was no stroll in the park. He could feel a slight trickle of blood at the corner of his mouth. *Better play it cool from now on. Better cooperate,* he thought. *These bozos are for real.*

For the next hour Taylor remained motionless, terrified, his imagination running wild. He forced himself to concentrate on his surroundings. The room contained the ramshackle bed, two wooden chairs, a small table, and a bucket in the corner of the room. A single candle was placed on the table, and the window had been boarded up from the outside. Oddly, they hadn't taken anything from him. He still had his wallet, wristwatch, and passport. Somewhere he had read that tourists ought to keep their passports with them, and he had stashed his in the overnight bag, which the man had thrown in a corner of the room.

Around six o'clock, the man who had forced

him from the car came into the back room. He rummaged through Taylor's overnight bag, retrieved the passport, and sat on the edge of the bed.

"Mr. Davis, I hope you will not give us any trouble," he said in impeccable English. "You will be treated well if you cooperate. If not, we will have no choice but to keep you restrained."

"Who are you?" Taylor demanded. "And why have I been kidnapped?"

"You are a prisoner of the Sendero Luminoso, Mr. Davis. We don't mean to harm you. We only intend to exchange you for some of our comrades."

The Sendero Luminoso. Taylor remembered that phrase from somewhere. Hadn't Senator Harding mention them during their meeting? Some kind of Maoist group operating out of Peru.

"I don't see that I have any choice but to cooperate," Taylor said begrudgingly.

"Very good. A sensible decision."

Taylor was wary of this man. He seemed too smooth, too calculating. "Are you going to keep me tied up like this?" Taylor asked.

The man untied both of Taylor's hands. "No, Mr. Davis. As long as you behave, you will not be restrained." He motioned toward the bucket. "That's for your personal needs, and food will be brought to you from time to time."

Taylor was curious. "Your English is very polished. Where did you learn to speak our language so well?"

"I grew up in Chicago, Mr. Davis. My father

was an immigrant worker in the steel industry, and he ruined his health earning enough money to send me to the University of Chicago where I took my degree. I learned very early to hate the system that exploited my father and others like him."

Taylor fished for more information. "Exploited? I don't understand."

"Come, come, Mr. Davis. You are an educated man. Surely you are aware of the dark side of capitalism and the wealthy class yourself. Tell me, what exactly does Western Datacorp do?"

He knows all about me. Somebody planned this whole thing. Taylor's mind was churning, trying to sort out the implications. "We're in the computer business, " he replied.

"Ah yes, computers. Wonderful devices. We have recently computerized our membership. What a time-saver."

"Glad to hear it," Taylor responded sarcastically. "You wouldn't be using Western computers by any chance?"

The man grinned. "No, I'm afraid not. We use only IBM. Big Blue is number one in our country also."

Taylor probed for more information. "I don't think I caught your name earlier."

He grinned. "I didn't throw it. My men call me El Jefe."

"El Jefe?"

"It means the chief. Even in a Marxist society, we need structure and discipline, Mr. Davis. Now .

. . just a reminder of our rules. You will not speak unless spoken to. You will not attempt to leave this room. You will cooperate with my men at all times. Is that understood?"

"I understand," Taylor said. "There's just one thing. How long will I be kept here?"

"That depends entirely on your government, Mr. Davis. The FBI captured five of our comrades during a drug raid in Miami, and all we ask is that they be returned to us. When that occurs, you will be released."

Taylor turned pale. It was well known that the U.S. adamantly refused to negotiate with terrorists. Hostages taken by the PLO in Beirut had languished in captivity for five, six, and seven years. For the first time during the long afternoon, Taylor realized he was in desperate trouble. "What if they refuse to deal with you?" he asked.

"They will deal, Mr. Davis. The American people will demand it." With that, El Jefe left the room.

Sometime around eight, one of the guards came into the room with a plate of beans and a tin can full of water. Taylor wasn't hungry so he left the beans alone, but he downed the water immediately.

He slept fitfully during the long night. Lying there in the dark, he kept going over the events of the afternoon. It was clear they hadn't picked him at random. Otherwise, how could El Jefe have known he worked for Western? He began to sort out the facts in his mind. *Who knew I was coming to Costa Rica? Senator Harding's office? Ridiculous. Our people?*

Impossible. The embassy, and of course, the hotel had my reservation. It has to be there somewhere. Could the Luminoso have somebody on the embassy staff? No way. It has to be the hotel. Somebody at the hotel gave them my name and date of arrival.

Satisfied that he had narrowed the possibilities to the most obvious source of information, Taylor realized that it meant nothing. So what? He was still their prisoner.

How will they try to make a deal? he wondered. *When?* He thought about Cyndi. *How will she find out about it? Poor girl, the shape she's in, and then discovering that I've been taken hostage by some loony group in the jungles of Costa Rica.*

The next morning, one of the guards brought in another plate of beans, this time with a little rice mixed in, and there was a stale tortilla. No coffee, though, only another tin can of water. "Hey, how about some coffee?" Taylor said. "Comprendo? Coffee?" The guard grinned. It was a stupid grin, and it irritated Taylor. "I thought you people were supposed to have some of the best coffee in the world."

After Taylor finished the beans, he started pacing the room, trying to figure out what to do. There was nothing he could do. He wasn't prepared for this. Wharton hadn't offered classes in how to be a hostage. His expertise at climbing the corporate ladder wasn't worth a plugged nickel in these mountains.

The bucket was stinking up the room. Taylor went over to the door and banged on it. "Hey. I want to talk to somebody." After five minutes of pounding on the door, he heard voices and footsteps, and the guard opened the door brandishing a machete in his hand. Taylor pointed to the bucket and pleaded with him. "Take that thing out of here." Eventually sign language prevailed, and the guard took it outside and emptied it.

Sometime after noon, El Jefe returned to the farmhouse and came into the back room with a Polaroid camera. "Well, Mr. Davis, are you comfortable?"

Taylor wasn't amused. "I don't know where I am or how long I'll be here, I've had nothing but beans to eat, the so-called toilet is stinking up the room, but other than that I'm fine, thank you."

El Jefe laughed uproariously. "I admit the accommodations are not what a man in your position is used to, but I'm afraid it will have to do for a while. If you will smile for the birdie, I'm going to take your picture."

"What for?" Taylor said sarcastically. "Your hostage album?"

"I think you can guess what we intend to use your picture for, Mr. Davis. Your government will want proof of our claim."

"When will they know about it?" Taylor asked, his expression betraying the fear that lay just beneath the surface.

"Oh, it shouldn't be too long," El Jefe replied. "Perhaps by the weekend."

Taylor was due back in Dallas on Friday afternoon. He had planned to attend "Night With The

Stars" with Cyndi, and she wouldn't miss him until then. She would be wondering why he hadn't called, of course, but even if he didn't arrive on Friday, she would assume he had stayed over for some business reason.

Taylor took advantage of El Jefe's ability with English to probe for more information. "Look, El Jefe or whatever your name is, why don't we sit down and talk about a deal. My company will probably pay a ransom for me. You know the U.S. government will never do a hostage exchange."

"Mr. Davis, we're not interested in money. You capitalists think money will solve any problem. It is our comrades we are concerned about. There will be a deal, or else."

A shiver raced down Taylor's spine. "What do you mean, or else?" he asked.

"Your politicians ignore the wishes of the people until the press screams loud enough about an issue; then they respond. You are going to be famous, Mr. Davis. The people will be clamoring for your release . . . according to our terms, naturally."

"I still think we could arrange a ransom," Taylor said weakly.

"No chance," El Jefe insisted. "We want our comrades returned, and the publicity will be good for our cause. It is the only way the people can be shown the truth about their so-called leaders."

El Jefe took four photographs. When he was about to leave the room, he asked Taylor if there was anything he needed.

Better drop the sarcasm, Taylor thought. "Yes, there is, as a matter of fact. I'm dying for a cup of coffee, and isn't there any way I can go outside to . . . you know . . . use the toilet?"

"I'm afraid we can't let you leave the house, but I will instruct my comrades to bring coffee with breakfast. You might as well enjoy our famous coffee while you are our guest." He grinned and then left the room.

Taylor flopped down on the bed and stared at the ceiling. It was fashioned from crude wooden planks cut by hand, and here and there a spider web hung from the wooden surface. He counted the webs. There were eight in all.

What day is it? he wondered. *It's Wednesday. I arrived on Monday, was taken hostage on Tuesday, and today is Wednesday.* As long as Taylor had his watch, there would be no problem knowing the day and time. Time moved slowly in this god-forsaken place.

Cyndi was surrounded by a group of her friends, basking in the warm glow of their congratulations. This year's version of "Night With The Stars" had been a smashing success, and she had reserved Armando's for a party after the show.

Blair came over to offer her congratulations. "Where's Taylor? He hasn't missed your big night, has he?"

"He's been in Costa Rica all week," Cyndi explained. "He was supposed to be in this afternoon, but apparently he was delayed for some reason. He probably left a message on the recorder, but I haven't had time to call in."

"Costa Rica? What on earth for?"

"Business, Blair. It's always business with Taylor."

Just then someone shouted Cyndi's name. "Cyndi, come over here quick." The voice came from the bar where a small group of people were frantically waving for her to come over. She edged her way through the crowd, and by the time she got to the bar, the whole room had gone quiet. Everyone was focused on the television mounted on the wall. Ted Koppel was reading a bulletin at the end of his *Nightline* program.

"This late breaking bulletin has not, I repeat, has not been confirmed by U.S. government officials. To repeat the bulletin once again, ABC has learned that an American businessman from Dallas has been missing from his hotel in San Jose, Costa Rica, since Tuesday. A local group, calling itself the Sendero Luminoso, has informed the AP by telephone that Mr. Taylor Davis, an executive with Western Data-corp in Dallas, has been taken hostage. The Sendero Luminoso, a Maoist guerrilla group operating out of Peru, is demanding the release of five prisoners held in Leavenworth on drug charges. At this hour, we have not been able to confirm the existence of such a group with the State Department."

There was an awkward silence in the room. Cyndi was stunned. "It must be a mistake," she said. "This is impossible. What else did he say? Somebody, please. What else did he say?"

Blair said, "That's all, Cyndi. What you heard at the end was it."

"But this is impossible," Cyndi said, her voice quivering. "Hostages are taken in the Middle East, not in Central America. There has to be a mistake."

Blair put her arm around Cyndi's waist. "Let me take you home. We'll get on the phone and find out what's going on."

The others agreed. Armando's was buzzing with talk of what had happened. The story was being retold around the room, each with a different portion emphasized or embellished. Cyndi just stood there, not knowing what to do next.

"Come on, Cyndi. We'll get to the bottom of this." Blair was insistent. "Better let me drive, honey. I'll get someone to drive my car home." Cyndi was limp, unfeeling, as she obediently handed over her keys.

At the apartment, Blair made a couple of drinks while Cyndi sat on the couch, repeating over and over, "I don't understand. There must be a mistake."

"Cyndi, we've got to think," Blair said. "We've got to figure out what to do. Why don't you call the AP in Washington and get the whole story?"

"You're right," Cyndi agreed. "We can't do anything until we know exactly what happened. I'd better check the recorder first."

There were no messages from Taylor. "I thought it was kind of odd that he hadn't called since he left. He always calls when he's away on business."

Cyndi got the number for the Associated Press from her address book. After working her way through the receptionist and a couple of flunkies on the night shift, she finally got the news desk.

" This is AP Washington," a voice said. "How can I help you?"

"This is Cyndi . . . I mean Mrs. Taylor Davis. I just heard about the kidnapping in Costa Rica, and I was hoping you could tell me exactly what happened."

"Did you say Mrs. Taylor Davis? Are you his wife?"

Cyndi was impatient. "Of course, I'm his wife. Now what is going on down there?"

"I'm terribly sorry, Mrs. Davis. All I can do is read the dispatch to you."

"That's fine," Cyndi replied. "Please hurry."

The wire report was exactly as Ted had reported, except for a little more detail on the Luminoso and their involvement in the drug cartel operating in South America. Their demand was clear-cut. Taylor would be released in exchange for the five Luminoso members presently held in the federal prison at Leavenworth.

"Is that all you have?" Cyndi pleaded. She yearned for any scrap of information that might make sense out of this nightmare.

"I'm afraid so, Mrs. Davis. I'm terribly sorry."

"Thank you," Cyndi said. "I appreciate your help."

No sooner had she hung up the phone when

she began to get calls from friends who wondered if she had heard the news. Cyndi patiently told each caller that yes, she had heard and no, she didn't know any more than what had been reported. After a half-hour she stopped taking calls, but left the recorder on in case Taylor called.

At half-past twelve, the caller identified himself as Agent Robeson from the Dallas FBI office. Cyndi hurriedly picked up the receiver and identified herself.

"Mrs. Davis, I assume you have heard the news report about your husband."

"Yes, I've heard it," she replied. "Can you tell me what's going on?"

"We've contacted the embassy in San Jose, and they know nothing about it. According to our information, the AP office in San Jose received a hand-delivered package containing two Polaroid snapshots of your husband, or at least we assume it's your husband, and a note demanding the release of five of their men from one of our federal prisons. I don't suppose you have heard from Mr. Davis?"

"No, I haven't heard from him since he left last Monday. He called from Houston just before his flight left, but nothing since then."

The agent paused, taking notes as they talked. "Does he usually keep in touch when he's away on business?"

"Yes," Cyndi said. "Almost every night. It's very unusual for him not to call."

"I see," the agent said. "We've checked with

his hotel and they say he never checked out. Nobody has seen him since Tuesday, and his bed apparently hasn't been slept in since then. Until we have information to the contrary, I'm afraid we'll have to assume foul play."

Cyndi was on the verge of tears. "You aren't suggesting . . . ?"

"Mrs. Davis, we're in no position to suggest anything except what we know. Your husband is missing, and this Luminoso group claims they have taken him hostage. The AP is faxing the photograph of your husband tonight. Would it be all right if we come by first thing in the morning for a positive identification?"

"Yes, of course," Cyndi said. "Do you have my address?"

"Ten-o-seven Turtle Creek, number five?"

"That's correct."

"Thank you for your help, Mrs. Davis. I'll be out around eight."

Cyndi hung up the phone and stared at Blair. "They have his photograph. They took his picture, Blair. It must be true." Cyndi began to weep.

Blair sat next to her and held her tightly. "It's going to be all right, honey. The government will get him out, I just know they will. It'll be all right."

Taylor had developed a bad case of diarrhea. It had started on Thursday, and Saturday he was wasted and weak. He hadn't been able to eat anything for a couple of days, and the guards ignored his complaints. El Jefe had been gone since Wednesday, and

Taylor was unable to convince the two goons that he needed some medicine. Personal hygiene was a dim memory. There was no water, no soap, and no change of clothes except for one pair of shorts and a shirt he had packed in the overnight bag. There was the shaving kit and toothbrush he had packed, but they were useless without water. He was lying on the bed, staring at the ceiling and feeling sorry for himself. For the first time in a long time, Taylor began to weep.

This isn't fair, he whined. *Why should this happen to me? I haven't done anything to deserve this. If there is a God, why would He let this happen to me?* Taylor hadn't thought about God in years. Maybe he should pray. But what would he say, and how would he know anybody was listening? "God, please help me," he whispered.

He thought about Cyndi. Did she know by now? Surely, she did. El Jefe had implied that something would happen by the weekend. Cyndi would have called the hotel when he didn't show up last night. But what could they tell her? That he hadn't checked out yet? Maybe she would call the embassy. Janet would have reported his disappearance on Tuesday. By now there would be swarms of CIA or FBI looking for him. It was just a matter of time.

Blair had insisted that Cyndi get some sleep but she hadn't slept, and when Blair checked on her around seven, Cyndi was just stepping out of the shower.

"Cyndi, there's a mob scene outside. All three

networks and both stations in Dallas are here, not to mention the newspapers. What shall I tell them?"

"Great," Cyndi said. "That's all I need. Can't you just ask them to please leave?"

"I tried, but you know how they are. You'll have to give them some kind of statement."

"All right," Cyndi replied, exasperated. "Just give me a minute to get my act together."

When she stepped outside a half hour later, the crowd began to push and shove and shout. "Mrs. Davis, have you heard from your husband?"

"Can you tell us what happened?"

"How do you feel, Mrs. Davis."

"Ladies and gentlemen, I know you have stories to write and deadlines to meet. I'm going to make a statement, and then I will ask you to please leave. I first heard about my husband's disappearance on *Nightline,* and when I called the AP in Washington, they confirmed basically what Koppel had reported. I talked with an FBI agent last night, and he said the terrorists had included a photograph of Taylor with their demand note. The hotel in San Jose says Taylor never checked out of his room. That's all I know at this point. Now I would appreciate it if you will leave me alone."

Cyndi's statement only generated more questions. "Can you tell us what your husband was doing in Costa Rica?" someone shouted.

"He was there on business," Cyndi replied.

"What kind of business? What company does he work for?"

"Taylor is chief financial officer for Western Datacorp," Cyndi replied.

"Does your husband have any connection with the CIA or the State Depart-ment?"

"Of course not," Cyndi said impatiently. "That's ridiculous."

"Mrs. Davis, what are your plans now?"

Cyndi paused to think for a moment. "I don't know, to tell you the truth. I guess I'll get in touch with somebody in Washington and try to find out what they're doing to get Taylor released."

There was more clamoring for answers that she didn't have, more pushing and shoving. Just then, a man in a dark suit pushed his way through the crowd of reporters and introduced himself to Cyndi as agent Frank Robeson with the FBI. "Can we go inside for a moment, Mrs. Davis?"

She let him in the apartment amid more clamoring and shouting from the news people, although a few of them rushed off to meet deadlines.

Robeson showed Cyndi his identification and then produced the photograph. "Is this your husband, Mrs. Davis?"

Cyndi stared at the photograph, trying to discern something about Taylor's surroundings. She could see that he was seated on a metal bed, but that was all.

"Yes, it's Taylor."

He returned the photograph to the folder he was carrying and said, "Thank you, Mrs. Davis. We won't trouble you any further."

"Wait a minute," she said. "You can't just leave without telling me what's going on. What are you people doing to get Taylor released?"

"Mrs. Davis, kidnapping on foreign soil is not in our jurisdiction. We have only been asked to make the identification."

Cyndi was confused and angry. "Well, who is responsible?" she demanded.

Robeson looked puzzled, as if Cyndi had breached some rule by asking for information outside his area of responsibility. It was the look you get from clerks at city hall who act put upon when you ask for information about some other department.

"I don't know," he replied. "I suppose the State Department handles these situations."

"I see," Cyndi said. "Thank you, Mr. Robeson. If you do receive any new information, I would appreciate a call."

Cyndi showed him to the door, and the throng of news people surged forward to discover who this man was and what he knew about the kidnapping in Central America.

Late in the afternoon on Saturday, Taylor heard the van drive up outside the farmhouse. He recognized El Jefe's voice. There was a lot of commotion outside. The door to the back room opened. El Jefe and one of the goons pushed a young man into the room, gagged and blindfolded just as he had been.

El Jefe was pleased with himself. "Mr. Davis, we have brought you some company." They untied him and removed the blindfold and gag, then left them alone in the room.

At first they just stared at each other. He was young, perhaps twenty or twenty-one, and he was muscular and well-built, like a running back.

"Hi," he said weakly. "My name is Jeff Richards."

Taylor lifted himself off the bed and stood rather unsteadily to shake hands with his new roommate. "I'm Taylor Davis. I assume you've also been brought here against your will?"

"It looks like it," Jeff said. "I've been working with a medical team outside Alajuela, and when I rode my bike into town for some supplies, this van came along. The next thing I knew, I had been taken captive.

El Jefe returned to the back room with Jeff's knapsack. "Here are your things, Mr. Richards. I will let Mr. Davis explain our rules to you. He has been a model guest, and I trust that you will not spoil our record." El Jefe raised the Polaroid into position. "Now, Mr. Richard, if you will look this way, I will capture this moment for posterity."

Before Jeff could react, El Jefe had taken two snapshots and left the room. Taylor told him how he had been taken from outside the café and how long he had been there at the farm house. When he mentioned his diarrhea, Jeff reached into his knapsack and handed Taylor a bottle of pills.

"Take one of these; it'll help."

Taylor gratefully swallowed one of the pills without any water. "You look a little young to be a doctor, Jeff."

"I'm not a doctor," Jeff replied. "I just work with a group of medical missionaries."

Taylor was curious. "Really? What kind of work?"

"Grunt work, mostly. You know . . . odd jobs, cleaning up, whatever they need."

Taylor was mystified. Why would anybody choose to do charity work in these backwater mountains? "Are you a missionary?" he asked.

Jeff laughed. "No, not really. I just decided to take my summer break working with Agape Missions, and they assigned me to Costa Rica."

"Agape?" Taylor had never heard of it. "Is that some kind of denomination?"

"It's Greek for love," Jeff explained. "Actually, it means unconditional love. You've never heard of it?"

"No, I haven't."

" Anyhow," Jeff continued, "I thought it would be interesting to spend the summer doing volunteer work before I finish my work at Stanford."

Stanford. Taylor knew Jeff's name sounded familiar. "You're the Jeff Richards that plays tailback at Stanford?"

"That's me," Jeff smiled. "Are you a football fan?"

"Sure," Taylor replied, "although I mostly keep up with the Southwest Conference since I've lived in Dallas. And, of course, the Cowboys. Well, I'll be. Fancy meeting you here, Jeff. I'm sorry you got into this mess, but I can't say I don't appreciate having somebody to talk to."

They spent the rest of the evening comparing notes and talking about their situation. Taylor briefed him on the routine, the food, and the two goons who were guarding them. They indulged in endless speculation about what might happen next, talked about the possibility of escape, and wondered what was being done back home to gain their release

Finally Jeff said, "Well, at least we know God isn't panicked by our situation."

Taylor looked up, wondering what Jeff meant, but decided not to pursue it.

CHAPTER ELEVEN

Cyndi stayed home from work on Monday and Tuesday. The press staked out the apartment until the story about Jeff broke, and then left her alone except for occasional phone calls. The Luminoso had repeated their demand for an exchange, the two hostages for their five Luminoso brothers at Leavenworth, but this time they set a two week dead-line.

When Cyndi heard about the deadline, a deep sense of foreboding settled over her. The networks showed a clip of the State Department spokesperson reading a prepared statement, and it left her feeling weak and angry. It was a carefully crafted series of paragraphs designed to make it appear that they were bringing the full force of the government to bear on the case, but it in fact said nothing.

By Wednesday, she couldn't stand being cooped up in the apartment any longer, so she returned to work. A telephone message from the bank's attorney was waiting on her desk. Cyndi returned the call immediately, hoping for a break, something new, or anything.

"This is Cyndi Davis returning Mr. Connally's call."

"One moment, please," the receptionist droned.

Howard Connally was a senior partner in the bank's law firm. After asking how she was holding up under the strain, he said, "Mrs. Davis, the bank has instructed us to do whatever we can to assist you in this trying situation. We've been in touch with the State Department, and I have some information that you might find helpful."

Cyndi's heart was beating faster. "Thank you. I would appreciate anything you can tell me."

"I talked with the undersecretary for Latin American Affairs, and he gave me some information about the Sendero Luminoso. They're primarily a drug-running operation, and State believes they're tied in with the Colombian cartel, but they also have a political agenda. They claim to represent the peasants in Peru and have recently spread their operations to Costa Rica. To our knowledge, this is the first time they have taken U.S. citizens hostage, so there's no way to predict their next move with any certainty."

The attorney's information wasn't making Cyndi feel any better. "What about their demands?" she pleaded. "Did the undersecretary say anything about a making a deal?"

"I'm afraid not," he said matter-of-factly. "The administration refuses to negotiate with terrorists, as you know, but he did say the CIA is working their sources to see what they can dig up. Nobody knows for sure where they're being held. We assume they are still in Costa Rica, but they could be anywhere between Mexico and Peru by now."

"Wonderful," Cyndi said sarcastically. "State knows nothing, the CIA knows nothing, and we know nothing. For all I know, Taylor could be dead by now." Cyndi felt helpless and defeated.

"I'm sorry, Mrs. Davis. This must be a terrible ordeal for you. Please contact us if we can be of any help . . . any help at all. I promise to call you the minute we know anything."

Cyndi was ashamed of herself. The man was trying to help her. "Mr. Connally, I really appreciate everything you've done. It was good of you to go to the trouble."

"Think nothing of it," he said. "Always glad to be of service."

Howard Connally hung up the phone and keyed the appropriate billing classification into the firm's client services system. The telephone system was integrated with a computer, which automatically kept track of time the firm's lawyers spent talking with clients, and all he had to do was key in the code that determined the billing rate. The display indicated he had been on the phone with Cyndi for three billable units—a minute and a half.

Connally muttered to himself as he keyed in the code. "Let's see, high-level government sourcing, that's code twelve. Five hundred dollars flat."

Cyndi was working on the stack of thank-you letters she always sent out the week after "Night With

The Stars" when she was interrupted by a familiar voice. It was Sharon.

"I don't want to disturb you," she said, "but I tried to call several times during the weekend and kept getting a busy signal. It must have been a zoo, huh?"

Cyndi felt comfortable with Sharon. Although she had never really had a close girlfriend growing up, she had always wanted to, and Sharon made her feel like it was possible.

"It was a zoo, all right," Cyndi replied. "Reporters on my doorstep, network people on the phone, everyone crazy for information when there was no information, asking the same questions over and over. It was awful, to tell you the truth."

"I'm really sorry about Taylor," Sharon said. "Are you holding up okay?"

"I guess so. How do you ever know how you will handle something like this? It's so unexpected, so . . . unpredictable."

"I know," Sharon said. "You read about hostages and watch it on the news, but when it happens to someone you know, it doesn't seem real."

Cyndi appreciated the chance to talk. "Would you like a cup of coffee?" she asked, hopeful that she could stay for a while.

"Sure. I don't have anything pressing."

Cyndi buzzed her secretary and asked her to bring in two coffees. "And Ceil, please hold my calls, okay?"

Sharon asked Cyndi if she knew anything other

than what had been reported on the news.

"Not really," Cyndi replied. "I just heard from the bank's attorney. He talked with somebody at the State Department, but all he could do was give me some information about the terrorists."

"Who are they?" Sharon asked. "What would they want with Taylor?"

Cyndi tried to explain. "They're part of the Colombian drug cartel, but they also claim to be some kind of liberation movement. Apparently they just picked Taylor at random. It's incredible. You're doing a routine business deal one minute, and the next minute you're a hostage."

"What about the FBI?" Sharon asked. "Have you heard from them?"

"An agent came out Saturday morning to have me identify Taylor's photograph, but he said they have nothing to do with crimes in other countries."

"What about the CIA?" Sharon asked. "Don't they get involved in these things.?"

"Who knows?" Cyndi replied. "If they are, they're keeping it pretty quiet."

Sharon was quiet for a moment, thinking about an old hurt she thought she had put to rest. "Reminds me of the MIA situation after Vietnam," she said pensively. "Thousands of men were never accounted for, and the government still classifies them as missing in action, even after all these years. My sister's husband was an MIA."

"Really?" Cyndi said, surprised by the revelation. "I didn't know that. I'm terribly sorry." Cyndi felt stupid. How could she have known; she hardly knew Sharon.

"It's a terrible thing," Sharon said. "Bonnie can't get her pension because they won't declare him officially dead. She has written hundreds, thousands of letters to the Pentagon, the State Department, the president, and every senator and congressman she can think of, all to no avail. Sometimes the government can be really stupid."

They sat quietly for a moment, then a tear began to work its way down Sharon's cheek. "Poor Bonnie. The worst part is not knowing for sure after all these years. Maybe they are still holding prisoners. Maybe he has amnesia somewhere. She can never put it to rest."

Cyndi reached over and took her hand. "I'm terribly sorry. It must be awful."

Sharon sat up straight on the couch. "I'm sorry, talking about my brother-in-law when you've got this terrible situation facing you. I don't know what got into me."

"Don't apologize," Cyndi said. "I'm glad you told me. It helps put my problem in perspective to hear about someone else."

"I guess you're right. Thanks for understanding." Sharon finished her coffee and placed the empty cup on Cyndi's desk. "What are you going to do now?"

"There isn't anything I can do. Staying home nearly drove me crazy. I guess I'll try to get some work done."

As Sharon was leaving, she had a thought. "Cyndi, do you remember the Friday morning group I told you about?"

"Yes, I think so," Cyndi replied. "You're talking about the group that meets here at the bank for Bible study or something?"

Sharon said, "I'd like to add your name to our prayer list if you don't mind."

Never in Cyndi's life had anyone asked if they could pray for her. It felt odd. She'd never thought of prayer in a personal sense, except for vague recollections of a childhood prayer at bedtime. "Now I lay me down to sleep . . ." it came back to her now. Funny how long-forgotten memories pop up as fresh as if they had just happened. She remembered that the prayer had a line in it that frightened her. "If I should die before I wake, I pray the Lord my soul to take." When she realized she was talking about dying, she wouldn't say it and her mother had just shrugged her shoulders and told her to go to sleep.

'If I should die before I wake.' In a sense, that's what happened to my baby. He never had a chance to wake up at all. Cyndi wondered, *Do unborn babies have souls? Or do they receive their souls at birth? If he already had a soul, where would he be now? Surely in heaven. Will I meet him some day? Will he remember what I did to him?*

The feeling of despair, which had been her companion since the abortion, covered her like a storm cloud which suddenly appears in the east and blots out the sun. *Oh God, I've got to stop thinking like this.*

"Cyndi?" Sharon was standing at the door, waiting for her response. "Are you all right?"

"I'm fine. I was just thinking about someone."

"You poor dear, you must miss him terribly."

"Yes, I do." Cyndi knew Sharon was talking about Taylor, and she did miss him, of course. But in truth she was thinking about him, or her. Her baby. Their baby. How could she miss him? She never got a chance to know him. "I'm sorry, Sharon. What were you saying?"

"About the prayer list."

"Of course. I'd be flattered to have my name on your prayer list. There certainly isn't much else we can do. Maybe a prayer or two will help."

Sharon had a sudden idea. "Would you like to go with me Friday morning?"

"You mean to the prayer group?"

"Uh huh. Maybe we could sort of function as your support group during this crisis."

Cyndi hadn't thought of herself as needing support until the last couple of months. She had always been strong, determined, self-reliant. One of her father's favorite expressions had been, "Nobody else can do it as good as you can, Cyndi." But her father had never been in this situation, either.

"Thanks for asking," she replied. "I'll think about it."

"Okay," Sharon said cheerfully. "I'll call you tomorrow afternoon. Is there anything else you need?"

"I don't think so. All I can do is wait for something to happen."

Wednesday and Thursday kind of ran together, like a dream that is so vivid and then disappears the minute you wake up. Cyndi spent both days at the office, appearing to function normally, but she was going through the motions, acting on instinct.

When Sharon called on Thursday, Cyndi figured she had nothing to lose, so she agreed to go to the prayer group the next morning. There was no point hanging around the television since the story had disappeared from the network news. It was as if it had never happened.

The Friday group met in a conference room on the third floor of the bank. Someone had brought coffee from the break room, and there was a box of donuts and sweet rolls on the end table. Cyndi didn't recognize anyone except Jim Peterson, although several people seemed to know her.

Jim opened his briefcase, took out a stack of small booklets, spread them around the conference table, and called the group to order. They were obviously enjoying the informal conversation and seemed reluctant to bring it to a conclusion, but soon took their places around the conference table. Jim was clearly a leader, but there was a softness, a winsomeness about him.

"Before we get started," he said, "I want to welcome Cyndi Davis this morning. Sharon invited her, and I'd just like to say that we're glad you joined us, Cyndi. Obviously, we all know about the terrible strain you've been under this past week, and I want you to know we've been praying for you, and especially for Taylor."

Cyndi wasn't sure he really meant it, but it was comforting to hear that she wasn't alone. "Thanks," she replied. "I appreciate it."

Jim directed their attention to the booklets he had spread around the table. "Before we spend a few moments in prayer, let's continue our discussion in the book of Romans. If you will turn to page twenty-two, I want us to think about the first few verses of chapter eight."

Cyndi picked up the booklet and looked at the cover. It was called "God's Road to Life . . . The New Testament Book of Romans."

Jim read aloud. "There is therefore now no condemnation to them which are in Christ Jesus, who walk not after the flesh, but after the Spirit." He looked up at them and asked, "What do you think he means by condemnation?"

There was a moment of silence, then one of the men said, "To condemn means to criticize or denounce."

Sharon said, "It's like a sentence in court. You know, the jury finds the defendant guilty of murder and he's condemned to die in the electric chair."

One of the men saw an opportunity for some good-natured ribbing and said, "Why does it always have to be a he? Why couldn't it be a she-murderer?" They all laughed, and Cyndi was surprised to see how loose they were. She had always thought religious people were stiff-necked and humorless.

Jim steered them back to the question. "Those are good comments. Does anybody else want to take a crack at it?"

Someone said, "I think it just means guilty. There is therefore now no guilt for those who are in Christ Jesus."

"That's a good way to put it," Jim said, "but I think we need to define what we mean by guilt." This comment set off a lively discussion about false guilt, guilt feelings, and the concept of legal guilt. It reminded Cyndi of Sharon's comment at the Adolphus that day at lunch, about true guilt being the result of breaking God's law. It also made her feel uneasy because of the guilt feeling she had suffered since the abortion.

After a few minutes, Jim brought the discussion back to the verse. "I think the closest we've come to a definition of the guilt in view here is the talk about legal guilt, the result of breaking the law. The Bible speaks of man as a transgressor, which means that when he breaks God's law, he becomes a lawbreaker from God's point of view. And it's important to understand that from God's point of view, lawlessness isn't a relative matter."

Someone asked, "What do you mean, Jim?"

"We think of crime in a relative sense," he answered. "In our mind, someone who breaks the speed limit isn't as bad as a thief. We divide crimes up between misdemeanors and felonies, and we believe a thief deserves harsher punishment than a speeder. From God's perspective, though, the issue is couched in more cosmic terms. God is holy and perfect and he created a perfect universe, but he gave his man-creation the right to choose lawlessness, or imperfection if I can put it in those terms."

"Adam and Eve chose to disobey God's law, and the result according to the Bible was estrangement between God and his man-creation. Because of their rebellion, all of their descendants were born with dead spirits, and mankind has been unable to relate to God the way it was intended. Disobedience is the crime, and the amount or relative character of the disobedience isn't the issue."

One of the girls from teller operations interrupted him. "Jim, this is getting a little heavy. Can you make it a little more simple?"

"All right," Jim said. "Let me see. If an unsigned check shows up in operations, what do you do with it?"

"We return it," she replied. "No signature, no pay."

Jim had used an illustration that would make sense to any banker. "Does it matter how much the check is for?" he asked.

"No," the teller replied.

"So as far as the bank is concerned, an unsigned check for a penny is just as bad as one for a million?"

The questioner's face lit up. "I see what you mean. As long as the rule is broken, it doesn't matter how bad it was broken. Is that what you're saying?"

"Exactly. God gave Adam and Eve everything they needed for a complete and full life. But since he wanted them to return his love, he had to give them the option not to love him; otherwise, their affection would be meaningless. He gave them one simple rule by which they could demonstrate that they loved and respected him as their Creator God. They were not to eat the fruit of one particular tree."

"Of course, you know what happened. They chose to disobey God, and that choice destroyed their relationship with him, literally killed it. The Bible says the minute they turned their backs on God, they died spiritually and then passed on dead spirits to their descendants after them." Jim smiled. "But the good news is that God didn't walk away and leave man in his estranged condition. He provided a way back."

Cyndi's mind was racing ninety miles an hour. She'd never heard the Adam and Eve story explained like this, and she was captivated by Jim's explanation. Before she realized what she was doing, she blurted out, "What is it?"

"It's right here in the verse, Cyndi," Jim said. "Let's look at it again, shall we? There is no condemnation, or legal guilt from God's point of view, to them which are in Christ Jesus. That's the good news."

Cyndi was confused. "But isn't there a little bit of God in all of us? I guess I don't understand how we can be in Him, or in Christ as it says."

Jim appreciated her question. "There is a little

of God in all of us in the sense that we are created in God's image. That means we are spirit-beings as well as physical. According to the Bible, we are not the same as plants and animals, merely a higher form of life, but we have a spiritual nature that was created so that we might know God. That's where Adam and Eve blew it. Because of their deliberate rebellion, they lost their innocence and became rebels. As rebels they could only produce rebels, and they passed on a rebellious, or sin nature to the entire human race."

Someone interrupted. "What exactly does that mean, Jim? A sin nature?"

"It's the same as a dead spirit," Jim explained. "It means an inborn tendency to sin. Put a group of small children in a room together, and you will see what I mean. You don't have to teach them to be selfish. They are naturally selfish. They have a selfish nature. Do you see what I mean.?"

Nobody took issue with his illustration, so he continued. "What this scripture is talking about is God's plan of redemption. When we turned our backs on God, he didn't turn his back on us. Because he loves us so much, he designed a way that things could be made right again. Maybe I could describe it this way. Our first parents kicked God out of their lives in the Garden of Eden, and men and women have been doing the same ever since. So God made a way that we could invite him back into our lives, even though we don't deserve it."

Cyndi was fascinated. She had never heard

anything like this in her entire life, and had always thought of religion as a system of rules and rituals. The way Jim talked about the Bible, about God, and about man sounded logical. What he said about God's love especially caught her attention. She had never considered the possibility of a love relationship with God. He seemed too remote, too far off.

Jim continued. "Turn back to page nineteen in your booklets. Do you see verse twenty-three just above chapter seven? 'For the wages of sin is death; but the gift of God is eternal life through Jesus Christ our Lord.' Death there doesn't mean physical death; it means spiritual death, or separation from God. If you can remember a time when something happened between you and someone you loved that absolutely destroyed your relationship, and then multiply that by a million or so, that's what this death or separation means."

Cyndi thought about her forced separation from Taylor, a separation they hadn't chosen. It did feel like a kind of death.

Jim continued. "But look what it says. The gift of God is eternal life through Jesus Christ. So God's plan was to make a way that we could invite him back into our lives by accepting His gift. We receive God's gift of eternal life by receiving Jesus Christ as Savior. When that happens, the Bible says that God declares us not guilty, and from then on we are in Christ. When God looks at us after that, He doesn't see lawbreak-ers or sinners, He sees men and women He has declared okay because we are in Christ."

One of the men interrupted. "So that's why it says there is no condemnation for those who are in Christ."

"Exactly." Jim checked his watch. "This has been a very stimulating discussion, but we're about to run out of time. Let's stop there and pick it up again next Friday."

Cyndi wished they could continue. She had expected them to be a group of religious fanatics or weirdoes, but they were people just like herself.

Jim took up the booklets, then directed their attention toward the prayer time. "I thought we'd do this a little different today, if it's okay with Cyndi. Normally, we take several prayer requests, but Taylor and Cyndi's situation is so critical, I thought we'd concentrate all of the prayer time on them. Would that be okay, Cyndi?"

"Yes, of course," Cyndi replied, embarrassed but grateful for the group's interest.

"All right. We'll just have a time of prayer, each one talking to God about Taylor and Cyndi. If you want to pray out loud, it'll be okay, and in a moment I'll close out. Why don't we join hands around the table?"

It was quiet at first. Nobody moved or said anything. Cyndi was feeling a little uncomfortable; then someone began to pray.

"Father, thank you for bringing Cyndi to our group this morning. I know you love her, and I ask you to give her comfort and peace in this difficult time. Amen."

Someone else prayed, "Dear Lord, you are ruler of the universe. You know what's going on in Costa Rica as well as Dallas, and I ask you to send your ministering angels to protect Taylor. Thank you, Lord."

Cyndi was amazed and confused at the same time. Could a person ask God to send angels wherever they wished? She'd never heard of such a thing.

Sharon prayed, "Dear Jesus, will you be a special companion to Cyndi during this time? I know you love her. You proved it by dying on the cross for her, and for all of us in this room. So, Lord, I ask you to be very real to Cyndi today. Amen."

After Jim prayed, several people in the group came around and said something to Cyndi; how glad they were that she had come with Sharon, or how they would be praying for Taylor. The love and concern she sensed in their comments was touching. Nothing like this had ever happened to Cyndi, and she didn't know how to respond. She just kept saying, "Thank you."

On the way out she told Jim how much she had enjoyed the discussion, and how she would like to talk with him some time. "I have to admit I really didn't follow everything you were saying, Jim. I'm not into religion very much, and some of it was a little over my head."

"Sure, Cyndi. I'd love to. Maybe Marge and I could have you out some night."

"That would be fun," Cyndi said. "I'd like that."

Sharon and Cyndi were alone on the elevator, and when they got to Sharon's floor, Cyndi took her hand. "Sharon, I really appreciated your prayer. Thanks for inviting me."

"I'm glad you came," Sharon smiled. "We don't have the solution to all the problems of the world, but it sure does help to have someone who shares your burden."

"I know," Cyndi replied, tears welling up in her eyes. "Thanks again."

CHAPTER TWELVE

It had been a week since they brought Jeff to the farmhouse, and nearly two weeks since Taylor had been taken. The guards had relaxed their rules and taken them to a creek where they could bathe and wash their clothes.

There was a rock ledge overhanging the creek, and Taylor and Jeff sat on the ledge to wait for their clothes to dry while the guards watched them from the opposite bank. One had the assault rifle cradled in his arm, and the other had the forty-five. By this time, they were certain the guards could not understand English, so they talked freely.

Jeff playfully constructed an imaginary escape plan. "What do you think they'd do if we just started running up the hillside on this side of the creek?"

"Are you kidding?" Taylor said. "The one with the AK-47 would cut us down before we made three steps."

"Yeah, but what if we really put some moves on them?" Jeff grinned. "You know, like I did in the UCLA game last year."

Taylor was unconvinced. "Go ahead, Mr. All-American. But if you fail to score, instead of the ball going over on downs, you suit up for the pearly gates."

"That wouldn't be such a disaster," Jeff said pensively. "Sometimes I look forward to going home."

"Me too," Taylor said. "But I'm not talking about going home; I'm talking about buying the farm. Pushing up daisies. Deadsville."

Jeff realized he had been misunderstood. "I know what you mean," he said. "I was talking about heaven."

"You really believe there's such a place?"

"Sure, don't you?"

Taylor picked up a small rock and threw it into the creek, forming an answer in his mind. Heaven was an abstraction to Taylor, a fantasy place. Tiny pink angels flitting to and fro among cotton candy clouds. "I've never really thought about it much, to be honest. Religion always seemed like a cop-out to me, like living in a fantasy world. I believe in what I can see and feel. Show me a Polaroid of heaven and I'll believe in it."

"I can't show you a Polaroid," Jeff replied, "but I can show you a picture of it."

Taylor thought he was making a joke. "Really? With Saint Peter posing at the pearly gates, I suppose."

"I'm serious. When we get back to the farm-house, I'll show you." Jeff was talking about his

Bible. The guards had let him keep his knapsack, and he had spent a lot of his time reading from a paperback New Testament. A couple of times Taylor had started to ask him what he found so fascinating about it, but then decided to leave well enough alone. Anybody who would spend his summer vacation doing charity work in these mountains had to be a little weird, and the less he knew about Jeff's idiosyncrasies the better.

Taylor changed the subject. "Jeff, what do you think is going on? I mean, do you think they've contacted the government by now?"

"I don't know," Jeff said. "I've been thinking all week about the hostages in Lebanon. Some of those men have been there five years or more."

"That's a happy thought. Somehow, I don't believe El Jefe is willing to wait that long."

"Why do you say that?" Jeff asked.

Taylor had been trying to fit the pieces together ever since he was brought to the farmhouse. "This is different from the Middle East," he explained. "First, Costa Rica is a democracy and friendly with the U.S. In Lebanon, nobody knows who's in charge from one day to the next, and we certainly can't call them friends. Second, in spite of El Jefe's revolutionary rhetoric, I have a hunch it's primarily a drug operation."

"So?" Jeff wasn't tracking with him.

"So . . . they're not loony like the Hezbollah or the other PLO groups. When the government refuses to deal, El Jefe will fall back to a ransom position to salvage something from the operation."

Jeff was still puzzled, although fascinated by Taylor's theory. "I still don't see the difference in our situation."

Taylor explained, "Western will be willing to cut a deal where the government isn't. We even have a provision for this sort of thing in our insurance coverage."

"You're kidding," Jeff replied.

"No . . . I'm not kidding," Taylor said. "Up to five million for corporate officers, of which happily, I am one."

Jeff let out a low whistle. "That's amazing. I've never heard of such a thing."

Taylor remembered how surprised he'd been when he found out about it. "It's not widely known for obvious reasons," he explained. "Not ever within the company."

"I don't know what in the world they thought they could get for me," Jeff said. "My dad drives a bus in San Diego. I wouldn't even be in college if it weren't for football."

Taylor was embarrassed that he had completely ignored Jeff with his analysis. "I don't think you need to worry. They wouldn't have any reason to keep you. Besides, our people will insist that they release us both."

Jeff smiled. "Oh, I'm not worried. My fate is not in the hands of these guys. God isn't unaware of my situation, and He's still in control of the universe, the last I heard."

Taylor decided not to pursue that. It just confirmed his cop-out theory. *Poor sucker*, he thought. *He really believes that stuff.*

The guards stood up and motioned for them to gather their things and head back up to the farmhouse. Reluctantly, they obeyed. Being confined in the back room did not compare favorably with spending time at the creek, just being out of doors and washing in the creek made them feel human again. Their prison seemed even worse after spending a couple of hours outside.

As soon as they were back in the farmhouse, Jeff got his New Testament, dog-eared a page near the end, and handed it to Taylor. "Read chapter twenty-one and you'll see what I was talking about. It's a picture of heaven."

Taylor took the book and looked down at the page. The chapter heading was "The New Jerusalem." It was confusing and strange to his ears, but it wasn't gibberish. It talked about God, angels, and future events. It said the first earth would pass away, a city called the New Jerusalem would come down out of heaven, and God would dwell with men. It said there would be no more tears, death, or pain. Everything would be new. It described the New Jerusalem as being brilliantly constructed from gold and precious jewels. It mentioned a spring called the water of life, and said that whoever was thirsty would be given this water without cost. It also talked about a Lamb, and it said that no impure person would enter the city, but only those whose names were written in the Lamb's book of life. Taylor looked up at Jeff.

"Didn't I tell you?" Jeff said. "Isn't that a picture of heaven?"

Taylor gave Jeff his auditor's expression, a look that indicated caution, even outright skepticism. He had used it hundreds of times when examining financial statements that professed to state the position of an enterprise, when he knew from experience that management had probably finessed the numbers to hide any problems.

"Jeff, this sounds like the Grimms' fairy tales. The good prince overcomes the evil witch and they all live happily ever after."

"It's not a fairy tale, Taylor. It's the actual work of God."

"How can you know that?" Taylor responded. "Anybody can write something and claim it's from God. The world is full of nuts who think they're Jesus Christ, and they go around making ridiculous claims about what God told them to do."

"That's a fair question," Jeff said. "Let's talk about the Bible itself before I try to answer that, and I'll use a simple three-part argument. First, I believe the Bible is the word of God because it claims to be. It claims divine authorship in many places, the clearest being in Second Timothy where it says all scripture is inspired by God. Second, it seems to be. Let me ask you a question. If we brought the world's ten most respected economists together and asked them to describe the best way to deal with the budget deficit, do you think they would agree on a solution?"

"Highly unlikely," Taylor agreed. "You'd probably get ten different solutions, maybe more than that."

Jeff continued. "Think about the Bible. It's not a book, really; it's a collection of sixty-six books with forty different authors from all walks of life. It was written over a fifteen hundred year period, and it covers not one but hundreds of controversial subjects—subjects like the origin of the universe, where we came from, and our purpose in life. And yet, there is an amazing consistency and agreement that runs throughout its pages. Wouldn't you agree that the Bible is at least a unique book, unlike anything else that has ever been produced?"

Taylor had never heard these things. He thought the Bible was written by first century monks who were codifying church doctrines.

Jeff repeated his question. "Well? Would you agree that it's at least unique?"

"If what you say is true," Taylor said cautiously, "then I agree it would be a unique book."

"Okay. The third point is that it proves to be. Millions of people who accept it as the word of God have found that it changed their lives drastically."

Taylor didn't understand Jeff's last point. "I don't think I follow you," he said.

"When I met you last week, you were in pretty bad shape with Montezuma's revenge. Imagine that you had never heard of diarrhea and you had no clue what was wrong. All you knew was that you were suffering. Now suppose I had given you a box of pills with a booklet of explanation and instructions, and you read the booklet. It not only explained what was wrong with you, but it prescribed the pills as a cure. To carry the illustration one step further, assume that I told you the booklet was written by your creator. Presumably, the one who created you would know how to make you work properly, right?"

"I follow you. Go on." Taylor was skeptical, but he was intrigued by Jeff's illustration.

"Suppose the instructions said you had to take the pills to be cured. You take the pills, and by sundown the next day you're completely cured. Now here's the point of my crude illustration. When I gave you the box of pills with the instructions, it claimed to be a cure. It said so right on the box. Then as you read through the instructions, it seemed to be a cure. It described your symptoms perfectly, explained the origin of the disease, and prescribed a course of treatment designed by your creator. Finally, you acted on what you had learned. You took the pills and they proved to be a cure. You personally experienced the truth about the cure."

Taylor appreciated the logic of Jeff's illustration, even if he was skeptical of the application. "I see your point, but there's just one problem with it."

"What's that?"

"How can you know that the men who wrote the Bible were actually writing what God said?"

Taylor was still holding the open New Testament in his hand, so Jeff told him to turn back to the beginning of the Revelation. "Read the first three verses of chapter one out loud."

Taylor looked skeptically at Jeff, then down at the New Testament. Turning the pages until he came to chapter one, he started reading. "The revelation of Jesus Christ, which God gave him to show his servants what must soon take place. He made it known by sending his angel to his servant John, who testifies to everything he saw, that is the word of God and the testimony of Jesus Christ. Blessed is the one who reads the words of this prophecy, and blessed are those who hear it and take to heart what is written in it, because the time is near."

Taylor looked quizzically at Jeff. "Okay. What's the point?"

"The book of Revelation was written by John the apostle," Jeff explained. "Skip down to verse nine and read that paragraph."

Taylor found the place and read aloud. "I, John, your brother and companion in the suffering and kingdom and patient endurance that are ours in Jesus, was on the island of Patmos because of the word of God and the testimony of Jesus. On the Lord's day I was in the spirit, and I heard behind me a loud voice like a trumpet, which said write on a scroll what you see and send it to the seven churches, to Ephesus, Smyrna, Pergamum, Thyatira . . ."

He stopped reading and looked up at Jeff. "Okay, he heard a voice. A lot of people hear voices. It's a mental disorder called paranoia."

Jeff was undaunted. "Keep reading."

Taylor continued to read. "I turned around to

see the voice that was speaking to me. And when I turned I saw seven golden lampstands, and among the lampstands was someone like the Son of Man, dressed in a robe reaching down to his feet with a golden sash around his chest . . ."

Jeff interrupted. "Stop right there. The phrase 'Son of Man' refers to Jesus. He often called Himself by that name. Clearly, John didn't just hear a voice. When he turned around, he saw Jesus standing there. Skip down to the last paragraph."

Taylor found his place and read the remaining portion. "When I saw him, I fell at his feet as though dead. Then he placed his right hand on me and said do not be afraid. I am the first and the last. I am the living one. I was dead, and behold I am alive forever and ever. And I hold the keys of death and Hades. Write therefore what you have seen, what is now and what will take place later."

Jeff stopped him again. "Would you at least agree that John claimed what he wrote in the Revelation came directly from Jesus Christ himself?"

"All right, " Taylor said. "But that doesn't prove it did."

"No, it doesn't," Jeff agreed. "I'm only giving you an example of my first point; the Bible claims to be the word of God. Let me ask you something, Taylor. What exactly do you mean by proof?"

Taylor paused. He'd never thought about proof as an abstract concept. He had always considered it in accounting terms, balances and accounts, which were proved by analysis and calculation.

"I suppose I think about proof in the scientific sense."

Jeff said, "The scientific method, huh? I'm not surprised, considering your accounting background, but the scientific method isn't the only way to get at the truth."

Taylor was puzzled. "What do you mean?"

"There are two methods for proving the truth, Taylor; the scientific method and the historical method. Some things can be measured in a laboratory, but others can't. For instance, historical events. You can't prove in a laboratory that Lincoln actually delivered the Gettysburg address because that event isn't repeatable. You can't do it over again. The only way to discover the truth about it is to find some eyewitnesses who can testify to what they saw and heard. That's how you get at the truth in a courtroom. You find some witnesses and have them tell what happened."

Taylor wasn't convinced. "But how do you know which witness is telling the truth?"

"Before I get into that, would you agree that some things can't be proven or disproved by the scientific method?"

"All right, I'll give you that much."

"And would you agree," Jeff continued, "that the issue with the historical method is the reliability of the witnesses?"

"That's one issue," Taylor said. "But a reliable witness could be mistaken."

"That's right. It's possible. That's why it's

important that the Bible was written by at least forty different eyewitnesses. Why do you think there are four gospels which cover essentially the same events in the life of Christ?"

Taylor didn't know there were four gospels, but he didn't want to let on. "I suppose you're going to tell me it's like having four witnesses confirm the same story in a courtroom."

"Exactly," Jeff replied. "There's a more important way to get at the truth, though, than either the historical or the scientific method.""

"What's that?"

"Let me show you something," Jeff said. "Hand me the New Testament for a minute."

Jeff took the New Testament and flipped back through the pages until he found what he was looking for. He dog-eared the page and handed it back to Taylor.

"When Paul the apostle was in Athens, he went to a gathering of local philosophers who met to debate the latest ideas. The Greeks worshipped a lot of different gods in those days, and on the way to the meeting Paul noticed a statue to the unknown god. Apparently, they were trying to cover all the bases. When they asked him if he wanted to speak, he stood up and told them about this unknown god, and he said that he was the one who created everything, and that he was in fact the only true God. Then he finished his talk with a very interesting comment. Read verse thirty-one and you'll see what I mean."

Taylor was fascinated by Jeff's ability to

remember and find things he was looking for in the Bible. He found the verse and read, "For He has set a day when He will judge the world with justice by the man He has appointed. He has given proof of this to all men by raising Him from the dead."

He looked at Jeff with a quizzical expression. Jeff tried to explain. "Did you notice the word 'proof'? It says God proved His existence and power by raising Jesus from the dead."

Taylor was stuck. Obviously, if such a thing had occurred it would be overwhelming proof. "Okay, what's your point?" he asked impatiently.

"My point," Jeff said slowly, "is that revelation from God is the ultimate way to determine truth. Taylor, there are two important questions in life. First, is there a God? Second, if there is, has He said anything? God is infinite, and we are finite. Therefore, the only possible way for us to know God is by revelation. He would have to reveal Himself to us. Does that make sense?"

Taylor was uncomfortable. Jeff's logic was poking holes in some of his cherished beliefs. Taylor believed in God, but he didn't think of Him in personal terms, or in terms that required any commitment or action. To him, God was an abstraction, a pleasant idea. Perhaps He was only a word.

Jeff continued. "I'm only trying to show you that if God did raise Jesus from the dead, then that would prove His existence and power. Christianity stands or falls on the resurrection, Taylor. If it really happened, then it proves Jesus is who He said He was and that whatever He said is the way it is."

Taylor saw an opening in Jeff's argument. "But what if it didn't really happen? How can you be sure?"

"Because of the witnesses," Jeff responded. "There were quite a few people who said they saw Jesus after he had been killed by the Romans, five hundred at one time according to Paul. The resurrection sets Christianity apart from all other world religions. No other religious leader in history predicted his own death and resurrection and then pulled it off. Buddha is dead, Mohammed is dead, they're all dead."

Taylor was deep in thought. Jeff was right, of course. If the resurrection really happened, then Jesus would be God, and He deserved to be ruler of the universe. His words would be completely authoritative.

"Taylor?"

"Sorry, Jeff. I was just thinking about what you said. This is all very interesting, but I'll have to think about it."

"Hey, I understand," Jeff said. "Why don't you read through the gospel of John? It tells who Jesus is and why he came to earth."

"Maybe I will. By the way, there was one thing I didn't understand in that part I read from Revelation."

"What's that?"

"Where it talked about a Lamb."

"That's a reference to Jesus," Jeff explained.

"If you read the gospel of John, you'll see where John the Baptist pointed to Jesus one day and called him the Lamb of God who takes away the sins of the world. The Jews of that day understood that he was referring to their promised Messiah, but that's another story."

"I'd like to hear about it some time."

"Sure," Jeff replied. "Looks like we're going to have plenty of time on our hands."

CHAPTER THIRTEEN

After Taylor was taken hostage, Cyndi constantly watched the newscasts, hoping for some new piece of information, some clue to Taylor's condition. After the first week, they dropped the story as if it had never happened, but then on Wednesday of the third week it returned with a vengeance. Cyndi had left work early to catch the five-thirty news. All of a sudden, Taylor and Jeff's pictures appeared on the screen.

"There was a new development in the Costa Rican hostage story late today." The screen changed to the anchorman. "The terrorists holding the two American hostages have issued an ultimatum. The Associated Press in San Jose reported today that they had received a telephone call from someone claiming to be a spokesman for the Sendero Luminoso. The caller said if the five Luminoso prisoners at Leavenworth are not released by tomorrow night, one of the hostages will be executed for unspecified crimes against the people. A State Department spokesman would neither confirm nor deny the report, but continued to state the government's policy of refusing to negotiate with terrorists. ABC's Phyllis Brown spoke with Mr. and Mrs. William Richards, parents of Jeff Richards, one of the hostages and a star football player at Stanford. This is her report."

The screen faded to Phyllis interviewing Jeff's parents in their living room.

"Mrs. Richards, how do you feel about the ultimatum issued by the terrorists?"

Cyndi couldn't believe it. It was the ultimate dumb question. *How do you think she feels, you idiot?*

Jeff's mother smiled. "Naturally, we're very concerned for Jeff's safety, and we continue to pray for his release."

Phyllis was clearly not satisfied with her response, so she turned to Jeff's father. "And what about you, Mr. Richards? Have you heard from the State Department?"

"No, we haven't," he replied. "We're a little numb, I guess you'd say. We knew nothing about it until you called earlier."

Phyllis was determined to get an emotional reaction, something that would play well on television. "As Jeff's parents, how do you feel about the government's refusal to negotiate for his release?"

Jeff's father looked like an ordinary working man in his bus driver's uniform, but there was a sense of calm strength that came across on television. "I'm sure they're doing all they can, but we're not trusting in the government for Jeff's safety."

Phyllis was puzzled. "I'm not sure I under-stand."

"We have a strong faith in God," he replied, "and we know that Jeff's fate is ultimately in His hands."

Phyllis hadn't expected that response, and she seemed flustered. "I see. Uh . . . thank you for speaking with us this evening."

The screen switched to Phyllis standing in front of the Richards' home. "That's the story from here, Peter. No word from the State Department, and Jeff's parents have nothing to hold on to now except their religious faith. This is Phyllis Brown, ABC News, reporting from San Diego. Back to you, Peter."

The anchorman appeared and said, "Thank you, Phyllis. We'll be back after this word."

Cyndi's heart rate increased as the commercial began to roll. She clicked the remote back and forth between CBS and NBC, but they had already aired the story.

"Oh my God," she whispered. "Somebody has to do something."

Just then the telephone rang. It was Sharon. "Cyndi, did you see the news?"

"Yes, just now."

"Do you want me to come over?"

"No, I'll be all right. I need to make some calls and try to make some sense out of this."

"Okay. If you change your mind, call me."

"Thanks, Sharon. I appreciate it more than you know."

Cyndi hung up the phone and dialed G. Preston's private number at Western. She had talked to the wolf right after the story broke, and he had assured her the company was doing everything it could to get Taylor released, but she hadn't heard from him since then.

G. Preston always made her feel like she had interrupted some earth-shatteringly important meeting, speaking in choppy bursts with mostly one-syllable words. "Cyndi . . . good to hear from you . . . everything all right?"

"No sir, I'm afraid there's more bad news," she said.

"More news? About Taylor?"

"Yes sir. I just saw it on ABC. The terrorists are threatening to kill one of them if their demands aren't met by tomorrow night."

There was a pause on G. Preston's end, then he said, "I wouldn't worry about it, dear. They're probably bluffing."

Probably bluffing? Cyndi couldn't believe what she'd heard. Did the wolf think this was a poker game? "I don't think so, Mr. Wilson. I'm terribly worried about Taylor, and I was wondering if you'd heard anything since we talked last week."

"We're doing all we can, Cyndi. I put Forbes Barrett on this as soon as we heard. Forbes spent a hitch with Army Intelligence, and he's been checking with some of his contacts. Let me put you through to him, and he'll brief you on the status of his investigation."

He's delegated this just like he would any business problem, she thought. *He's going to pass me off to an assistant.* "Thank you, Mr. Wilson. I appreciate your help."

"Glad to be of service," he said condescendingly. "Hold on while I connect you with Forbes."

After a couple of clicking sounds, Forbes came on the line. "Forbes, this is Mr. Wilson. Cyndi Davis is on the line and I want you to brief her on your investigation."

"Certainly, sir." The wolf clicked off the line. "Hello, Cyndi. How are you holding up?"

"As well as could be expected," Cyndi said. "But there's been a new development."

"Really? What sort of development?"

Cyndi told him about the ultimatum. "Can you tell me anything, Forbes? I've been going crazy trying to find somebody who knows something . . . anything."

"I talked to an old friend at the CIA, and he told me the State Department refuses to discuss a swap. Technically, they couldn't agree to a deal anyhow since the prisoners at Leavenworth are under the jurisdiction of the Justice Department. State did ask the CIA to check their sources in Costa Rica, but so far they've come up with a big zero."

Cyndi felt like she was mired in play-dough. This whole episode was obviously an embarrassment to the government, and they were passing around the Davis matter like a hot potato, doing their best to make sure it was on somebody else's desk when it blew up. Obviously, the people at Western had done the same.

"Thanks, Forbes," she said. "If you hear anything else, please call me."

"As soon as we know anything," he replied, "I'll be in touch."

Cyndi hung up the phone and felt absolutely, totally alone. It reminded her of an incident during her childhood when she got separated from the rest of her family during a camping vacation in the Adirondacks. She had left the campsite to pick a bouquet of flowers for her mother, and instead of taking the path back to the camp, she had mistakenly headed the opposite direction. After a half hour, the trail disappeared. Instead of reversing direction, she had plunged ahead, finally settling down under a huge tree after becoming hopelessly lost. They had found her after a couple of hours, but Cyndi had never forgotten how helpless she felt under that tree.

If only her mother could hold her like she did then and make it all go away, but Cyndi's mother died suddenly during her sophomore year at SMU, and her father had never remarried. Tears filled her eyes, and on impulse she picked up the telephone and dialed Providence.

The housekeeper answered. "Franklin residence."

"This is Cyndi Davis. Is my father home yet?"

"Mrs. Davis, how nice to hear from you. I'm afraid he's still at the store. Would you like to try him there?"

"Yes, I will. Thank you."

Cyndi found the number in her address book and after a couple of rings, she heard her father's voice. "This is Burke Franklin."

"Burke, it's Cyndi." Cyndi's father had always insisted that she address him by his first name. The sound of his voice caused the tears that had been welling up in her eyes to let loose, and she began to sob uncontrollably.

"Sweetheart, what's the matter?"

"Did you see the news tonight?" she asked.

"No, honey. I've been in a merchandising meeting since three. We only broke up a few minutes ago. What is it?"

Cyndi blubbered out the news. "The terrorists say they're going to kill one of the hostages if their demands aren't met by tomorrow night."

"Sweetheart, that's just a bluff. I'll bet you they're negotiating this very minute, and this is just their way to turn up the heat a little."

"I wish I could believe that," Cyndi said, gaining control of herself. "One of the executives at Western has a contact at the CIA, and he said the government refuses to even discuss it. He also said the CIA has done some checking down there and they've drawn a blank."

"Sweetheart," he purred, "I know it looks bad, but you have to pull yourself together. You have to be strong . . . especially now."

Cyndi heard disappointment in her father's voice. Not disappointment at the news about Taylor, but at her inability to be strong and self-assured. Cyndi's relationship with her father had always kept her off-balance and unsure of his acceptance. Femininity, softness, and vulnerability were not traits he admired, and she had done her best to suppress those attributes and pattern herself after the hard-charging executives he admired. She desperately wanted him to drop everything and come to Dallas to be with her, but he would surely view such a request as weakness.

"I know, Burke," she admitted weakly. "I thought I was doing pretty well until today. I'm sorry."

"Sweetheart, I've got catalog meetings for the next three days. If it weren't for that I'd come down to Dallas and spend a couple of days with you. It's just that the timing is impossible. You do understand, don't you?"

"Of course," she lied. "Don't worry about me. I'll be okay. It's just that . . ." Her voice trailed off and she started crying. The unbridled display of emotion compounded her feelings of inadequacy, but there was no stopping it.

"What is it, Cyndi?" her father asked.

"It's just that I don't see what would be the big deal about trading five crummy dope peddlers for Taylor and that college student."

"Cyndi, you know it's impossible. If the government made a deal with this group, it would just encourage every other would-be savior of the world to do the same thing. We'd have a hundred new kidnappings within a week."

"So what am I supposed to do?" she demanded. "Offer up Taylor as a sacrifice for the government's precious policy? This isn't some theoretical exercise. We're talking about my husband."

Cyndi's father tried to soothe her feelings as best he could over the telephone. "I know, sweetheart. But it won't do any good to get angry or upset. All we can do is wait."

She was embarrassed by her outburst. " I know, Burke. I'm sorry to dump on you like this."

"It's all right," he said. "Listen, I've got to run. We're trying to get Liz Claiborne to take ten pages in the catalog, and I'm having dinner with her numbers man tonight. Wish me luck."

"Sure," Cyndi replied. "I'll call as soon as something happens."

"Bye, sweetheart."

"Goodbye," she said reluctantly. "I love you."

Cyndi hung up the phone and tried to sort out her mixed-up feelings—concern for Taylor, desire to please her father, fear of the unknown, anger at the turn their lives had taken these last few months. They all combined to overwhelm and push her under like a swimmer turned end over end by crashing surf.

The phone rang, and Cyndi instinctively answered it. A coarse female voice said, "Is this Mrs. Davis?"

"This is Cyndi Davis."

"Mrs. Davis," the voice said. "This is the *Times Herald* calling. I assume you've heard about the ultimatum?"

"Yes, I heard about it."

The reporter said, "I was wondering if you could give us a statement for the morning edition?"

Cyndi was irritated by her impersonal manner, not even identifying herself. "Who is this?" she demanded.

"I'm sorry. This is Evelyn White with the *Dallas Times Herald*."

"Evelyn," Cyndi barked, "I don't have a statement. Print whatever you wish."

"Uh . . . okay. Sorry I disturbed you, Mrs. Davis."

Idiot press. Cyndi was angry. *Do they think I enjoy having my innermost feelings plastered all over the front page? How do I even know what I'm feeling? Why is this happening to me?*

An ugly thought surfaced in her mind, one she had flirted with a couple of times but then immediately suppressed. What if this was punishment for killing her baby? A life for a life. Wasn't that in the Bible somewhere? A dark presentiment of evil welled up from deep in her gut. It was a heavy depressing sensation, pressing down on her like a huge weight.

"Is this the kind of God you are?" she mumbled angrily. Cyndi was startled by her boldness. She had never attempted to talk directly to God, and she was embarrassed by the accusation in her question. She waited for a moment but heard nothing, felt nothing. Her words hung suspended in space, unanswered, unacknowledged. "Maybe God doesn't talk to murderers," she whispered.

She had another thought. *I'll call Sharon. I've got to talk to somebody.*

Cyndi dialed Sharon's number, hoping that she was still at home. When she answered, Cyndi took a deep breath and plunged ahead. "Sharon, I think I would like to have some company tonight."

"I'll be right over."

"No, I'd better come to your place," Cyndi said. "My phone will be ringing off the hook."

Cyndi scribbled directions on the back of an envelope, turned the recorder on, and headed north in the BMW. Sharon lived in a small apartment complex in Farmer's Branch, just north of LBJ Freeway. The Foxmoor was nothing special. It was like a hundred other developments that clung to the freeways and major arteries around Dallas, home to the exploding singles population. Sharon had decorated her one-bedroom apartment simply but tastefully. Family pictures were prominently displayed in the living area, and a beautiful afghan was draped over the couch.

Cyndi eyed the afghan. "Did you make it?"

Sharon smiled. "I wish. Give me some numbers to calculate and I'm a whiz, but I'm hopeless with my hands. One of my aunts did it for me. When Mother died, my aunt sort of took me on as a project, and she's always sending things. Isn't it beautiful?"

Cyndi admired the intricate pattern and beautiful color scheme. "It's gorgeous," she said.

Sharon went to the kitchen and poured two

coffees. "Have you had supper?"

"No," Cyndi replied, "but don't worry about it. I don't think I could hold anything on my stomach right now. Coffee will be fine."

They fiddled with small talk for a few minutes, talking about the weather, the bank, Sharon's apartment—everything but the matter at hand. Finally, Cyndi blurted it out. "Sharon, something is driving me crazy and I've got to have an answer."

"All right," Sharon said, puzzled by the abrupt change in conversation. "I don't know if I can help, but I'll certainly try."

"Do you believe God causes everything that happens?"

Sharon wasn't surprised by Cyndi's question. "Are you thinking about what happened to Taylor?"

"Yes. Do you believe God is responsible?"

"No, Cyndi. I don't. When God created man, He gave him a free will, the ability to make his own choices. I believe the terrorists who kidnapped Taylor made their own choice, and they're responsible for their actions."

Cyndi wasn't satisfied. "But couldn't God have stopped them, if He wanted to?"

Sharon paused. "Cyndi, you have just asked one of the hardest questions in the world. What you're really asking is how could God, if He is all-loving and all-powerful, allow suffering and evil to exist? Isn't that what you're really asking?"

"I guess it is," Cyndi admitted.

"God didn't introduce suffering and evil into

the world," Sharon said calmly, choosing her words carefully. "Man did. You remember what happened in the Garden of Eden?"

"I know the basic story." Cyndi had always thought the Eden story was mythical, but she wanted to hear what Sharon had to say, especially after Jim's discussion about Adam and Eve at the Friday group.

"God created a perfect universe with no suffering and no evil. But when He created Adam and Eve, He gave them the ability to choose their own destiny. They could live in harmony with God and His creation, or they could set about to destroy it. It's like two cars driving through a beautiful forest. In one car the people choose to protect the environment, but in the other they indiscriminately throw trash out the windows. Adam and Eve chose to trash their relationship with God, and they littered the universe with the effects of sin."

Cyndi couldn't get one question out of her mind. "But why didn't God inter-vene?"

"He did," Sharon replied, "but not in the way you're thinking about. You need to remember that we're not robots. God made us unique and special, with the ability to love Him or not love Him. We're not puppets on a string. Can you make your employees do exactly as you say any time you wish?"

Cyndi smiled. "Sometimes I wish I could."

"But you can't because they have a will of their own."

"That's true," Cyndi agreed. "But I'm not God, either."

"No, you're not. Would it help you understand if you knew that God had the power to do whatever He wished, but He chose to limit His power when He created man?"

"I'm not sure I—"

Sharon interrupted her in mid-sentence. "God created man to be a creature who could know Him and love Him in a way that the plants and animals never could. But in order for man's love to have meaning, God had to give up something. He had to give man the right to reject His love so that love would have meaning. Does that make sense?"

"Yes, I think so," Cyndi replied, absorbed by Sharon's explanation. The way Sharon and her friends talked about God and man in terms of a relationship was completely new to her, and she was fascinated by the thought that she could know God like she knew Taylor or one of her friends.

Sharon continued. "Earlier you asked why God didn't intervene and straighten everything out, and I said in a way he did. Let me explain what I meant."

Sharon went out to the kitchen and returned with a Bible. "Cyndi, listen to this." She turned the pages until she found what she was looking for, and then read, "You see, at just the right time, when we were still powerless, Christ died for the ungodly. Very rarely will anyone die for a righteous man, though for a good man someone might possibly dare to die. But God demonstrates his own love for us in this. While we were still sinners, Christ died for us."

She turned back a few pages and read another

passage. "For God so loved the world that He gave His one and only Son, that whoever believes in him shall not perish but have eternal life."

Sharon looked up. "I could just as well have read it this way. For God so loved Cyndi Davis, that He gave His one and only Son. To go back to your original question, if God decided to eliminate all evil from the world at midnight tonight, don't you see that you and I would be included?"

"What do you mean?" Cyndi asked curiously.

"Compared with God, anything less than absolute perfection is evil. Would you say that you have lived a perfect life, never once doing anything wrong?"

"Of course not."

"And neither have I," Sharon said. "Nobody has. Therefore, if God decided to get rid of all the evil in the world, He would have to destroy every person on earth."

All of a sudden Cyndi understood. "I've never thought of it that way," she muttered.

Sharon continued. "God's solution is redemption, not destruction. Man chose a path that leads to destruction, but God intervened with a plan of redemption. When Jesus died on the cross, God accepted His death as payment for your sins and mine because Jesus lived the only perfect life. Rather than destroy mankind and start over again, God chose to provide individual redemption to any person who will believe in Jesus and accept him as Savior and Lord. That way, God makes it a matter of individual choice and He doesn't violate our free will."

Cyndi had never understood the death of Jesus in this light. She blurted out, "But . . . why would he do such a thing?"

"That one I can answer," Sharon replied. "Look at it for yourself." She handed the open Bible to Cyndi and asked her to read verse sixteen aloud.

"For God so loved the world that He gave His one and only Son . . ." Cyndi looked up at Sharon with eyes that understood.

Sharon could see that she understood. "He loves you, Cyndi. That's why He did it."

Cyndi bowed her head and tears flowed gently down her cheeks. The ugly scene at the clinic was plastered on the screen of her mind like a giant billboard, inviting one and all to gape at the terrible thing Cyndi Taylor did. "I don't see how he could love me after what I did," she whimpered.

"What are you talking about?" Sharon asked.

"I think this thing with Taylor is God's way of getting even with me for something terrible I've done," Cyndi explained.

Sharon reached over and took both of Cyndi's hands in hers. "I don't know what you've done, but the Bible says that no sin is too big for God. Jesus died for all sin. Nothing was excluded."

Cyndi sobbed and shook uncontrollably, and her ugly secret spilled out. "Not even abortion? Does God love me even though I killed by baby?"

Sharon held her tight and said, "Cyndi, God loves you unconditionally. Nothing you have ever done in the past or might do in the future will drive Him away. His love derives from His own character, and it isn't based on your performance or worthiness."

Cyndi got up and searched for a tissue to wipe away the remainder of her tears. "Thanks," she sniffled. She told Sharon how she and Taylor had decided on the abortion as a matter of convenience, about the terrible scene at the clinic, and the feelings of guilt that had dogged her.

Sharon smiled. "What you've done is not a trivial thing, Cyndi, but the more important issue is where you stand in relationship to God's love and forgiveness. Have you ever received Jesus as your Savior?"

Cyndi looked at her with a puzzled expression. "I'm not sure I understand what you mean."

"A moment ago I mentioned God's plan of redemption, the death of Jesus on our behalf. The Bible says that anyone who receives God's gift of salvation through Jesus Christ has forgiveness for sin and literally becomes a new person. Have you ever consciously done that?"

"I guess not. To be honest with you, I've never heard it explained before, and I still don't quite understand it."

Sharon explained the experience called the new birth, but she could see that Cyndi was having a hard time. "Cyndi, do you have a Bible?" she asked.

Somebody gave me one years ago," Cyndi replied. "But I don't have any idea what happened to it."

"Why don't you stop by the Galleria on your way home? There's a bookstore called The Good Word on the second level, and they have the newer translations. Ask for the New International Version, and start reading through the gospel of John. The more you read about the life of Christ, the more sense it will make."

Sharon's suggestion had an elegant simplicity about it. Why not learn about the most important life ever lived? If God really did come to planet earth in the person of Jesus Christ, wouldn't it be important to read about it from the original source? "All right. I'll do it," Cyndi said.

Cyndi left The Good Word and headed for the Galleria's north parking garage, but as she walked past the entrance to the Westin, she decided to detour by Armando's to see if any of her friends were still around. The happy hour crowd had thinned out somewhat, but Blair was still there.

Blair had heard about the Luminoso's ultimatum. "Cyndi, you poor dear," she said. "Let me buy you a drink."

They settled into a booth, and Cyndi was bringing her up to date on the situation with Taylor when Blair noticed the package Cyndi had absent-mindedly placed on the table.

"What kind of shop is the Good Word?" she asked innocently.

Cyndi was embarrassed to admit that she'd been shopping for a Bible. "Oh. . . . it's just a bookstore."

Blair's curiosity was aroused, and she wasn't about to let Cyndi get away without finding out what was so important that she had make a special trip to the Galleria to buy it. "What is it?" she asked.

"Oh, it's nothing."

"Come on, Cyndi. Don't keep secrets from Blair."

Cyndi was trapped. "If you must know, it's a new version of the Bible."

Blair's mouth dropped open. "Cyndi. . . . sweetheart. . . . don't tell me this thing with Taylor has turned you to religion."

Blair's tone of voice irritated Cyndi. What if it had turned her to religion? Why should it be of any concern to Blair? "No, I'm not turning to religion," she frowned. "I just decided to buy myself a new Bible."

Blair could see that Cyndi was offended by her remarks. "I'm sorry, Cyndi. I didn't mean anything by it. I was just surprised, that's all."

Cyndi finished her drink and gathered up her things. "I've got to run, Blair. See you later, okay?"

There were several messages on the recorder from friends who had seen the news. After returning the calls, Cyndi made herself a sandwich and settled down on the couch with her new acquisition, a handsome leather ultra-thin edition of the New International Version Bible. The fifty-dollar price tag had surprised her a little, but Cyndi and Taylor had grown used to nice things, and she had instinctively chosen the most expensive version in the store.

She opened it to the table of contents, found the New Testament book of John, and started reading. "In the beginning was the Word, and the Word was with god, and the Word was God. He was with God in the beginning." *Sounds like the Word was a person. Is he talking about Jesus?* she wondered. "Through Him all things were made; without Him nothing was made that has been made. In Him was life, and that life was the light of men. The light shines in the darkness, but the darkness has not understood it."

Cyndi had the strangest sensation that she was reading truth. About the middle of the first chapter, a phrase jumped off the page and captured her attention. It said "grace and truth came through Jesus Christ." Grace and truth. *That's what we're all looking for,* she thought. *That's what the mad rush is really about.*

She read about John the Baptist, how he introduced Jesus to the people as the Lamb of God, how Jesus called His first disciples to follow Him, and how He changed water into wine at a wedding feast.

In chapter three, she read about a religious leader named Nicodemus. Jesus told him he would never see the kingdom of God unless he was born again, and then explained that He was talking about a spiritual birth. Then she read, "For God so loved the world . . ." Cyndi paused and repeated something Sharon had said. "For God so loved Cyndi Davis . . . For God so loved Cyndi Davis."

She finished the sandwich and went to the

kitchen for a glass of milk. Returning to the couch, she fluffed up some pillows, stretched out with the Bible, and continued to read. It was fascinating. There was an encounter with a Samaritan woman, a healing by a pool, prophecies about future events, feeding of five thousand people with a few paltry loaves and fishes, and an incident where He reportedly walked on water. As she read, a portrait formed in her mind of a kind and good man, a compassionate man who identified with hurting people and went out of His way to help them. He was a wise man who spoke words of truth and had no patience with phoney religion. He was a man with supernatural abilities, a worker of miracles, even raising a man called Lazarus from the dead by simply calling out his name.

Then the story took a dark turn. He also had enemies, and they accused Him of sedition and treachery before the Roman governor. Incredibly, even though Pilate didn't believe the charges, he let them crucify Jesus on a cross. Cyndi felt anger welling up within her. He didn't deserve to die. Then she came to the Easter story. Cyndi had grown up thinking of Easter as one of the best retailing seasons of the year, especially for the fashionable apparel sold in her father's store. She was vaguely aware of the religious aspect, but to read it in black and white as one would read the thrilling climax of a good novel made it fresh and new. She almost felt like cheering.

Toward the end of chapter twenty, she was arrested by another passage. It said, "Jesus did many other miraculous signs in the presence of the disciples, which are not recorded in this book. But these are written that you may believe that Jesus is the Christ, the Son of God, and that by believing you may have life in His name."

Cyndi placed the open Bible over her heart. *Life in his name,* she mused. In one of those flashes of insight that appear in odd moments, she understood. Jesus loved her so much that He had died in her place. She deserved to die, not Him. It was an act of incredibly unselfish, unconditional, undeserved love, and she could receive His gift of grace and truth by believing in Him. Cyndi sat up, placed the Bible on the coffee table, and slipped to her knees next to the couch.

"God, this is Cyndi," she said. "I know I don't deserve Your love, and You know that I've done many wrong things, especially taking my baby's life. But if what I've just read is true, You're offering me forgiveness and a new life. I do believe in Jesus and accept Him as my Savior, and I want You to have my life from now on. I want to be born again too."

She waited for tears but none came. She expected to have a spectacular feeling, but nothing happened. There was simply a calm, but firm assurance that what she had done was right, and that it would change her life forever.

Cyndi got up and called Sharon.

"Hello," Sharon answered.

"Sharon, it's Cyndi."

"Cyndi . . . what's wrong? It's nearly twelve

o'clock."

"I know," Cyndi said excitedly. "But I had to call and tell you I did it."

Sharon was awake now, and she knew that late-night calls were usually bad news. "Did what? What are you talking about?"

"I bought a Bible, and I read through the book of John."

Sharon paused, wondering if Cyndi had called to ask a question or debate something she'd read. "Cyndi, I'm so glad you followed my advice. What did you think of it?"

"Sharon, I do believe in Jesus. I asked Him to be my Savior tonight. I guess that makes me a Christian, huh?"

"Oh Cyndi, I'm so happy for you," Sharon replied. "Yes, it does make you a Christian. The Bible says it's like being born again."

"I know," Cyndi replied. "I read that part again. I must admit, though, I didn't feel anything."

"That doesn't matter," Sharon explained. "The new birth is based on God's promise, not your feelings. Just keep telling Him 'thank you,' and He will make it real to you in His own good time."

"Thanks, Sharon. And . . . thank you for being a real friend."

CHAPTER FOURTEEN

El Jefe parked the van near the Plaza de la Cultura. He walked around the corner and headed for El Chivo, a seedy bar near the central bus terminal. Janet was waiting in a booth near the back. She was dressed like a tica, her deep tan making it difficult in the semi-darkness to tell that she was a gringo. He sat opposite her in the booth and ordered a beer.

"Do you have any information for me, gringo lady?

"They need more time," she said. "It is very difficult to make decisions in our government. Many people have to be consulted, and it takes time."

El Jefe tried to remain calm. "Your government is very foolish. Did you tell them we are serious? That the execution will take place as scheduled?"

Janet could see he was in no mood to negotiate, but her instructions were to stall. "They absolutely refuse to release your friends," she reported. "But there are alternatives that we feel you may find interesting."

"Our demands are not negotiable," El Jefe growled. "If our comrades are not released by noon tomorrow, one of the hostages will be executed, and your government will be responsible for his death."

Janet knew he wasn't bluffing, but she made one more try. "The only thing that can move our government is a groundswell of public opinion," she explained. "It takes time for such a thing to develop."

El Jefe made no attempt to hide his contempt. "That's the trouble with capitalists. You are only moved by the prevailing political winds. The welfare of individuals means nothing."

Janet was incredulous. This half-baked Maoist was lecturing her on the worth of the individual? Did he understand even the rudiments of Marxist-Leninist doctrine? Millions of individuals had perished in Stalin's gulags, and other millions had been sacrificed to the rampaging Red Guards during the latter years of Mao's rule in China.

She started to set him straight, but this wasn't the time or place for political debate. Besides, she knew that even in a democracy there were times when individuals were sacrificed for the common good. Hadn't Churchill known in advance of the Luftwaffe's raid on Coventry during the war? Had he warned Coventry's hapless citizens, though, the Nazis would have realized that Britain had cracked their communications code and the war would have dragged on, resulting in the loss of many more lives.

At least, that was the rationale. It was a matter of arithmetic, actually. The citizens of Nagasaki and Hiroshima had been traded for the presumed millions who would have perished in a lengthy assault on the Japanese mainland. Now the lives of Taylor Davis and Jeff Richards hung in the same balance. Two lives versus who knows how many others.

El Jefe downed the remainder of his beer. "You know how to reach me if your government changes its mind. Remember, gringo lady, tomorrow at noon."

He left Janet in the booth, walked through the smoky haze toward the front entrance, and then he was gone. Janet paid the bill and headed the opposite direction. Her Washington contact would be waiting for a report.

When Janet returned to her apartment, she took the lap-top computer from its case, plugged it into the telephone jack, and dialed the CIA's computer at Langley.

After a short wait, the display came to life with the standard request. "Please enter your identification code." Janet responded with the nine-digit number that had been assigned to her for this project.

Langley's computer requested the password. In order to forestall attempts to sign on the system with a series of random guesses, the communication protocol allowed only seven seconds for a password response. Janet quickly typed the password, "Goforth."

Another query appeared on the screen. "Do you wish this message encrypted?"

She typed Y_E_S and waited, staring at the blank screen. Finally, a message appeared at the top of the screen. "You may enter the system."

Janet typed, "To: Admiral. From: Fleet. El Jefe stands by original demand. I think he means it. Unable to stall any longer. Do you have further instructions?"

Even though Janet could read what she had just typed on the laptop, the electronic impulses transmitted over the telephone were garbled by the encryption routine in the communication software. They would only make sense after Langley's computer decrypted it on the other end. She had signed onto the system in the two-way mode, which indicated she was waiting for an answer. After about ten minutes, the screen came to life.

"To: Fleet. From: Admiral. Message received. Disengage from project."

Janet calmly returned the lap-top to its case and changed into tennis gear for her game with the ambassador's wife at four.

Senator Harding was furious. In spite of the kidnappings in Costa Rica, Congress had done nothing, and to make matters worse the press had failed to keep the story alive. He decided to rattle their cage a little, so he placed a call to the president of NBC News.

Mike Barnett was not a newsman. He had been recruited from Paramount to head up the news division after NBC fell into third place in the ratings. His reputation had been made by a succession of wildly successful shows that had vaulted ABC into first place in prime time, even though the critics had panned them, calling them shallow, exploitative, and in some cases, trash. Mike had simply taken the day-time soap opera formula, casted some name stars, and added a little glitz.

Mike answered in his usual manner, direct and up front. "Senator," he said cheerily. "This is Mike Barnett. What can I do for you?"

"Mike, it's about this hostage thing in Costa Rica. I don't understand why you people aren't giving it more play. Everybody knows the President is cozy with the Sandinistas, and now it looks like he's protecting those terrorists. I would have thought you'd put a full-court press on this story."

"Senator, the public is bored with terrorist kid-nappings. The PLO still has seven hostages in Lebanon, and to be honest with you, that story in Central America hardly made a blip in our ratings."

Harding had very little regard for news people, and he didn't try to hide his contempt. "Mike, some of my colleagues are beginning to think your liberal bias is showing. One of the Democrats holds a press conference to criticize the administration's position on the freedom fighters, and you give him three or four minutes. But when the Sandinistas and their friends take two Americans hostage, proving what the president has been saying about communist influence in Central America, you give us a big yawn."

"Senator," Mike replied, "I only give the people what they want. Tell me a nuclear plant is leaking radiation into the surrounding counties, or massive forest fires have destroyed half of Yellowstone Park, and I'll put them on the air. Hostage stories are old news. That's just the way it is, Senator."

Senator Harding ended the conversation with a veiled threat. "I don't need to be told the way it is, Mike. I've been in this town a long time, and I can tell you that things have a way of coming back around." Having issued his warning, the senator ended the conversation. He wasn't pleased by the way the kidnappings had been handled. The State Department had fumbled the ball from the beginning, shifting responsibility to the Justice Department, and the White House had been invisible except for the usual press communique deploring the hostage-taking and vowing to punish the perpetrators. He picked up the phone and dialed Bill Powers's private number at the CIA.

"Bill, this is Prescott Harding."

"Senator Harding. How are you?"

"This is not a social call, Bill. I want to know what's going on with the hostage situation in Costa Rica."

Powers was cautious. "We're going through the usual drill, Senator. Why do you ask?"

"The press has all but ignored this story, and I think it's because the administration hasn't made a big deal out of it. Have you heard from the White House?"

Senator Harding had been used as a White House spokesman on Central America in the past. He had expected to do the same in this case, appearing on network interviews, expressing outrage and otherwise looking statesmanly. His determination to roll back the communist menace south of the border gave him an edge in the race for secretary of state.

Bill Powers was a technocrat, not a politician, but he had learned how to make the right political moves in his rise to the top of the CIA. He was also a long-time friend of the president.

"The White House is very concerned about the kidnappings, Senator, and a strongly worded statement has been relayed to the presidente. Of course, he claims no knowledge of the Luminoso and says there is nothing he can do."

Senator Harding wasn't satisfied with Bill's non-answer. "What about a noise from the oval office?" he asked. "Why hasn't the president used this incident to attack the Democrats who've been holding up aid to the freedom fighters?"

Bill wasn't about to be dragged into the middle of that argument. "Senator, I'm afraid you'll have to query your own sources on that one."

"All right, Bill," he sighed. "Just one more thing . . . do you think the ultimatum is credible? Will they carry out their threat?"

"From what we know of the Luminoso, they probably took the second hostage with this threat in mind. They may kill one in order to turn up the heat, hoping it would force us to negotiate for the remaining hostage."

The senator paused for a moment, calculating

the effect on the press. "Well, at least the networks will have to get off their duffs if the Luminoso executes one of them."

"You're probably right, Senator."

Taylor and Jeff had just finished supper when they heard the van drive up outside. There was a commotion, voices, and then footsteps. El Jefe came into the back room and instructed them to stand with their arms behind their backs. Then his two goons tied their hands with leather cords. Taylor was frightened. He had more or less settled into the daily routine, and he felt threatened by this abrupt change.

"What's this all about?" Taylor asked.

El Jefe was noncommittal. "We are going for a little ride."

"I think it's about time you told us the truth," Taylor demanded. "What are you planning to do with us?"

"Your government has given us no choice," El Jefe replied. "They refuse to take us seriously, so we are forced to resort to a little piece of drama to prove our point."

Taylor didn't like the sound of things. "What do you mean? What sort of drama?" he pleaded.

El Jefe took two playing cards from his shirt pocket. "This, my friends, is the most important game of cards you will ever play. One of you will be executed tonight, sacrificed on the altar of your government's procrastination and stupidity. I have two cards in my hand, the ace of spades and the ten of diamonds. The one who chooses the ace of spades will have the honor of dying for our comrades in Leavenworth."

This is a game, Taylor thought. *He's just trying to intimidate us.*

El Jefe dramatically shuffled the two cards and then pushed them face down toward Taylor. "Please take one of the cards in your mouth, Mr. Davis." Taylor obediently took a card. El Jefe offered the remaining card to Jeff. As they stood there with hands tied behind their backs and the playing cards clenched between their teeth, El Jefe started to laugh.

"It is a momentous occasion, is it not?" he roared. "Which one will be honored tonight? Which one will appear on your network newscasts tomorrow night? Let us announce the results, shall we?"

El Jefe took Taylor's card and turned it over. "Well, well. Mr. Davis has chosen the ace of spades, gentlemen."

Taylor felt faint. His knees buckled and he sat back on the edge of the bed. "You can't do this," he protested. "I am an American citizen."

El Jefe swung around and back-handed Taylor with a crushing blow to his face. "Shut up, American citizen! I am the law here. You have been duly tried and convicted of crimes against the people, and at midnight you will pay with your life."

Jeff had said nothing to this point. Then he spoke deliberately and calmly. "Let me take his place."

El Jefe turned toward Jeff, unbelieving. "What's this? You want to take this coward's place?"

"Yes," Jeff said calmly. "If you keep Taylor, you can trade him for five million dollars. His company has an insurance policy that covers kidnapped executives."

El Jefe was skeptical. "Are you stupid as well as naïve, college student? You are offering to give your life for this stranger, this capitalist businessman?"

"Yes. I want to take his place."

El Jefe turned to Taylor. "Is this true, gringo? Is there such an insurance policy?"

Taylor figured Jeff was stalling for time. He couldn't believe Jeff really meant to take his place, but he had to go along. "Yes, it's true."

El Jefe paused for a moment, calculating the relative worth of his two captives. "All right, Mr. Richards. If you insist, then we will allow you the honor of dying for our comrades."

He motioned to the two guards, and they took them outside and pushed them into the back of the van. El Jefe and one of the guards rode in the front, and the other guard sat in the back with the AK-47. After traveling over the twisting, bumpy road that led from the farmhouse to the highway, they turned east toward San Jose.

As soon as they were on the main highway, El Jefe handed a small, dark bottle to the guard in the back and told Jeff to drink it. The guard removed his gag and held it up to his lips. Jeff was frightened, and he held the liquid in his mouth for a moment before swallowing it.

Taylor waited for his share, then realized it was intended only for Jeff, the designated sacrifice. In a few minutes Jeff's eyelids drooped and he slumped to the floor of the van, but he was still breathing.

Taylor's mind swirled with conflicting thoughts and images. He thought of Cyndi and tried to visualize what it had been like for her these past weeks. He thought about the company. Had G. Preston tried to seek his release? Was the ransom ready to be paid? He thought about Jeff's offer to take his place. *Why did he do it?* he wondered.

They hit a rough spot in the highway, and Taylor was thrown against the side of the van. He cursed under his breath, but then felt a metal object under his arm. Watching the guard closely, he shifted his body until he could grasp it with the fingers of his right hand. It felt like . . . an ax! It had been left there with other tools that had not been in the van the day Taylor was taken outside the roadside café. When they were shoved in the van, he had noticed some tools and a length of nylon rope, but he hadn't seen the ax.

My God, what a break, he thought. *I may be able to cut through the leather cord around my hands. But then what? What am I going to do about the goon with the assault rifle?* Taylor's mind was racing now. *Don't worry about that, just get busy with the ax.*

While the guard in the back dozed, Taylor rubbed the binding against the business end of the ax. After a while he felt the leather thong give way slightly. He figured they would be in San Jose in another two hours. Whatever he was going to do would have to be done there. It was his only real chance.

The constant rubbing against the ax had parted additional threads in the leather binding, and Taylor started to believe that he might actually escape. But what about Jeff? Could he save his own neck and leave Jeff to whatever fate would have been his own if Jeff hadn't intervened? The analytical part of his brain kicked into gear. *Don't even think about it, Taylor. It's every man for himself. Besides, there is nothing you can do. It's the law of the jungle. Survival of the fittest.*

Taylor's guess that they were headed toward San Jose proved to be correct. The van had slowed considerably, and streetlights passing like silent sentinels told him they were in the outskirts of the city. Taylor put some pressure on the binding, and it felt like it had been worn through to the point where a sudden jerk would snap the remaining threads.

Although Taylor knew nothing about San Jose except for the little he had seen near the Ministry of Finance and the area around the Cariari Hotel, they seemed to be on one of the main streets. He couldn't have known that El Jefe had planned the most daring execution in the Luminoso's history.

The van was headed up the Avenida Central toward Sabana Park. When they dead-ended at the park, the driver jumped the curb and headed the van into the wooded area, a favorite spot for daytime strolls. El Jefe told the driver to stop the van and turn off the ignition. Taylor figured it was around midnight, although he couldn't be sure until his hands were free.

"Ahora!" El Jefe barked, and he and the driver opened the front doors and came around to the back. The one with the AK-47 opened the back door, reached for the coil of nylon rope, and tossed it to El Jefe. He climbed out of the van. Then the three of them pulled Jeff out the back door by his legs and carried him about a hundred feet to a medium-sized hardwood tree.

They failed to close the back door of the van, leaving Taylor in a position to see what they were doing. When El Jefe took the coil of rope and threw it over one of the lower limbs, he panicked, suddenly realizing they meant to hang Jeff. Taylor sat up as straight as he could and snapped the leather thong with a mighty outward thrust of his arms.

Now what? Try to help Jeff? Impossible. I've got to get out of here now. This is my only chance, he reasoned. *Can't leave by the back door, they'll see me for sure. Got to get out the front.* As quietly as possible, Taylor moved to the front seat, hunkered down as he slipped out the door on the passenger side, and then crawled toward a clump of bushes off to his right. Once he was safely in the brush, he turned and looked back toward the shadowy figures just as the three of them were hoisting Jeff off the ground with the rope around his neck.

The two goons held Jeff in place while El Jefe took the loose end of the rope and secured it around the base of the tree. At his signal they let Jeff go, and the full weight of his body collapsed toward the ground. At first there was nothing. Then Jeff stiffened and jerked, gasping for one last breath. Then it was over. Taylor felt like he was going to be sick. He had never seen anything so horrible, so barbaric.

I've got to get out of here, he thought. *As soon as they see that I'm gone, they'll search the area.* Taylor slipped out of the brush and headed for the darkest part of the woods. He could hear their excited, bewildered voices and he started to run. A jogging trail appeared, and he followed it to the southern edge of the park where he collapsed into a clump of bushes, gasping for air. *Got to stay here,* he thought. *They may circle around. Stay hidden till morning, then find the embassy. Oh God, thank you. Thank you.*

Ray Hargrove, the bureau chief for Associated Press in San Jose, was awakened by the telephone. "Hello?" he moaned, half-asleep.

"Senor Hargrove?"

"This is Ray Hargrove. What time is it?" He squinted at the bedside clock. It was one-thirty.

"This is the supreme leader of the Sendero Luminoso, and I have an exclusive for you. Are you interested?"

Ray sat up in bed. He had been following the hostage story and wondered when there would be a break. "Go on, I'm listening," he replied cautiously.

"One of the capitalists has been tried and convicted by the people's court, and execution was carried out at midnight. You will find the criminal in Sabana Park. Tell the Americans that we will not rest until our comrades are free."

"Wait a minute," Ray shouted. "How do I know you're for real? What is your name?"

El Jefe said, "I am the supreme commander of the Sendero Luminoso. That is all you need to know." Click.

"Wait a minute!" Ray demanded. It was no use. He dialed his office and waited for an answer. AP offices around the world were staffed twenty-four hours for obvious reasons, but he couldn't remember who was on duty. Raul answered the phone after several rings, having been aroused from a deep sleep.

"Raul, is that you?" Ray said excitedly. "Get your duff off that couch and take this down. Get a photographer and have him meet me at the office in twenty minutes. You got that?"

"Si, senor. I will call Ricardo. What is it, Senor Hargrove?"

"Never mind," Ray said. "Just get him there pronto."

Ricardo was waiting at the office, loaded down with cameras and equipment bag. Ray grabbed a minicam, telephoned the police and told them about the call, then hustled Ricardo down the stairs and into the car. He wanted to be sure they got there before the police.

They got to the park just as the police arrived and followed the main search party into the wooded area. It didn't take long before they found Jeff. Ray Hargrove had seen it all in the news business, but he was never really prepared for the ugly face of violence. Jeff's body hanging from the tree sickened him, but he was a professional. He calmly filmed the frenzied activity of the police as they took the body down and searched the area. Ricardo also took pictures from every possible angle. Since Ray had taken the call from El Jefe, the captain asked him to come to headquarters to give a statement. An ambulance had arrived by now. As Jeff's body was loaded onto the stretcher, Ray walked over for a close look. "What a shame," he muttered. "He was so young."

The next morning, Taylor crawled from his hiding place and hailed a taxi. When they pulled up at the embassy, he had the driver wait until he found someone to pay the fare. He presented himself at the guard's desk just inside the door. The guard made several calls, someone came with a file that contained Taylor's photograph, and he was led upstairs to a suite of offices to wait for the ambassador. While they were waiting, Taylor asked about Janet.

The ambassador's aide was puzzled. "Janet Dempsey? The young lady in the commerce section? She left yesterday. Reassigned to Europe, I think."

"Commerce section?" Taylor said. "I thought she was the ambassador's executive assistant. She met me at the airport when I arrived."

"Executive assistant?" the aide responded. "You must be mistaken. Miss Dempsey was a communications clerk in the commerce section. Did you say she met you at the airport?"

"That's right," Taylor said. "I was told it had been arranged."

The aide paused a moment, looking as if he was arranging the pieces of a puzzle in his mind. "How odd. We knew nothing about it in this office. In fact, we didn't know you were in Costa Rica until we heard the news about your capture."

Something's wrong, Taylor thought. *Something is terribly wrong here.*

The ambassador arrived within the hour. Taylor told him the whole story about Janet, about the Luminoso, the farmhouse, and about the tragic episode in Sabana Park. The ambassador was shocked to hear about the hanging and immediately telephoned the police. After an extended conversation in Spanish, he hung up the phone and confirmed that a young man identified as Jeff Richards had been hanged in the park sometime around midnight. When the police heard that Taylor was at the embassy, they insisted he wait there until they could send someone to question him.

While they were waiting for the police to arrive, the ambassador's secretary came into the room with a copy of The Tico Times. The entire front page had been given to the story, with a picture of Jeff's body hanging from the tree prominently displayed in the center of the page. Taylor suddenly realized that the story would be on the networks at home.

"I have to call my wife," Taylor said.

"Of course, Mr. Davis. You can use the telephone in the next office."

The media mob was outside the apartment again. The story had broken on the *Today* show, and

Cyndi had immediately called Sharon and asked her to come over. Even though it rang constantly, she was afraid to take the telephone off the hook in case something new developed. Sharon answered every call, repeating the same line about Mrs. Davis having nothing to say until she knew something further about Taylor's condition. One of the calls, however, caused Sharon's face to light up with a broad smile.

"Cyndi . . . it's Taylor."

Cyndi grabbed the telephone and blurted out, "Taylor? Is it really you, sweetheart?"

"I'm okay," Taylor said. "Have you heard the news about Jeff?"

"It was on the *Today* show this morning," Cyndi said, tears of joy streaming down her cheeks. "I've been going nuts ever since. Where are you? What happened?"

"I'll tell you all about it when I get home. I was able to escape last night, and I'm at the embassy in San Jose. There's some red tape to clear up, then I'll be on the first flight to Dallas."

"Oh Taylor, it's a miracle. I can't wait to see you."

"I know," he said softly. "Me too."

They talked for a few more minutes, then Taylor said he had to meet with the police. He promised to call back as soon as he knew which flight he'd be on.

Cyndi and Sharon hugged and cried, then Cyndi remembered the press outside the apartment. "I guess I'd better let the news people know about this," she said reluctantly.

Taylor's escape was a bigger story than the original kidnapping or execution. Cyndi spent nearly an hour with the media people outside the apartment. The rest of the morning was jammed with calls and requests for interviews. One call wasn't from a newsperson, however. It was from Jeff's father. Cyndi hadn't even thought of Jeff in her excitement over Taylor's escape.

"Hello. This is Cyndi Davis," she said tentatively.

"Mrs. Davis, this is Bill Richards, Jeff's dad. We just wanted you to know how happy we are that Taylor was able to escape."

Cyndi tried to think of something appropriate to say. "Thank you" didn't seem quite right. "Mr. Richards, I'm so sorry about Jeff. I don't know what to say."

"That's all right," he said. "We've all been through quite an ordeal. We just wanted you to know our prayers of thanksgiving are with you and your husband."

His prayers are with me? Shouldn't this be the other way around? Cyndi was embarrassed. "Thank you, Mr. Richards. I appreciate your call more than you know, and I want you to know that we share your heartache also."

Cyndi hung up the phone and told Sharon what had happened. "What kind of people would be giving thanks at a time like this?" she wondered aloud.

"Must be special people," Sharon replied.

CHAPTER FIFTEEN

Pan Am two-forty-three from San Jose to Houston lifted off the runway at ten minutes after three. Taylor missed the previous day's flight because of the extensive police interviews. When he told the police he could identify El Jefe, they had exchanged worried glances and suggested that he spend the night at the embassy. From that moment on a clinging, creeping fear had been Taylor's constant companion. He had even insisted that one of the embassy guards accompany him to the airport and see him safely aboard the flight.

Taylor took the Tico Times from his briefcase. When he looked at the gruesome photo of Jeff hanging from the tree, he saw himself. *I could be dead right now,* he thought. *This very instant I could be . . . what? . . . where? Why did he do it? Why would he give up his life, his football career? Jeff could have made millions in the NFL.*

"Would you like coffee or tea, Mr. Davis?" The flight attendant recognized Taylor. His photograph had been on the networks several times, and the crew was aware that he was the one who escaped.

"Black coffee," he replied.

Taylor knew he was still at risk. They could follow him anywhere, even to Dallas. For all he knew, his assassin could be on this very flight. His mind was spinning with the implications . . . Maybe the government will provide me with a bodyguard. We'll have to move to a more secure apartment. A pleasant business trip had turned into a nightmare that was threatening to change his life in unpredictable ways. Taylor's cleverness and analytical skills were useless against this threat. He felt small and vulnerable.

When they landed at Houston, the flight attendant came back to warn Taylor that a crowd of news people was waiting for him. It wasn't unexpected, and since he had over an hour before his connecting flight to Dallas, he agreed to take their questions in the VIP room. Nothing in Taylor's past had prepared him for the scene that followed. They were rude, loud, and some of the questions were obviously designed to elicit negative comments about the State Department's policy on hostages.

"Mr. Davis, can you tell us exactly how you were kidnapped?" someone shouted.

"I was taken from a car by three armed men."

"Where were you at the time?"

Taylor paused. *How much should I say about Janet Dempsey. Be careful, Taylor.* "I was driving to the coast with a friend, and we had stopped at a roadside café in the mountains. I was waiting in the car while my friend went inside, and three men drove up behind the car and forced me to go with them."

"What did your friend do when he found you missing?"

Taylor cursed under his breath. How to get out of this? Taylor wisely took another question from the back of the room.

"Were you and Jeff Richards taken at the same time?"

"No," Taylor explained. "Jeff was brought to the farmhouse about a week after I was taken."

"Can you tell us something about the conditions in the house? How were you treated?"

Taylor launched into a lengthy description of the farmhouse, the back room, the diet of beans and rice, their daily routine, and descriptions of the three men.

"Were you present when Jeff Richards was executed?" Taylor paused. "Yes. We were bound and gagged and driven to the park around midnight. When they took Jeff from the van, I was able to get my hands free and slip into some bushes nearby. After I reached cover, I turned just in time to see them securing the rope. Jeff was drugged, so I don't think he felt anything."

They furiously took down his comments and the television crews pressed in closer. Someone asked, "Do you have any idea why they chose Jeff for the execution?"

Taylor had already decided that he would keep Jeff's sacrifice to himself. No purpose would be served by making it public, and he was afraid it would make him look foolish if he told what happened in the cabin that night. Allowing Jeff to take his place would no doubt be perceived as cowardly. It was a secret better kept to himself. "I have no idea how they decided," he lied.

"Mr. Davis, can you tell us how you felt when you saw them hang the other hostage?"

"I felt terrible. How do you think I felt? It was horrible."

A voice yelled from the back. "Mr. Davis, how do you feel about the State Department's refusal to negotiate for the release of political hostages?"

Taylor was cautious. "I don't want to get into political questions. Obviously, my viewpoint is colored by my own experience as a hostage."

"But don't you think Mr. Richards might be alive tonight if the government had acted sooner?"

"I can't answer that," Taylor said. "It would only be speculation."

More questions were shouted as the airline representative called the conference to a halt and led Taylor from the room.

"Have you talked to your wife?"

"What were her first words when she discovered you were safe?"

"Will you ever go back to Costa Rica?"

Taylor waved goodbye and left the VIP room headed toward the gate for his flight to Dallas. His encounter with the press made him feel like a swimmer attacked by sharks. As soon as one of them drew blood, the others became frenzied, crazed, and determined to finish him off, to tear him limb from limb. *My God,* he wondered. *What must they be doing to Jeff's parents?*

The press scene was replayed in Dallas. They were waiting when he stepped off the plane. Television crews surrounded Taylor and Cyndi and recorded their tearful reunion for the six o'clock news. Taylor was upset. "Can't you people give us just a minute of privacy?"

His frantic plea only increased the jostling and pushing. Cyndi snuggled close to him and tried to calm him down. "They're only doing their job, sweetheart. I don't care if the whole world knows it . . . I love you."

"I know," he said. "It's just that I've already been through this in Houston."

There was no stopping them. Taylor finally agreed to take a few questions. It was nearly a word-for-word repeat of the scene in Houston, and it was another hour before they were able to head for home. A car was waiting outside the baggage area, and when Taylor realized Cyndi was headed toward the car, he stopped in his tracks.

"What's this?" Taylor demanded.

"He's with the FBI, sweetheart. They wanted to ask you a few questions and besides, I thought he could help us get through the press people outside the apartment."

"You mean I have to go through that again?"

"I'm afraid so. They've been camped there off and on for the last two weeks."

At the apartment, they were able to push through the reporters and get inside without too much difficulty. While Cyndi made a pot of coffee, Taylor briefed the agent on his ordeal. He started from the beginning and told him the whole story, except for the part about Jeff offering to take his place. He even told him about Janet Dempsey.

"You say she was the ambassador's executive assistant?" he asked.

"That's what she told me," Taylor replied. "But at the embassy they said she worked in the commerce section."

"Hmmmmm . . . interesting," the agent said as he scribbled a note. "I'll do some checking. Did they say where in Europe she had been transferred?"

"No. Just somewhere in Europe."

The agent spent most of the interview asking questions about El Jefe. He quizzed Taylor extensively on his physical appearance, speech patterns, habits, and anything that might help them prepare a profile.

Taylor remembered something. "Wait a minute. I think he said he was educated in this country. That's it. The University of Chicago."

"But you have no name other than El Jefe?"

"No. That's all they called him."

The agent scribbled a few additional notes on his pad and then returned it to his briefcase. "Thank you, Mr. Davis. You've been a big help."

Long after Cyndi had dropped off to sleep, Taylor was still awake and restless. He couldn't stop thinking about the events in Costa Rica, especially Jeff's offer to take his place. *Why?* he wondered. *Why did he do it? It doesn't make sense. Stories about soldiers who throw themselves on live grenades to protect their buddies are just legends. Nobody does that kind of thing in real life.*

Taylor sat straight up. "What's that?"

Cyndi was aroused by his voice and mumbled, "What's the matter? What is it?"

"That noise. Didn't you hear it?" Adrenaline raced through Taylor's veins and pushed his pulse rate to the stratosphere. He jumped out of bed and crept through the apartment. Nothing was disturbed. He turned on all the lights, looked in every closet, checked outside, and finally returned to the bedroom. *It's just nerves,* he thought. *I've got to get control of myself.* When he returned to their king-sized bed, Cyndi moved over to his side, snuggled against him, and said, "It's okay, you're safe now. It's going to be okay."

Cyndi had never been physically expressive, and Taylor liked feeling her warm body snuggled close to him, especially now. Intimacy was not a word he used very often, and the closeness that characterizes understanding between special friends was not part of Taylor's experience. He'd never known intimacy like that, at least not that he could remember, and it hadn't been present in his home.

In Taylor's world, relationships were used to gain advantage. His parents had always entertained clients of the firm, or people whom his father had targeted as potential clients. He had learned early the skills of expediency and manipulation. His whole life had been spent in the pursuit of the next advantage, and to his generation, relationships meant networking and collecting business cards. That's why he couldn't get Jeff's sacrifice out of his mind. What could possibly have motivated Jeff to give his life for a stranger?

The next morning, Taylor called Jeff's parents. They were glad he had escaped, of course, but they wanted to know about Jeff: his last hours, whether or not he suffered, what he said. Taylor didn't mention Jeff's sacrifice, but he did tell them what a special son they had, and how brave Jeff had been during the time he was held captive. He also promised to attend Jeff's funeral in San Diego the following Tuesday.

It was a brilliant day. The southern California sun combined with cool Pacific breezes to create the ambiance that had attracted generations of easterners escaping the smokestacks of Pittsburgh and Cleveland. Taylor and Cyndi had flown in on Monday night, and they were seated with hundreds of mourners in the sanctuary of Community Church. It was a pleasant tile-roofed structure patterned after the Spanish missions of early California. A section had been reserved near the front for the Stanford football team. Their youth and energy added a distinct poignancy to the occasion.

Network crews had positioned their cameras across the street from the church, ready to capture something, anything, with their intrusive telephoto lenses. Their presence reminded the mourners that Jeff's death carried a significance beyond one family's private grief.

After the family was seated, a young woman stepped to the microphone and sang a selection titled "Because He Lives." Then Jeff's pastor stood to give the eulogy. Actually, it was more a sermon than a eulogy since he used so much scripture. Taylor thought it was out of place at first, but then he got interested in the message. It was about life and hope as contrasted with death and despair.

"If Jeff was truly dead," the speaker said, "this would be a sad occasion, and we would have cause for despair. But Jeff lives, just as surely as the Savior lives. Listen to these words from the letter Paul wrote to the church at Corinth. 'But Christ has indeed been raised from the dead, the firstfruits of those who have fallen asleep. For since death came through a man, the resurrection of the dead comes also through a man. For as in Adam all die, so in Christ all will be made alive. But each in his own turn. Christ the firstfruits; then, when He comes, those who belong to Him.'"

Jeff's pastor was confident, self-assured, and had a strong voice. "Paul speaks of Jesus as a pathfinder," he continued, "when he calls him the firstfruits. He simply means that those who have received Christ as Savior and Lord are assured of personal resurrection by virtue of the fact that Jesus was Himself resurrected from the dead. I emphasize the word fact because Jeff's faith wasn't based on religious tradition or philosophy, but on the supreme fact of the universe, the resurrection of Jesus Christ in space and time. The resurrection is not a mystical ideal or a mythological relic. It is one of the most widely attested events in history. In the passage I just read, Paul says that Jesus appeared to many people after His resurrection, including a group of five hundred on one occasion."

Taylor had never thought of Jesus as a man who really lived and died and then came back to life. He wasn't sure what he thought about him. Was He just a myth perpetrated and kept alive by zealous followers? Was He a legend on the order of King Arthur? Jeff's pastor was presenting Jesus as unique in the history of the world, the only man ever resurrected from the dead. If it was true, then He was no King Arthur, and He was no myth.

Taylor pushed those thoughts from his mind and focused on the eulogy just in time to hear Jeff's pastor quote a vaguely familiar line.

"'Where, O death, is your victory? Where, O death, is your sting? The sting of death is sin, and the power of sin is the law. But thanks be to God! He gives us the victory through our Lord Jesus Christ.' The terrorists in Costa Rica thought they were taking Jeff's life, but Jeff Richards lives. He won't be walking among us as before, but he lives. He's just gone home a little early."

A scene appeared in Taylor's mind. He and Jeff were relaxing on the ledge overlooking the creek. The Luminoso goons were watching from the opposite bank, and Jeff was saying something about going home. What was it? They were talking about the impossibility of escape because of the guard with the assault rifle, and Jeff had said he sometimes looked forward to going home. Taylor thought he meant San Diego, but Jeff was talking about heaven.

". . . . just gone home a little early."

The pastor closed his Bible and sat down on the front pew. There was absolute quiet. Nobody moved. Every person in the room was thinking about his closing words . . .

"just gone home a little early."

CHAPTER SIXTEEN

Friday morning, Cyndi got up early and was dressed and ready for work by six-thirty. Taylor was still asleep when she came in to kiss him gently on the cheek.

"Where are you going so early?" he mumbled

"Sweetheart, I've got a breakfast meeting at the bank. I put some toaster waffles out for you, okay?"

Taylor sat up in bed, rubbing the sleep from his eyes. "What kind of meeting?"

Cyndi's first reaction was to lie. No need to tell Taylor about the prayer group she had been meeting with on Friday mornings. It had become a priority in her life since that night she decided to become a follower of Jesus, but she had dreaded Taylor's reaction. Would he think she had lost her mind? Gone religious? Changed in some way that would threaten their relationship? Besides, how could she explain it to him? He was so analytical.

She took a chance. "It's sort of a support group."

By now, Taylor was wide awake. Cyndi had

never been a morning person, and he had assumed that it was a business meeting.

"Support group? What kind of support group?"

Cyndi sat down on the edge of the bed and held Taylor's hand. "I nearly went crazy while you were being held hostage, and Sharon Dillow invited me to a prayer group that meets at the bank every Friday morning. I thought it might help, so I went. Jim Peterson leads it, and it's a really neat group."

"Who is Sharon Dillow . . . and Jim Peterson?" Taylor didn't recognize either name. What was going on? You didn't become a part of Taylor and Cyndi's crowd without going through an unwritten ritual of initiation, and if you couldn't bring something to the table you didn't get in.

Cyndi knew the rules. "Sharon is a trust officer," she said. "And Jim Peterson is one of our senior vice presidents. I've really got to run, sweetheart. I'll tell you all about it later, okay?" She kissed him and fled, leaving Taylor sitting up in bed, wondering what was happening to her.

"Don't forget to lock the front door," he shouted.

Taylor shuffled to the kitchen and poured himself a coffee, ignoring the waffles Cyndi had placed next to the toaster. He retrieved the *Times Herald* from the front walk, bolted the door, and settled down in the living area with the paper. His eyes wandered over the front page, but his mind wouldn't accept the transition; it was already engaged.

Had Cyndi gotten involved with some kind of cult? Taylor realized that she had been under incredible stress while he was in Costa Rica, but a prayer group? Prayer was for old ladies and weaklings. Even when he feared for his life that night in the cabin, it had never occurred to him to pray. In Taylor's world, every man was his own savior. If you couldn't get what you wanted by your own will power and skill power, by clever negotiation, or by manipulating others with persuasion and perks, then you didn't deserve it.

Admittedly, his philosophy had been severely challenged in the mountains of Costa Rica. Nothing in his background and training had prepared him for the utterly helpless position he had been in. If Jeff hadn't taken his place that night, Taylor's life would have ended in Sabana Park. The fast-track whiz kid, the youngest executive ever appointed CFO at Western Datacorp, would be a fading memory. His replacement would be seated at his desk this very minute, happily planning moves calculated to push the memory of Taylor Davis even farther into the background.

If Jeff hadn't taken my place, he mused. *Why did he do it? It was a stupid thing to do. He probably saw it as a grand gesture, something that would impress God . . . or the gods . . . whatever.* A question that had been purely theoretical in the past suddenly surfaced in Taylor's consciousness as very real and practical, demanding to be answered. *Do I believe in God? I mean, do I believe there is a God?*

Taylor hadn't bought Darwin's solution, primarily because the evolutionary theory ignored the big question. Evolved from what? The evolutionists theorized that life began in a primordial slime, and some went even farther back to swirling gasses that supposedly caused the big bang. But nobody could explain where the slime or the gasses came from. To believe that a being as complex as Homo sapiens had been crafted by a series of accidental mutations was nonsense, sheer speculation. Taylor's financial mind demanded something more systematic, more logical.

All right, wise guy . . . what's the alternative? Taylor put the paper aside, sipped the last of the coffee, and stared out the window. *Creation, of course. If the universe didn't evolve, then it was created. Those are the only choices. But created by what . . . or whom?*

In a flash of understanding, Taylor realized that he did believe there was a God. If he didn't buy the evolution story, then by his own calculation he had to believe in creation. But what kind of God? Obviously, he would be powerful . . . and infinitely brilliant . . . and, of course, creative! Was God still hanging around? He would have to be, Taylor figured, since the kind of God it would take to create and run the universe would have to be indestructible. Was He a person? Person seemed to be the wrong word. Was He like a person? Could He communicate with men?

Suddenly, Taylor remembered something Jeff

said one night in the farmhouse. He said there were two critical questions in life. Is there a God? And if there is, has He said anything? They were talking about whether heaven was a real place or not, and Jeff showed him some verses from the book of Revelation. It all came back to him now. He could recall that scene as clear as if it were taking place in the present moment. Jeff was saying the Bible was the revelation of God to men. He had been so young, so sure of himself, so passionate about his beliefs.

Of course, Taylor thought. *If God created man, and if He wants to communicate with us, then the Bible must have His message in it. And if God is a person or if He is personal, then prayer would be a way of talking to Him.*

The sheer simplicity of it appealed to Taylor. But did it make sense? Was it logical? Would it "compute"? *Probably not,* he thought. *The whole thing has to be taken on faith, and what's the difference between faith and wishful thinking?*

Taylor shelved his questions, picked up the sports section and read that the Mavericks had returned from a twelve-day road trip. Somehow they were hanging on to second place even though Perkins had been sidelined with an injured knee.

CHAPTER SEVENTEEN

For several weeks following his escape, Taylor suffered from intense anxiety. A debilitating fear of the Luminoso drained his energy and gutted his confidence. He couldn't sleep, he was unable to concentrate, and the simplest decisions loomed above him like monsters. He bluffed his way through meetings at the office, hoping nobody would notice. Cyndi did her best to help, but she didn't really understand what he was feeling. How could she? She hadn't seen Jeff hanging from that tree, drugged and helpless, a brilliant football career ended by a few zealots. And for what? What had they proved? How could Jeff's death advance their glorious revolution?

Cyndi had been a comfort though, even if she didn't understand what he was feeling deep inside. She seemed different to Taylor. She talked less about herself and her career, and seemed to be more focused on him. There was something new he couldn't quite define, a softness . . . no, more like a confidence that all was well in spite of the turmoil around her. There had been moments when he wished he could share his fear with her, to let her into his private world, but too many years of training in maleness had closed off that possibility. To share what he was feeling was too risky, too likely to be perceived as weakness.

Taylor thought about seeing a shrink, but in spite of the fact that being in analysis was a trendy thing in north Dallas, he couldn't bring himself to do it. Cocktail party chatter about co-dependency, getting in touch with your feelings, and understanding your inner child sounded like psychobalbble to Taylor. Besides, he found it incredibly boring.

Taylor's mother had been in analysis for years, and it had cost his father a small fortune. At gatherings in their home and at rare family dinners, she talked endlessly about the new insights "Antoine" had shared in that week's session. Dr. Antoine Van Zandt had always sounded like a stage name to Taylor, a goofy combination of French and German. Why would any man want to be known as "Antoine?"

The point was, she was just as neurotic after years of analysis, and Taylor had never been able to figure out why his father put up with it. He never had understood the relationship between his parents. At times it resembled a business arrangement, at others a complicated dance between two people who were desperately trying to appear as if they knew what they were doing when it was perfectly obvious that they were reading from different scripts. If for no other reason, Taylor wouldn't go near a psychiatrist because of what he remembered about his mother.

Taylor was an only child, and he sometimes

wondered if his mother swore off babies after he turned out to be more trouble than she had anticipated, even with a nanny. Growing up without siblings had been a mixed blessing. He got all the attention, of course, and he never lacked for anything, but he also felt that he had missed something important. There were times when he found it impossible to cultivate common friendships, and he had always wondered if things would have been different had he grown up in a real family.

Western was Taylor's family now. Ever since he could remember, he had used relationships with institutions as a substitute for family, and after making his mark at Wharton, the corporation had become his source of security and purpose. Stepping off the elevator at the eighteenth floor was like returning to the womb. He was safe there. He had identity on the eighteenth floor. The corporation would protect him, stand up for him, and take care of him in old age. At least that's what he had thought until two unexpected visitors appeared on the eighteenth floor one Tuesday morning.

Jenny buzzed him on the intercom and said there were two men from the Justice Department to see him. "Justice Department?" Taylor asked. "You mean like in Washington?"

There were muffled voices as Jenny confirmed her understanding. "Yes sir, they want to ask you a few questions."

Taylor tried to figure out what this could be. Something to do with the recent stock issue? No, that would be the SEC. The visit with Senator Harding? Not likely. Nothing he thought about made sense. "All right, Jenny. Bring them in."

Two dark-suited, well-groomed men walked into Taylor's office and flashed cards that identified them as special agents assigned to the commercial investigations branch of the Justice Department.

They occupied themselves with small talk about the weather and the Cowboy- Redskins game the previous Sunday while Jenny brought three coffees. Under normal circumstances, Taylor would have played the harried executive game, busy corporate officer interrupted from important matters by government functionaries. But circumstances hadn't been normal since Costa Rica, and he could feel beads of sweat under his collar and on his forehead. His mouth was dry, and a hurried swig of coffee didn't seem to help.

"Mr. Davis, we understand you are the chief financial officer of Western Datacorp."

"Yes, that's correct," Taylor answered.

"Have you recently made a trip to Costa Rica?"

Taylor relaxed slightly. "You must be here about the kidnapping. I've already told the FBI everything I know about it."

One of the agents said, "This isn't about the kidnapping, Mr. Davis. Did you meet with the minister of finance while you were in San Jose?"

So that's it, Taylor thought. "Yes, I met with Senor Pedrano about our joint venture in Costa Rica.

There had been a misunderstanding with the new government about repatriation of profits."

The agents stood to their feet. "Mr. Davis, I'm sorry to inform you that you are under arrest. You have the right to remain silent . . ."

Taylor's mouth dropped open. This wasn't happening, not in his office, not during business hours. It couldn't be.

". . . . you have the right to an attorney, and you have the right to know that anything you say may be taken down and used as evidence against you."

Taylor was stunned. "There must be some mistake. I don't understand," he pleaded. "What's the charge?" *Think, Taylor. Get you mind in gear. There's been a colossal bureaucratic screw-up, and you'll have to straighten it out.*

"The twenty thousand dollars you gave to Senor Pedrano was a criminal violation of the Foreign Corrupt Practices Act," the agent explained. "Section five specifically prohibits the giving of bribes to foreign officials."

"Bribe?" Taylor shouted. "That was no bribe. We were simply meeting the official requirements of their government." *Brilliant, Taylor. You just admitted that you gave him the twenty thousand. You better get your act together . . . quick!* His mind was searching, looking for the right combination of relevant facts. "There must be a mistake," he offered weakly.

One of the agents moved around the desk and produced a pair of handcuffs that had been concealed under his coat. "Please stand up," he said calmly.

"We don't like to do this, but it's regulations."

Taylor obediently stood to his feet as the agent secured the cuff on his right hand, then expertly clasped the left as well. "Don't I have the right to call my attorney?" he asked.

"In due time. Shall we go now?"

Taylor felt totally out of control, free-falling through space, the victim of a macabre joke that had gone terribly amiss. When they stepped from his office into the waiting area, he was momentarily blinded by televisions lights.

Jenny was protesting and trying to explain at the same time. "Mr. Davis, can you tell us what the charge is? Why are you being arrested?"

The agents slowed momentarily, then hustled him out of the office and toward the elevators with newsmen and cameras in pursuit. As they waited for the elevator, Taylor could hear one of the reporters at the end of the hall. "Channel five news has learned from usually reliable government sources that Mr. Taylor Davis, chief financial officer of Western Data-corp, has been arrested on charges of bribing a foreign official. Mr. Davis was recently involved in the kidnapping in Costa Rica, having escaped from the terrorists who were holding. . . ."

The elevator door opened and they stepped in. Mercifully, the agents barred the newspeople from joining them. At the first floor, they pushed through another crowd that had obviously heard something was up, a group that included people from his old department. Taylor was whisked to a waiting car and pushed into the back seat.

As they made their way to the Federal Building eight blocks away, Taylor kept turning two questions over in his mind. How did the Feds know about his meeting with Senor Pedrano, and who tipped the press to his arrest?

It all became clear at the arraignment. The judge obviously had advance knowledge about the case, and when the prosecutor described the charges, it all fell in place. It had been a sting operation! Taylor hadn't met with Senor Pedrano, he had met with a federal agent posing as the finance minister. They suckered him with the demand for a bribe, and then videotaped the meeting. They also tipped the press in order to get maximum exposure for the operation.

Paying "grease money" to foreign officials was a commonly accepted business practice in international operations, and the government very well knew it, but it was technically a crime after Congress passed the Foreign Corrupt Practices Act in a knee-jerk reaction to the Lockheed scandal. The Justice Department knew they couldn't enforce the law, but by arranging highly–publicized sting operations, they reminded the business community that big brother was watching.

When they arrived at the Federal Building, Taylor was taken before the judge, who explained the charges against him.

"Mr. Davis, how do you plead?" the judge asked.

Taylor answered, "Not guilty, your honor.

The prosecutor didn't ask for bail, since the government was primarily interested in the publicity. They weren't pretending that Taylor was a menace to society.

"Very well," the judge said. "In that case, I will release the defendant on his own recognizance. Mr. Davis, you will be notified of your trial date as soon as we have it on the docket. You are free to go for the moment."

For the moment? Taylor thought. *This isn't a game, and it isn't a nightmare. Taylor, you are in big trouble, and you'd better get the big guns out. Nobody can push Western Datacorp around like this, not even the government. Heads will roll when G. Preston hears about this.*

Jenny had called Cyndi and she was waiting outside the courtroom, genuinely perplexed by the proceedings. "Sweetheart, what's going on? What's it all about?"

"It's a huge misunderstanding," Taylor said. "Let's get out of here and I'll tell you all about it."

It was nearly five by the time they picked up Taylor's car, and since he didn't want to face anybody at the office just yet, they drove straight home, arriving just in time to see the arrest on the five-thirty news. It was awful. They were stunned by the spectacle of Taylor being taken from his office in handcuffs. At the end of the piece, a reporter interviewed Fred Hartwell, who was identified as a spokesman for the corporation. "Mr. Hartwell, we understand that Mr. Davis was in Costa Rica on company business. Can you tell us the extent of Western's involvement in this affair?"

Taylor's confidence disappeared as Fred effected a sanctimonious look, putting on his best "who me?" face. He knew what Fred was about to say.

"The company knows absolutely nothing about the alleged wrongdoing," Fred said, looking straight into the camera. *At least he emphasized "alleged,"* Taylor thought. Fred continued. "I can assure you that we will investigate this incident thoroughly, and if company policy has been breached, requisite measures will be taken."

"Requisite measures?" Taylor muttered aloud. When Fred was in public situations or conferences with relative strangers, he always sprinkled his conversations with two-dollar words, a habit that had always irritated Taylor.

Cyndi was completely in the dark, mystified by Jenny's call, the courtroom appearance, and now this spectacle on the evening news. "Taylor, what is this all about?" she pleaded.

"It's about covering your rear," he replied sarcastically. Taylor explained about the meeting with Senor Pedrano and the twenty thousand dollar fee. "It was a straight business deal, something that happens all the time. In Central and South America, you sometimes have to pay a fee to get public officials to do what they're supposed to do anyhow. It's called grease money, or mordida."

"Mor . . . what?"

"Mordida," Taylor explained. "It means the bite."

Cyndi was still puzzled. "But if it's not illegal in Costa Rica, why are you being charged here?"

"They're using an obscure law called the Foreign Corrupt Practices Act. Nobody pays any attention to it because it's virtually unenforceable."

"Then why did they charge you?" Cyndi asked impatiently. "I still don't understand."

It was all very clear to Taylor now. "From time to time, they make a big public deal out of some case, just to remind everybody that big brother is watching. The IRS does it every year in February or March. A well-known person will be hauled into court for tax-evasion, and the IRS hopes the press will make it a big story. Then all the ordinary taxpayers have it fresh on their minds when they sit down to do their own taxes."

Cyndi was frightened. "So they happened to pick you. Doesn't that mean you're in trouble?"

"No way," Taylor said bravely. "Number one, it was a corporate transaction. I was just the delivery boy, just carrying out orders. Number two, it was a sting operation."

"A what?" Cyndi asked, still puzzled.

"They set me up," he explained. "It was a federal agent pretending to be the finance minister. That's entrapment, and it'll never stand up in court." Taylor conveniently ignored the fact that the FBI had gotten a conviction with a sting operation in the Abscam trial.

He continued. "Number three, the wolf is going to be hot about this. It makes the company look bad, and I guarantee you he will bring the full force of Western's resources to bear on it."

"But what about Fred's statement?" Cyndi asked.

"What do you mean?"

"He just said the company knew nothing about it."

Taylor paused for a moment, considering the possibility that he might indeed be thrown overboard. "That's just a statement hurriedly thrown together by public relations. It doesn't mean anything."

The group gathered in G. Preston's office was not in a happy mood. They had just watched the five-thirty news on a portable TV that Miss Roberts had brought in, and they were waiting for the chairman's reaction. He glared at the TV, as if he could will the story to go away by staring it down.

Ryan spoke first. "This is terrible. Who let those news people on the eighteenth floor? Has anybody checked with security?"

"It's too late for that," the chairman grunted. "The fact is it happened."

Forbes sensed a golden opportunity to destroy the one obstacle to his own career goals, but he had to determine where G. Preston stood first. "Does anybody know how this happened?" he asked innocently, carefully watching the chairman's reaction.

"He was acting on his own," G. Preston responded. "Today was the first I knew anything about it. Apparently Mr. Davis thought he could cut a few corners and get away with it."

"Wow, that's too bad," Forbes offered. His implied concern for Taylor's well-being didn't fool anybody in the room.

"The question is, what do we do about it?" Fred added. "We've got a bona fide public relations thing on our hands, and whatever we do has got to be done quickly. We've got to contain the damage. What do you think, Ben?"

In addition to the executive committee members, G. Preston had asked Western's in-house counsel to attend the meeting. Ben Thompson was as conservative as they come, and he could always be counted on to articulate the worst case scenario. Ben automatically opposed every acquisition Western considered on grounds of real or imagined potential liability. The other officers called him "Play it Safe" Thompson.

"I think we need to be sure of the company's position first," Ben answered. "Has anybody checked the actual transaction? The press will want to know how twenty thousand dollars could be sent down to Costa Rica without anybody knowing about it."

They all watched the chairman, wondering if he knew the answer. He did. "I've already had the auditors check it out, and it's really very simple," G. Preston explained. "Taylor prepared a disbursement authorization before he left for San Jose, instructing accounts payable to wire transfer twenty thousand to San Jose for a currency hedging transaction. As you know, anybody in this room can authorize up to fifty thousand without another signature. Except, of course, for Ben here."

There was nervous laughter at G. Preston's implied joke about the trustworthiness of lawyers, but Ben ignored it and continued his analysis of the company's position. "The legal situation is quite clear, then. Taylor was acting completely on his own and the company has no potential liability that I can see, either civil or criminal. Of course, we might be accused of lousy internal controls . . ."

Fred Harwell interrupted. "Then it's public relations, pure and simple. We've got to have a story by tomorrow morning, or the press will keep this thing alive. Seems to me the first thing we do is tell them Taylor has taken a leave of absence while we investigate it thoroughly. Then after a week or so, we announce the results of the investigation and say that Taylor has resigned to pursue other interests."

It was obvious by Fred's detailed recommendation that he and the chairman had already discussed the situation before the meeting and arrived at this conclusion. This wasn't the first executive committee meeting that had been convened in order to officially bless a decision that G. Preston and Fred had already made, and the chairman's silence was the signal that this was one of those decisions.

"Are we talking paid or unpaid leave?" Ryan asked. He was disturbed by this ruthless exercise of power, even though he had seen it hundreds of times in his career. Truth was, he would rather be out selling adding machines and calculators than participating in this blood-letting.

G. Preston didn't even hesitate. "Unpaid. How would it look if we agreed that our numbers man is a criminal, then said we're going to take care of him until they lock him up?"

That was it. The decision was set in concrete, and the only thing left was to take care of the paperwork. Fred left the meeting to call Taylor.

Taylor and Cyndi hadn't planned to take any calls, a concern that was unfounded, since there weren't any. They had expected a deluge after the news, but none of their friends had the courage to call and say they'd seen it.

"Funny how people react to this kind of thing," Taylor mused aloud. "It's as if we announced that we both have terminal disease." What had happened was a no-no in their crowd. It was all right to cut corners, even legal corners, but it was not okay to get caught.

When the telephone did finally ring, Taylor answered it out of curiosity. "This is Taylor Davis."

"Taylor . . . Fred. Just wanted to call and let you know how concerned we are about what happened today. Mr. Wilson wants you to know that we'll do everything in our power to straighten this out."

"Thanks," Taylor sighed with relief. "It was quite a surprise, obviously. Before I knew what was happening, I was standing before the judge. The whole thing is a ridiculous government screw up."

"That's our thinking, too," Fred said. "The

chairman would like to see you tomorrow morning. Can you be in at nine?"

"Sure," Taylor responded. "I'm as anxious as anybody to get this straightened out. Thanks for calling."

"No problem," Fred cooed.

Taylor hung up and turned to Cyndi. "There's nothing to worry about, sweetheart. The wolf will teach the government to mess with Western's CFO . . . you watch."

Brave words, but they didn't help Taylor sleep. He tossed and turned most of the night, trying to put it all in place, constructing and discarding scenarios in his mind and then starting over again.

Cyndi lay in the darkness composing a prayer. *God, this is Cyndi again. I don't understand the first thing about the trouble Taylor is in, but I know we need your help. Please get us out of this mess.*

In his wildest imagination, Taylor couldn't have expected what happened the following morning. Miss Roberts told him the meeting was in Fred's office, and he expected to find Fred and G. Preston waiting for him. Instead he found Fred, Ben Thompson, and a security guard from downstairs.

Fred was the spokesman. "It was good of you to come in, Taylor. Please have a seat." He cleared his throat and began his little speech. "We're all terribly upset about what happened yesterday. It must have been quite an ordeal."

"It's not on my list of favorite things to do," Taylor replied, trying his best to remain calm.

Fred continued. "Obviously, the company is in a no-win situation, Taylor. On the one hand, we want to make sure your rights are protected, but on the other, we have to take measures to mitigate the damage your unfortunate decision has inflicted on the corporation."

Taylor could see where this was headed. "Wait a minute, Fred. You make it sound like I was the Lone Ranger in this thing. I didn't make this decision, the chairman did. I was only carrying out his instruction." *Where's the wolf?* Taylor wondered. *Why isn't he in this meeting?*

Fred abandoned his feigned concern for Taylor. "Mr. Wilson knew absolutely nothing about this affair. The auditors have examined the transaction slip and confirmed that you personally authorized the transfer of funds to Costa Rica . . ."

Taylor was stunned. G. Preston had covered himself by having the disbursement authorization prepared with Taylor as approver. Clever. The wolf was throwing him to the wolves.

" . . . and Mr. Thompson has advised us the best thing to do is place you on leave until this unfortunate incident is cleared up."

Ben looked surprised, unable to believe that he was being blamed for the decision, but Taylor wasn't fooled by the tawdry display of buck-passing. He understood what was happening. The company needed a scapegoat, and he was elected.

"What's the timing?" Taylor asked with resignation.

"Immediately," Fred responded.

"For how long?" Taylor asked. He still couldn't believe the chairman would hang this on a senior officer. Normally, the ax fell lower down on the tree. But then he was the one who had been arrested and he was the logical target.

"Until it's cleared up," Fred said.

"What about legal help?" Taylor asked, trying to salvage something out of the meeting.

Fred smiled. "Our attorneys will be available to help you in every way possible. We don't abandon our own, Taylor."

Don't abandon our own? Taylor couldn't believe it. Fred was trying to close the meeting with a pleasant benediction, all for one and one for all. It made him feel sick.

If the arrest the day before had been humiliating, being escorted from the premises by security was far worse. The government agents had been aliens, an outside force. This was like being forced out of your home by your parents. Taylor protested, but the guard told him he was only following orders.

He drove aimlessly for an hour, first heading out North Central toward home, then west on LBJ, then back south on Stemmons. His emotions gyrated wildly from anger to self-pity to despair, then back to anger. How could this happen to him? His life had been so charmed, his career so well-planned and executed. If anything, he felt more out of control now than he had in Costa Rica. The Luminoso had been an evil force, a chance happening like a collision with a drunk driver. Western was no drunk driver; it was his home, his foundation, his security, and the thing thing gave his life meaning.

Drop the fantasy, Taylor, he whispered to himself. *The wolf operates by the law of the jungle, and it was either the company or you. No question who loses that game. You've got to start planning your next move.*

The hope that Western would somehow rescue Taylor from his predicament had been smashed to pieces by little men meeting in an office on the eighteenth floor, and there was nothing he could do about it. Taylor turned north on the tollway and headed for home.

CHAPTER EIGHTEEN

Taylor spent the rest of the day thinking about what had happened. He examined it from every possible angle, constructed scenarios step by step, and tried to figure out a sensible conclusion. One scenario had him taking the public rap for the company, but returning as a conquering hero after Western's attorneys made mincemeat of the government's case. He envisioned the wolf giving him a reward for his bravery, perhaps a trip to Hawaii to recuperate from his ordeal.

"That's it," Taylor said aloud as he picked up the phone to call Western's attorneys.

"Giddings, Ellis, and Marshall," the receptionist chirped on the other end.

"This is Taylor Davis. I'd like to speak with Dan Marshall, please."

Dan had been the lead attorney on Western's underwriting, and he and Taylor had spent a lot of time working together on the project. Even though Dan wasn't a criminal lawyer, Taylor valued his advice.

Dan sounded cautious. "Hello, Taylor. I've been expecting your call."

Taylor was embarrassed. "Yeah. . . . well, I guess I'm a household name after last night's news, huh?"

"Sounds like you've got yourself a legal problem. What's it all about?"

Taylor didn't want to talk about it over the phone, so he made an appointment with Dan for the following morning and then spent the rest of the afternoon trying to decide what to tell Cyndi about the meeting in Fred's office. When Cyndi got home at six, she was surprised to find him asleep on the couch.

"Mmmmm . . . sweetheart, is that you?" He sat up on the couch and tried to clear away the cobwebs. "What time is it?"

"It's after six. Are you feeling okay?"

"Yeah, I'm okay . . . sort of."

Cyndi took off her coat and sat down on the couch next to him. "What's the matter, sweetheart?"

"The company decided to put me on administrative leave," he replied, trying to make it sound like a routine matter.

"What for? I don't get it."

"The arrest yesterday." Taylor was trying to place the company's decision in the best light. "They have to take a public stance, so I've been elected to take the heat."

Cyndi was genuinely perplexed. "But what does it mean? Have you lost your job?"

"No, nothing like that," he assured her. "They want it to look like they're taking action until the legal issues are settled. I'm meeting with the attorneys in the morning, and I have no doubt they'll have it settled within a week or two at the most. It just means I won't be going to the office until this blows over."

Taylor did his best to maintain a positive attitude, but an unmistakable pall hung over the rest of the evening. A quiet dinner interspersed with Cyndi's what-if questions was followed by a fitful evening of switching back and forth between television channels. The only bright spot was Cyndi snuggling next to him and assuring him that whatever happened, they would face it together.

The following morning, Taylor's brave façade was severely cracked by the morning paper. The story was still on the front page, and it contained fresh quotes cranked out by Western's public relations department. "Fred Hartwell, executive vice president of Western Datacorp, told the Times Herald that Mr. Davis has been placed on unpaid leave until further notice. When questioned about Western's knowledge of the alleged bribery, he said the company has launched an internal investigation to determine the facts, and continued to insist that Western knew nothing about the incident before Mr. Davis was arrested on Tuesday."

"Unpaid leave?" Taylor blurted out. "Fred didn't say anything about suspending my salary."

Cyndi knew intuitively that this was more serious than Taylor had pretended. She wasn't unschooled in the nuances of corporate behavior, and she certainly understood the public relations problem Western had on its hands. "When the wolves circle the cabin, you throw them some meat and hope they'll go away," she said sarcastically.

Taylor looked up from the paper. "What did you say?"

"Nothing," she replied angrily.

Taylor was kept waiting in the reception area at the attorney's office for nearly an hour. The receptionist kept offering him coffee and saying Dan was in a meeting.

When she finally ushered him into Dan's office, Taylor was introduced to one of the firm's criminal law specialists, and older member of the firm. Dan nervously asked him to brief Taylor on his options, clearly unhappy about having to sit through such an unpleasant meeting.

"Mr. Davis," he began rather formally, "it's our understanding that the government has a videotape of your alleged meeting with Senor Pedrano."

"That's what they claimed at the arraignment," Taylor answered. "Look, let's not beat around the bush, shall we? I paid the twenty thousand, but it was on Mr. Wilson's instructions and with his full knowledge. Besides, it was a straight business deal, something that happens all the time in Central America. Grease money is a cost of doing business in most of the world, and I don't see how the government can apply our standards of conduct to the rest of the world, much less call it a criminal act."

"Can you prove that Mr. Wilson knew about the transaction?" Dan asked.

Taylor was becoming a little irritated. "He approved it over the telephone . . . unfortunately for me as it turns out." Taylor was thinking about the doctored transaction slip. "Suppose I can't prove he authorized it. Isn't there a law against entrapment? And how can they charge me with something that was done in another country?"

The older man peered at Taylor over the top of his reading glasses. "You've been charged under a provision of the Foreign Corrupt Practices Act, which covers specified acts anywhere in the world, and unfortunately, the Abscam trial set a precedent on the entrapment issue."

"So where are we?" Taylor asked. "What do you guys recommend?"

"Mr. Davis, in a case such as this where the facts are virtually undisputed, we normally recommend a plea bargain."

"Plea bargain? You sound like I've already been convicted," Taylor snapped. "What kind of plea bargain?"

The older man explained in a calm but deliberate tone. "I spoke with the prosecutor on a strictly informal basis this morning, and he indicated the government would entertain a guilty plea to a lesser charge, perhaps obstruction of justice with recommendation of probated sentence."

Taylor was furious. It was obvious that this

meeting had been scripted in Fred Harwell's office, and the attorneys were simply playing the part assigned to them by a powerful client. "I only have one question," Taylor said. "What is your estimate of the fee?"

Dan cleared his throat, uneasy about his part in the meeting. "In the event of a plea bargain, Western has agreed to take care of our fee. Under other circumstances, we're led to believe that it will be your responsibility, and a full-blown defense could run as high as eighty or a hundred thousand."

"Well, it looks like Senor Pedrano isn't the only one being offered a bribe," Taylor said sarcastically. "Gentlemen, thank you for your time, but I don't think I'll be requiring your services." Taylor got up and stalked out of the room, leaving Dan and his associate staring at each other.

His last vestige of hope dashed in Dan Marshall's office, Taylor headed toward home, then changed his mind and drove to the Galleria. He sometimes walked around the Galleria while wrestling with a particularly thorny problem, hoping the distractions offered by North Dallas's monument to consumerism would clear his mind and spark a new idea.

The bright lights and myriad offerings only made him feel worse. The specialty boutiques, fashion displays, and electronic gadgets mocked him with mute arrogance. His generation had raised conspicuous consumption to new heights, demanding the latest, the best, the fashionable; now the products of their desires seemed cheap and tawdry. In spite of the things Taylor owned and the position he had attained, he was being victimized by the very system he had worked so hard to master. To the system there was very little difference between things and people. Western had treated Taylor much like it would a factory made obsolete by changing technology. Get rid of it. Start over with something new, something more profitable. Bad publicity had rendered him expendable—last year's technology.

Taylor headed for the parking garage as tears rolled down his cheeks. He quickened his pace, afraid that someone would notice. When he got to the car, it all broke loose. Long-suppressed feelings rushed to the surface like a diver gasping for oxygen, and his body shook as he sobbed uncontrollably. He had bet his whole life on the system, and it was grinding him under like trash.

He sat in his car for nearly an hour until he didn't feel anything anymore, then drove home and waited for Cyndi to arrive. There was no use pretending with her anymore. She deserved to know the truth, and after dinner Taylor told her the real story. "I've been dumped, sweetheart. I'm through at Western. It's just a matter of time until they make it official."

Cyndi had never seen Taylor so down, so whipped. He had always been such a fighter. "Taylor, this isn't the end of the world. You can get a good job somewhere else. We'll make it."

"Sure," he replied. "You heard of any good

openings at Leavenworth? If I'm lucky, I'll get to be a file clerk in the warden's office."

"Stop it," Cyndi pleaded. "We're going to beat this thing. I just know it."

"Thanks, sweetheart," he said. "It helps to know you're on my team."

Cyndi had a thought. "Taylor, we're not without friends. The Friday group has held us up in prayer through this whole ordeal. Why don't you go with me tomorrow morning?"

He had forgotten about the Friday prayer group. Why not? Even though he didn't believe in it, what could it hurt at this stage? "All right," he agreed. "I'll go with you. You sure they won't mind a skeptic joining in?"

"They won't mind," she smiled. "I've never felt as loved and accepted anywhere as I do with those people." Cyndi threw her arms around Taylor and pulled him close. He could feel tears forming in the corner of his eyes as she gently rocked him back and forth. "It's going to be okay, Taylor. We're going to beat this thing together."

Jim opened the discussion by reading from the New Testament book of Galatians. "I'd like to read verse thirteen from chapter three as a devotional thought this morning," he said. Then he read aloud, "Christ redeemed us from the curse of the law by becoming a curse for us, for it is written cursed is everyone who is hung on a tree. He redeemed us in order that the blessing given to Abraham might come to the Gentiles through Christ Jesus, so that by faith we might receive the promise of the Spirit."

Taylor was struck by a phrase Jim read. "Cursed is everyone who is hung on a tree." He was back in Sabana Park, hiding in underbrush, watching as Jeff hung from a tree, the life squeezed from his body by his own weight.

" . . . the expression hung from a tree," Jim continued, "is a reference to the crucifixion of Jesus. He was hung on a cross, of course, not from a tree as we think of a hanging. The important thought in this verse is that He became a curse for us, or that He took our place there . . ."

In a flash of insight, Taylor understood. Jeff had taken his place, too. Taylor had received the curse when El Jefe gave him the ace of spades that night in the farmhouse, but Jeff took it instead. *Why?* he wondered. *Why did he do it?*

Jim continued with his explanation. "When Adam and Eve deliberately chose to disobey God, they passed on to their descendants what the Bible calls a sin nature. We are born with this nature, a tendency to be our own god, and many people spend their whole lives acting as if God was irrelevant. . . ."

He's right, Taylor thought. *That's a perfect description of my life.*

"Since God is perfect," Jim said, "He couldn't ignore sin or He would be dishonest, a denial of His own character. So He redeemed us by taking the curse upon himself. God came to earth in the person of His Son, Jesus, and took the rap for us. We were under a sentence of death, we deserved punishment, but He took our place. He became a curse for us. Incredible, isn't it?"

The group was quiet until someone asked the question that Taylor wanted to ask—a question that had been more in the back of his mind ever since the night Jeff was killed.

"Jim. . . . I never have understood exactly why He did it. I guess I understand why a payment had to be made, but why did God make the payment for us?"

Jim smiled. "In the first place, we need to understand that we couldn't make the payment ourselves. What would we use? We have nothing of value to offer God—not good deeds, not wealth or fame. Nothing we can do or say is good enough. That's the bad news. The good news is that Jesus paid the price for us simply because He loved us. It says in the book of Romans that even though we had ignored God, Jesus demonstrated His love for us on the cross."

Taylor was deep in thought. *I've always wanted to be loved like that. Is that why Jeff took my place in Sabana Park? He didn't owe me anything. He didn't even know me.*

"Just to wrap this up," Jim was saying, "God won't force His love on us. We have to receive it. The passage says that redemption comes through Jesus, and by faith we receive the promise of the Spirit. That means God has left the decision with us. The price has been paid, but we receive redemption by faith in Jesus Christ. We're nearly out of time, but let's spend a moment in prayer, shall we? Does anybody have a special need you want us to remember this morning?"

Cyndi didn't hesitate. Everybody in the room knew about Taylor's situation already, but she wanted it included. "Please pray for us," she said. "As you all know, we're facing some very difficult days."

"Thank you," Jim said. "Anybody else?"

Several other concerns were mentioned, practical things like family relationships or difficulties at work. One man mentioned his son who was in a drug program.

Jim suggested that they join hands, and then he prayed. He didn't use stilted, archaic terms, but talked to God as if He were seated in the circle with them. Taylor felt like he was suspended in a time-warp waiting for Jim to finish talking to God. Nothing else in the world mattered except this moment.

Afterward, while everyone chatted over coffee and donuts, Taylor found an opportunity to speak with Jim privately. "Jim, I enjoyed your talk, but I honestly don't understand that last part about receiving the Spirit by faith."

Jim finished his coffee and said, "That is a mystery, isn't it? If you have time, why don't you come up to my office and let's talk about it?"

"I'd like that," Taylor said.

"Good. My office is on the tenth floor. I'll see you there in fifteen minutes."

Jim had already poured two coffees by the time Taylor arrived, and he directed him to a small couch.

"Let's sit over here, shall we?" Jim's office had a seating area with two easy chairs and a small couch, separated by a low coffee table. He had an easy manner about him, and Taylor felt comfortable even though they barely knew each other. "I'm so glad you joined us this morning," Jim said. "You must be feeling a lot of stress, Taylor. I hope this morning helped some."

"Stress is an understatement, Jim. I was just beginning to get over the kidnapping when this thing with the government came down on me. I'm a little traumatized to be honest, but this morning helped a lot. Thanks."

Jim got right to the point. "Taylor, you asked me about receiving the Spirit by faith. I assume you have never made that decision?"

"I guess not, since I don't really understand it," Taylor confessed.

"The Bible says we were born with dead spirits, Taylor, and we have no way to relate to God because of the tremendous gap between God and man. So God built a bridge over the gap, Christ's death on the cross, but we have to cross that bridge. When a person decides to receive God's gift of redemption, to commit his life and future to Jesus Christ, he crosses the bridge, and God makes him into a new person. The Bible says he becomes a new creation, a spirit-creature with the ability to know God and relate to him. His sins are forgiven, and he is assured of spending eternity with God. Have you ever heard the expression born-again?"

"Yeah," Taylor said. "Although in my circle,

it's not a very nice thing to say about someone. It usually implies hypocrisy."

Jim smiled. "I know what you mean. It's funny how we make such a big deal of hypocrisy when we're all guilty of it. That's really the point of the scripture I read this morning. Because of our hypocrisy, among other things, we are under a curse, but we can receive God's blessing through faith in Christ."

"I guess the faith part is my hang-up, Jim. I'm used to dealing with facts, and I don't see how wishful thinking can make something happen."

Jim chuckled. "You sound like one of the disciples."

"I don't understand," Taylor said.

Jim explained, "A couple of the disciples saw Jesus after He was resurrected. When they rushed back to tell the others, Thomas responded like you did just now. He said 'I'll believe it when I see it.'"

"You mean doubting Thomas?" Taylor responded. "I've heard that expression, but I didn't realize it was from the Bible."

"There's a lot of stuff in the Bible," Jim replied. "Do you know how Jesus responded to Thomas? He showed up at one of their gatherings and let him feel the scars in his hands and side. Thomas became a believer that night."

"That would be pretty impressive," Taylor said.

"Taylor, I understand your desire to see God in the flesh, but the truth is you believe all kinds of things you can't see with your physical eyes. You already live most of your life by faith. You get a piece of paper from a doctor you barely know, with scribbles you can't read or understand, and you take it to a stranger who claims to be a pharmacist. He gives you some pills you know nothing about, and you take them. If that isn't faith, what is it?"

"I guess you're right," Taylor smiled. "I hadn't thought of faith in those terms."

"Taylor, the evidence for God is all around us, and the existence of Jesus on the earth is a historically documented fact. On top of all that, God has given us the Bible as a road map. Do you think it makes sense to travel through life without consulting the only map that describes the way to eternal life?"

Taylor was deep in thought. He remembered how Jeff had talked about the Bible, describing it as the revelation of God to man. "No, that doesn't make sense," Taylor said.

Jim continued. "Faith is just acting like God tells the truth, Taylor. We have two basic choices in life. We can believe God and receive redemption on his terms, or we can go through life pretending we're our own god with the power to determine our own destiny. It's really not much of a choice, in my opinion."

They were silent for a moment. Taylor knew Jim was right. It was one or the other. All his life, Taylor had chosen to be his own god, making up his own values. Objection to faith was a flimsy screen he had erected to conceal self-worship.

Taylor broke the silence with something that

he now understood with exceptional clarity. "I think God gave me a sign like he did Thomas."

Jim was puzzled. "What kind of sign?"

"Nobody else knows this, but when Jeff Richards was hanged by the terrorists, it should have been me."

"What do you mean?"

Taylor told him about El Jefe's card game in the farmhouse that night, and how Jeff had offered to take his place. "Jeff was a Christian, and we had talked a couple of times about the Bible and about faith, but I didn't really understand why he took my place until just now. I think God wants me to understand that Jesus died on the cross for me . . . for Taylor Davis, skeptic. I'm like Thomas. I wouldn't believe unless I saw it."

Jim was surprised. "That's an incredible story, Taylor. God used a tragedy to show you something very precious."

"Yeah, I know," Taylor said. "Jim, thanks a lot for this talk. I think I understand what faith is now, and I promise you I'll give it serious consideration. I appreciate your help."

"Glad to do it. I'll be praying for you, Taylor."

Somewhere between Jim's office and the elevator, Taylor crossed the bridge. He decided to give up running his own life, acting as if he were his own god, and he consciously placed his faith in Jesus Christ. It wasn't an emotional thing, although he felt good about what he was doing. It was a decision, an action—a step of faith!

Taylor was unusually quiet at dinner. Cyndi figured it was because of the arrest and shabby treatment he had received from the company. He blurted out something so totally unexpected, she thought she must have misheard.

"Cyndi, I decided to become a Christian today."

"What?" she gasped.

"After the prayer group this morning, I spent some time with Jim talking about faith in Christ, and I decided to become a Christian. Are you surprised?"

Cyndi's heart beat faster and tears formed in her eyes. "I made the same decision while you were in Costa Rica. Sharon explained it to me one day, and I bought a Bible that very evening. I couldn't stop reading through John that night. When I saw what Jesus went through for us, I knew I had to respond. I've been on pins and needles since you got home, wanting to tell you but afraid of what you might think."

Taylor reached across the table and took Cyndi's hand. "Sweetheart, it looks like God wanted us in this together. I don't understand it all, but I can't help but feel that we've made the most important discovery in life. I'm glad we're doing it together."

Cyndi dabbed at the corners of her eyes with her napkin. "Me too. I feel like a new-born person. The things I've felt and thought these last few weeks don't seem like the old me at all. It's been wonderful."

They spent the remainder of the evening talking excitedly about what had happened and the events that led to their decisions. Taylor told her about Jeff's sacrifice, and how God used it to open his eyes to the purpose for Christ's death on the cross. She shared with him the terrible guilt she had felt about the abortion, and how the knowledge that she was forgiven had made her feel clean and pure. She even expressed hope that they would be united with the baby some day, and that it would be a joyful, wholesome reunion.

When Cyndi got ready for bed, Taylor told her he would be in later. "There's something I have to do before I can sleep tonight," he said. He sat down with his laptop computer and composed a letter to Jeff's parents. He told them about Jeff taking his place, and what a brave and loving thing it had been. He told them what a fine young man he was, and how he would be honored if he could have a son just like him some day. Then he told them about the part Jeff had played in his decision to become a Christian.

"God used Jeff to show me Himself," he wrote. "I don't know whether that will comfort you in your loss, but I believe it's one of the noblest things that could be said about someone . . . he showed me what God is like. I expect to see Jeff again some day, as I know you do, and I'm looking forward to thanking him in person. Yours truly, Taylor."

CHAPTER NINETEEN

The world seemed fresh and new to Taylor. The Bible was becoming a treasure. It was a daily source of knowledge about things that had always been mysteries. He and Cyndi had started attending Grace Presbyterian, Jim Peterson's church, and had found a warmth and fellowship there that neither of them had ever experienced. The most amazing thing was the peace Taylor felt in spite of losing his job and preparing for the trial.

Jim had recommended an attorney to Taylor. Mike Phillips was a member of Grace Presbyterian who specialized in criminal law. He and Taylor went over final preparations on the Monday before the trial started on Tuesday.

"We've got to convince the jury that you were acting as an agent for the company," Mike said. "We've got the telephone record that proves you called Mr. Wilson's private number from San Jose, but you could have been talking about the weather as far as the jury knows. We need something stronger."

"What about the transaction slip?" Taylor

asked.

"You mean the fact that it doesn't actually have your signature?"

"Yeah. Won't that help?" Taylor knew nothing about the rules of evidence, but the absence of his signature seemed important to him. Mike had obtained a copy of the disbursement authorization during the discovery phase and found that someone had typed "per Taylor Davis" on the signature line.

Mike wasn't happy with his case. As things stood, it came down to Taylor's word against Mr. Wilson's, and it was a fifty-fifty which one the jury would believe. "Taylor, what do you think really happened?"

"You mean the transaction slip?"

"Right. Who typed it, and who gave the order?"

Taylor had leveled with Mike from the beginning, partly because he trusted Mike, but primarily because he still didn't think he had done anything wrong. "I think the chairman set me up, Mike. I think after I talked to him on the phone that day, he had someone prepare the disbursement authorization with my name on it in case something went wrong."

"But who?" Mike asked

"You can be sure he had one of the top officers do it, and there's no way any of them would admit it. Does it really matter?"

"The law is a little vague on responsibility, Taylor. If we could prove that the order came directly from Mr. Wilson, then it becomes a corporate crime.

The corporation is deemed responsible."

"What's the penalty?" Taylor wondered how you could send a corporation to jail.

"Normally a pretty hefty fine and a cease and desist order, which forces a company to discontinue some practice or line of business. In some of the insider trading cases, the government forced a corporation to dismiss several of its top officers—the head man in a couple of cases."

Taylor pondered the prospect of G. Preston being forcibly removed from his lair on the eighteenth floor. "How the mighty are fallen," he mumbled.

"Of course, there's always the chance I'll be able to shake Wilson's testimony," Mike added.

"Don't count on it," Taylor responded. "I've seen him in action too many times."

"Yeah . . . well, you've never seen him on the witness stand under oath. It's one thing to shade the truth in a business deal; it's quite another to perjure yourself."

Taylor pensively tapped the eraser end of his pencil on the conference table. Mike's comments about cross-examination applied to him as well. How would he hold up? Would the prosecutor twist his answers, make him look like a fool before the jury? What if the jury was made up of blue collar types who wouldn't understand business matters? Would they even listen to his testimony?

"Mike, what do you really think of my chances?"

Taylor, I'll be honest with you. It comes down

to whether the jury believes you or Mr. Wilson. In an even contest I would be more confident, but the government's video will make you look like a crook before you even get on the stand. You'll be starting at minus ten."

Taylor appreciated Mike's candor. "Care to make a prediction?"

"I don't make predictions," Mike said. "But you're entitled to hear the worst case. If you're convicted, the judge will determine your sentence, and he's very tough on white-collar crime. They call him maximum Bob around the Federal Building."

"So spell it out," Taylor asked. "Am I looking at a prison term?"

"I'm afraid so. The maximum sentence is fifteen to twenty, which means you'd serve at least seven. It goes down from there."

Taylor stopped tapping the pencil and wrote some figures on the yellow pad in front of him. "That's only three thousand, two hundred and fifty-five days."

"All rise," the bailiff announced. "The federal district court is now in session with the honorable Robert J. Walker presiding."

Jury selection had taken three days. Mike did his best to impanel a jury that would be sympathetic to his case, but as Taylor scanned the seven men and five women, it was patently obvious that Mike had failed. There simply hadn't been enough white-collar, upper middle class types to choose from. The group seated in the jury box was not likely to empathize with, nor understand the complicated world of commerce and finance. All of the men were laborers, men who worked with their hands. Four of the women were working wives employed in clerical or sales positions. The fifth was the only pro-fessional.

The morning had been taken up with opening arguments from both sides. Now the government prosecutor was ready to present the strongest part of his case, the video tape. Two large monitors had been brought into the courtroom. There was one for the judge and jury, and another for the gallery.

"Your honor, this video tape is marked as exhibit three. With your permission, we would like to show it to the jury."

Mike was on his feet. "Objection, your honor."

"What is your objection, counsel?" the judge grunted.

Mike knew he had no chance of excluding the video, but he had to at least try. "Your honor, this tape is prejudicial to my client since it was made without his knowledge and consent. It may mislead the jury since it does not show the events preceding the meeting, namely my client's telephone conversation with Mr. Wilson, the chairman of Western Datacorp."

Taylor smiled at the clever way Mike had pre-introduced his case, and at the same time attempted to create a question of credibility in the jurors' minds. The judge didn't buy it.

"Objection denied, and I will caution counsel to wait his turn."

"Thank you, your honor." Mike sat down and watched the jury for their reactions to the tape. The video had a leader where the place, date, and time was established by the agent playing Senor Pedrano. The next sequence showed Taylor entering the office with the briefcase. The sound quality was not very good, and several of the jurors leaned forward to hear what was being said. Taylor was shocked at how cut and dried it appeared even to him.

"Did you bring the twenty thousand, Mr. Davis?" the agent was saying.

"Yes," Taylor replied. "Would you care to count it?" The film then showed him placing the briefcase on Senor Pedrano's desk, opening it, and turning it toward the agent.

"Everything seems to be in order, Mr. Davis. In return for twenty thousand dollars, I will use my good offices to assist your company in its problems with my government."

Good grief, Taylor thought. *The only thing missing is the word bribe.* He glanced at the jury, and there was no mistaking their reaction. It was a very damning piece of evidence. The prosecutor ran the tape several times over Mike's objections, just to make sure the image of Taylor delivering a briefcase full of money was burned into the jurors' minds.

Taylor turned to Mike and whispered, "They didn't show the first meeting."

Mike gave him a puzzled look. "Is it important?"

"I'm not sure," Taylor said. "But it might be.

When Senor Pedrano . . . uh, the agent . . . said it would cost twenty thousand, I think I said something about checking with the home office in Dallas."

"No wonder they didn't show it." Mike scribbled a note on his pad, reminding himself to bring it out on cross-examination.

The agent who had pretended to be Senor Pedrano was called to the stand next. The prosecutor walked him through the transaction step by step. One question that had dogged Taylor was partially answered by the agent's testimony when the prosecutor asked him how the sting operation was set up in the beginning.

"We had a tip that Mr. Davis would be meeting with the finance minister on the day in question."

Tipped off? Taylor figured it could only have been two people. *Senator Harding? Janet Dempsey? No, Janet wouldn't have had time. It had to be the senator.*

The prosecutor asked the agent a few technical questions about the placement of the camera, the equipment they used, and the steps taken to ensure the integrity of the film as evidence. He then turned him over to Mike for cross-examination.

Mike stood just in front of the bench and to the right of the witness stand, a position that allowed him to face the jury as he asked his questions. That way they were certain to catch his facial expression as well as hear the question clearly.

"Agent Parker, did the videotape shown to the jury include both meetings in the finance minister's office?"

The agent looked surprised. "I don't understand."

"You had two meetings with my client in the finance minister's office. Did the video include the first meeting?"

"Objection, your honor." The prosecutor was on his feet. "It hasn't been established that there were two meetings."

"Quite right, your honor," Mike replied. "If you will allow me to continue, I will establish that fact with Agent Parker's help." Mike was gambling that the judge would be just as curious as the jury about the first meeting.

"Objection overruled."

"Thank you, your honor." Mike looked at the jurors. He hoped he had planted a seed of doubt in their minds about the prosecutor's motive in concealing an important fact.

"Mr. Parker, didn't you meet with my client on two successive days, and isn't this video tape an account of the second meeting only?"

"Well, yes . . . but I don't see what that has to do with . . ."

"Thank you, Mr. Parker. I have no further questions, your honor."

Mike knew he couldn't force the prosecutor to show the first meeting to the jury.

He also knew the jury would now be curious about the meeting wondering if it contained evidence that weakened the government's case. He was also taking a risk. If Taylor's memory was flawed, and if the prosecutor took advantage of it by showing the first meeting on redirect, then Taylor's entire testimony would be suspect.

The government's final witness was Alicia Williams, Western's disbursements manager. The prosecutor entered the transaction slip into evidence, then asked her a few questions about Western's disbursement policies. He asked about who could authorize expenditures of this size, and the details concerning this particular transaction. Mike was surprised at this opening, and when his turn came, he jumped to his feet to take advantage of it. He lifted the transaction slip from the exhibits table and handed it to her, looking straight at the jury with his first question. "Miss Williams, have you ever seen this document before?"

"Yes sir."

"Did Mr. Davis give it to you?"

"No sir."

"How did it come into your possession?"

"I received it through the interoffice mail."

Mike paused, looking at the jury. "Can you tell this jury who sent it to you?"

"It came from corporate."

"Will you explain what you mean by corporate, Miss Williams?"

"It came from the eighteenth floor, from corporate headquarters."

"But which person on the eighteenth floor?" Mike asked pointedly.

She shifted nervously. "I don't know. It didn't say who sent it."

"Miss Williams, do you mean to tell this jury that you would prepare a disbursement for twenty thousand dollars without knowing who made the request?"

"Oh, I knew who authorized it . . . it was Mr. Davis."

"How do you know that?" Mike asked.

"His name was on the disbursement slip."

Mike spoke slowly and deliberately, making certain the jury understood his next point since it was the one flaw in the government's case. "Miss Williams, I ask you to look at the transaction slip in your hand. Will you please tell the jury whether or not it contains Mr. Davis' signature?"

She looked down at the form, then back at Mike, then toward the jury. "It doesn't have his actual signature, just his authorization."

"I'm sorry, Miss Williams. I don't understand the difference between a signature and an authorization. Will you explain that to us?"

"Sometimes we get disbursement slips from the eighteenth floor that don't actually have signatures. They just say per Mr. Wilson or one of the other corporate officers."

"Do Western's disbursement policies allow you to cut checks without a signature on the transaction slip . . . especially a transaction for twenty thousand dollars?"

Alicia was visibly upset at being maneuvered

into admitting she had done something against written policy. "It's standard procedure. We've never had a problem with it before."

"Miss Williams, do you know for a fact that Mr. Davis authorized the disbursement of twenty thousand dollars to the Banco Nacional in San Jose?"

"I was certain that he had . . ."

"Miss Williams, I asked you a simple question. Do you know for a fact that Mr. Davis authorized this transaction?"

Alicia stared down at her purse. "I guess not," she mumbled.

Mike looked straight at the jury, modulating his tone of voice for effect. "Please speak more clearly, Miss Williams. The jury is waiting for your answer."

"I guess not," she repeated.

Mike abruptly turned toward the witness stand. "Miss Williams, my client's freedom depends on whether or not he personally authorized this transaction, and he deserves better than guesswork. I ask you again, do you know for a fact that Mr. Davis authorized the transaction in question?"

Alicia was trapped. Hundreds of disbursements had been made on the basis of similar transaction slips, and she had always felt they were wrong. But who was she to question corporate officers?

"No, I do not know it for a fact."

"Thank you, Miss Williams." Mike turned and walked toward his seat. He sat down, looked over at the jury and said, "I have no further questions of this witness."

"Does the prosecution wish to redirect?" the judge asked.

The prosecutor stood to his feet. "Just a couple of questions, your honor."

"Miss Williams, are your company's officers aware that disbursement slips sometimes carry their authorization without actual signatures?"

"Yes sir, it happens all the time."

"Have you ever had an officer complain that a transaction slip with his name hadn't actually been authorized by him?"

"No sir. Never."

"That's all, your honor."

The judge said, "The witness may step down."

The government rested its case with Alicia Williams, the weakest part of its case in Mike's opinion. He had expected several of Western's officers to be put on the stand to affirm that Taylor was acting alone, but for some reason the prosecutor had decided to stand pat. Mike had hoped the prosecutor would call Mr. Wilson himself in an attempt to rebut Taylor's testimony before he could give it. Since they hadn't, he had been forced to subpoena the chairman as a defense witness, albeit a hostile one. Mike had planned a simple and complicated defense in an attempt to gain the jury's ear. Only two people knew what really happened that day—Taylor and G. Preston Wilson. He would put Taylor on the stand to tell his story, then try to weaken G. Preston's testimony that Taylor had acted alone.

During the noon recess, Taylor and Cyndi had lunch with Mike at the Adolphus since it was only a ten minute walk from the Federal Building. Jim Peterson was there with a customer. On his way out, he stopped at their table and handed Taylor a note.

"I thought you might need this," he said, then left with his guest.

Taylor unfolded the note and read it aloud. "You will be brought before kings and governors, and all on account of my name. This will result in your being witnesses to them. But make up your mind not to worry beforehand how you will defend yourselves. For I will give you words and wisdom that none of your adversaries will be able to resist or contradict. Luke twenty-one, twelve through fifteen."

"That's encouraging," Taylor said.

"Yeah," Mike added. "It would be a lot more encouraging if we had corroboration for your testimony that the chairman approved the transaction."

"What's that, Mike?" Cyndi asked.

"Corroboration? It's a principle of evidence. Testimony carries a lot more weight if it's confirmed by at least one other person."

Taylor had done pretty well up to this point, but the prospect of testifying under oath made him a little nervous. He was looking for assurance. "Mike, how do you think we've done so far?"

"I guess cautious optimism best describes my mood," Mike said. "The video was devastating without question, but we'll be able to offset it some with your testimony about the first meeting. And we definitely made points with the jury right before lunch.

"Yeah . . . I was watching them," Cyndi chimed in. "That business about the transaction slip without Taylor's signature didn't help the government at all."

"We've still got to make the jury believe you were acting under orders," Mike said. "It's our only real hope."

When Taylor took the stand, Mike skillfully led him through the events leading up to and during his trip to San Jose. He had Taylor describe the first meeting in Senor Pedrano's office; how he told him he'd have to call Dallas for instructions; how the chairman had approved the transaction; and how he returned the next day with what he considered "grease money," a questionable but not illegal practice in Central and South America. Then Mike tried something he knew would bring the prosecutor to his feet in protest.

"Mr. Davis, is it true that shortly after you left Senor Pedrano's office you were kidnapped by terrorists?"

"Objection," the prosecutor shouted. "This is irrelevant to this case."

Mike was looking for a sympathy hook, some reason for the jurors to identify with Taylor. He figured most of them had seen or heard about the kidnapping on the news. If they hadn't made the connection before now, he would help them a little. By bringing the kidnapping into Taylor's testimony, he hoped to cast him as a victim of crime, rather than a criminal.

"Counsel, is this line of questioning germane to the issue?" Judge Walker was frowning, but he had given Mike a second chance to make his point with the jury. Mike wasn't about to waste it.

"Your honor, my client's character is at issue in this trial. His actions during the time he was held hostage and the bravery he exhibited during his escape from those murderers tells us something about the kind of man he is"

"I object, your honor." The prosecutor was furious, knowing full well the points Mike was making with the jury.

"Counsel, I'm going to sustain the objection. This line of questioning is irrelevant. Please continue."

"That's all, your honor," Mike said.

The prosecutor had been making notes all during Taylor's testimony. As he stood up and moved toward the witness stand, Taylor whispered a prayer. *God, please help me say the right thing.*

"Mr. Davis, please tell the jury what your position is at Western Datacorp."

"I am . . . was the chief financial officer."

"And will you tell us your approximate annual salary?"

Mike was on his feet. "Objection, Mr. Davis's salary is irrelevant."

" Your honor, I'm trying to establish the level of authority Mr. Davis held in the corporation, a level that enabled him to initiate a transaction of this magnitude without anyone else's approval."

"Objection overruled. You may continue."

Mike had worried about this. The prosecutor was driving a cultural wedge between Taylor and the jury, positioning him as a corporate fat cat—someone who thought he could get whatever he wanted by ignoring rules and writing huge checks.

"Your annual salary, Mr. Davis?"

"Before I was terminated, I was earning about two hundred thousand a year including incentive bonuses."

The prosecutor paused, waiting for the jury to absorb this information. "And didn't you have a company car?"

"Yes, sir."

"And stock options?"

"That's correct," Taylor answered.

"Mr. Davis, most of the members of this jury are ordinary working people. Will you explain stock options for them?"

Mike was up. "Your honor, I object. This is a trial, not a lecture on investments."

The judge had allowed the prosecutor quite a bit of latitude to this point, and he was becoming impatient. "Counsel, I'm going to overrule your objection, but I will also warn the prosecutor to get to his point."

"Can you tell the jury what stock options are, Mr. Davis?"

Taylor shifted in the witness chair, trying to think of a way to keep his answer as simple as possible. "It's a way to let employees feel they own part of the company. A stock option allows you to buy stock in the company at a certain price during a specified period . . . usually two years."

"And the price is usually below the market price everybody else has to pay. Correct?"

Taylor knew what the prosecutor was up to, but he didn't know how to head him off. "Sometimes it is, sometimes it isn't."

The prosecutor turned his back to Taylor as he asked his next question. "Does every employee of the company get stock options?"

"No. Stock options are usually reserved for management."

He turned and shouted the next question at Taylor. "And only the very top people in management . . . right?"

The judge broke in before Taylor could answer. "Counsel, we've been very patient, but I think you've milked this cow dry."

The crowd broke out in laughter at the judge's colorful metaphor. Taylor was thankful for the slight break in tension. He knew the prosecutor was painting a picture of him in the jurors' minds, and there was nothing he could do about it. He had been a corporate fat cat. He had been given perks and advantages that the average working man or woman would never understand.

Having made his point, the prosecutor shifted gears. "Mr. Davis, what was the upper limit of your disbursing authority? How big a check could you write without someone else's approval?"

"Up to fifty thousand," Taylor answered.

"So you would be able to disburse twenty thousand dollars to an account at the Banco Nacional in San Jose without anyone else knowing about it?"

"I wouldn't say nobody else knew about it," Taylor protested. "A disbursement authorization has to go through several stages even though a corporate officer has approved it."

" But nobody else had to approve it. Is that correct?"

Taylor paused before he answered, realizing that the prosecutor had maneuvered him into tacitly admitting that he initiated the San Jose transaction.

"I could approve disbursements up to fifty thousand, but I didn't approve the money that went to San Jose . . . Mr. Wilson did, as I've already testified."

"Good boy, Taylor," Mike muttered under his breath. He knew what the prosecutor was up to. Mike had been dying a slow death at the defense table, hoping Taylor would catch on and reverse things.

The prosecutor walked over to his table and picked up a large black book. Turning back toward Taylor, he opened it to a previously marked page.

"Mr. Davis, as chief financial officer of Western Datacorp, you would be expected to be familiar with the Foreign Corrupt Practices Act. Would you not?"

"I remember when it was passed by congress."

"I will read from section five of the act, Mr. Davis. It says no person shall pay or offer to pay any foreign official to induce said official to perform an act beneficial to the offeror. It shall be deemed bribery, a criminal act punishable by a fine not to exceed five hundred thousand dollars and imprisonment for a period not to exceed twenty years."

The prosecutor held the book open and turned toward the jury. "Mr. Davis, were you under the impression this provision didn't apply to you for some reason?"

"Objection," Mike shouted. "He's badgering the witness, your honor."

"Sustained," the judge intoned.

The prosecutor was undeterred. "Mr. Davis, isn't it a fact that you initiated and carried out the transaction in question with the intention of currying favor with Mr. Wilson?"

"Your honor, I object," Mike screamed. "The witness has already testified that Mr. Wilson approved the transaction."

"Objection sustained."

It was too late. One glance at the jury told Mike the damage was done. The prosecutor had characterized Taylor as a young man with power, money, and advantages, acquired through selfish ambition and questionable practices. He made him seem like the kind of man that would do anything to enhance his position and prestige. He had successfully put Taylor's position and perks on trial, rather than the alleged offense.

The prosecutor knew he had reached his objective. "I have no further questions, your honor."

"The witness may step down."

Taylor walked over to the defense table and slumped in his chair. Cyndi had been seated in the front row of the gallery throughout the trial, just behind the defense table. She leaned forward and whispered, "You did great."

They had one last chance. Mike stood and announced his last witness. "Your honor, the defense will now call G. Preston Wilson to the stand."

There was a shuffle in the courtroom as everyone turned to see what he looked like. G. Preston had been waiting in the witness room since noon, and he was clearly in no mood to take part in these proceedings. Mike waited for him to take the oath, then approached the witness chair with his first question.

"Mr. Wilson, what is your position with Western Datacorp?"

"Chairman of the board and chief executive officer," he growled.

"Is there anyone higher than you in the corporate chain of command?"

"Only the board."

"But does the board make operating decisions?" Mike asked.

"Not really. They're more concerned with broad policy."

Mike looked toward the jury. "Is it fair to say that you have the final say in corporate actions?"

"Yes, that's correct." It was obvious that G.

Preston had been briefed by the company's attorney to give concise answers, offering nothing more than a bare response to the specific question.

"Mr. Wilson, did you approve Mr. Davis's trip to San Jose?"

The chairman was puzzled and wary. "What do you mean by approval?"

"Mr. Wilson, isn't it a fact that you sent Mr. Davis to San Jose to find a solution to your problem with the Costa Rican government, and that he carried a letter of introduction from Senator Harding?"

"Obviously, I knew about the trip . . ."

Mike turned up the heat. "Mr. Wilson, isn't it a fact that you made a special trip to Washington with Mr. Davis to speak with Senator Harding about this very matter, and that you subsequently directed Mr. Davis to go to San Jose and meet with the finance minister about the company's problem?"

G. Preston was clearly uncomfortable. "Yes, I authorized the trip."

"Mr. Wilson, the jury would like to know whether you in fact directed Mr. Davis to go to San Jose?" Mike looked at the jurors, seeking silent agreement that he was articulating their own questions. Several jurors nodded in agreement.

"I seem to remember saying that it would be a good idea," he offered weakly.

Mike had taken a calculated risk by calling G. Preston as a witness. He knew the chairman would deny approving the payment, a denial that would support the government's case. But if he was less than convincing, it would improve Taylor's credibility with the jury.

"Mr. Wilson, now that we've established the fact that you personally ordered Mr. Davis to go to San Jose, I would like to direct your attention to the afternoon of June fourth. You received a telephone call from San Jose . . . from Mr. Davis. Will you tell us about the content of that call?"

"I get hundreds of calls. I can't possibly remember each and every one."

"We appreciate the fact that you're a busy man, Mr. Wilson," Mike said sarcastically. "But, I'm certain you will remember this particular call. It has already been established from your company's telephone records that you received a call from San Jose on the afternoon of June fourth, a call that was directed to your personal number. Mr. Davis has testified under oath that he made that call, and that he spoke with you personally. I'm asking you to recollect that conversation for the jury."

G. Preston shifted nervously in the witness chair, absentmindedly reaching for a cigar and then replacing it in his coat pocket. "Well, yes, I remember Mr. Davis' call. He told me our problem in Costa Rica was taken care of, and I congratulated him on his work and then hung up."

Mike felt beads of perspiration forming on the back of his neck. The one thing he had feared most was a blatant lie, and he had served it up to the jury with his inept questioning. The prosecutor was smiling, fully aware of the terrible mistake Mike had made. If Mike continued to hammer on the point, and if G. Preston continued to lie as convincingly as he had just now, Mike would only be digging a deeper hole for himself. But he had to at least try.

"Mr. Wilson, isn't it a fact that Mr. Davis told you about the requirement for twenty thousand dollars, and that you personally approved it?"

"Absolutely not! I knew nothing about it until the day Mr. Davis was arrested."

Mike's gamble had failed. Worse than that, it had boomeranged. G. Preston was a convincing liar, just as Taylor had said, and his testimony was clearly a net minus for Taylor. Mike wrapped up his questioning with a few innocuous details about the corporation in an attempt to leave the jury with something other than the wolf's blatant lie ringing in their ears.

"Your honor, the defense rests." Mike was dejected and whipped. He had risked his whole case on a hunch that he could shake G. Preston's testimony, and he had failed miserably.

"Wait a minute!" someone shouted from the back of the courtroom. Taylor turned with everyone else to see a woman standing just inside the door, demanding to be heard. It was Miss Roberts!

Mike walked to the back of the courtroom and held a hurried, whispered conversation with her while the judge tried to restore order to the proceedings. Mike turned and announced, "Your honor, the defense wishes to call one additional witness, Miss Kathryn Roberts."

The prosecutor was on his feet. "Objection.

There is no Roberts on my list of witnesses."

"Mr. Phillips, will you please explain what is going on here?" the judge asked.

"Your honor, Miss Roberts has material information about this trial and has only just now come forward. I respectfully request permission to put her on the stand as a defense witness."

"This is highly irregular, counsel, but I'm going to allow it. The objection is overruled."

G. Preston had remained in the courtroom after his testimony and was clearly agitated. After Miss Roberts was sworn in, Mike established the fact that she was Mr. Wilson's executive secretary, had worked for him for twenty years, and then handed her the transaction slip that had been entered into evidence.

"Miss Roberts, have you ever seen this disbursement authorization before?"

"Yes I have. I typed it myself."

"Please tell the jury why you typed this particular transaction slip."

Miss Roberts turned toward the jury. "Mr. Wilson told me to fill it out and to put Mr. Davis' name as the approver."

A murmur swept through the courtroom. Taylor glanced at G. Preston. He was seething, something Taylor had seen many times. There was never any doubt when the wolf was angry about something. You could see his neck muscles tighten and the blood slowly rise, creating a pink hue in his neck and face.

Mike let the disturbance run its course and then

continued. "Miss Roberts, do you remember when this occurred?"

"Oh yes, I wrote it down on my desk calendar. It was the afternoon of June fourth. Mr. Davis had called Mr. Wilson from Costa Rica, and it was right after that telephone call."

"Miss Roberts, this is very important. Do you have any reason to know why Mr. Wilson told you to fill out the disbursement of twenty thousand to the bank in San Jose?"

Roberts looked straight at the wolf, unflinching in her determination. "Yes, I do. Mr. Davis told Mr. Wilson that it would take an additional investment of twenty thousand dollars to clear up the problem in Costa Rica. Mr. Wilson said he would approve it and have the money wired to the bank that afternoon. It was right after that call that he had me fill out the disbursement with Mr. Davis's name on it."

"Miss Roberts, how do you know what was said during that phone conversation?"

"I listened in."

"You heard the entire conversation between them?" Mike asked pointedly.

"Yes sir."

"Why did you listen in to this particular conversation, Miss Roberts?"

"I did it all the time. Mr. Wilson's memory wasn't always good, so I listened to his conversations to make sure I knew about important calls."

There were a few giggles, than laughter broke out in the gallery. Several of the jurors smiled broadly.

"Miss Roberts, let me see if I understand what happened that day," Mike continued. "Mr. Davis called Mr. Wilson from San Jose and explained about the twenty thousand dollars. Mr. Wilson approved the transaction over the telephone, and then had you fill out a disbursement authorization with Mr. Davis' name on the approval line. Is that correct?"

"Yes sir, that's how it happened."

Mike had one last question. "Miss Roberts, why have you come forward with this information?"

Roberts stared at G. Preston, but he was looking down at the floor. "Because it wasn't right what they did. They fired Mr. Davis because of the publicity, and then told the press he had resigned. And all because Mr. Wilson covered his tracks like a coward. It wasn't right."

Taylor had heard G. Preston called a lot of names, but never a coward . . . and certainly never to his face. It was extraordinary, unthinkable.

Mike turned to the prosecutor and said, "Your witness, counsel."

The prosecutor stood to his feet, obviously surprised and shocked by Kathryn's testimony. He considered for a moment how he might be able to weaken it on cross-examination, and then decided against it. "We have no questions, your honor."

The jury had taken less than an hour to bring in a verdict of not guilty. Taylor and Cyndi were standing in the hall outside the courtroom talking to Kathryn Roberts. G. Preston burst through the door and when he saw them he shouted, "Roberts, you're fired!"

"You can't fire me," she said calmly. "I turned in my resignation before I left the office."

"You'll be sorry for this," he sputtered. He walked hurriedly out of the building.

"Miss Roberts, I can't thank you enough," Taylor said. "What you did took a lot of courage. I'm sorry about your job."

"Don't be," she answered. "I've hated it for years and just wouldn't admit it to myself. I've always wanted to start my own answering service, and I guess now's the time to try it."

Cyndi hugged her and wished her well. Kathryn turned and hugged Taylor. "Don't worry about your future, Taylor. You'll find a place."

"Thanks," Taylor responded. He was struck by the incongruity of the scene—Taylor Davis hugging Miss Roberts in the main hall of the Federal Building. In one of those rare moments when you understand something keenly, he realized that she wasn't just "Roberts," the wolf's secretary. She was Kathryn Roberts, fellow human made in God's image, a unique personality with her own hurts, hopes, and dreams. It was right that they should be hugging in the main hall of the Federal Building.

Outside on the front walk, G. Preston was surrounded by a mob of newspeople shouting questions and pushing microphones in his face. Taylor and Cyndi hesitated for a moment, then skirted around the crowd, which totally ignored them, and strode arm in arm away from the noisy scene.

As they left the courthouse, Taylor noticed a familiar saying chiseled into the border around the upper part of the building: "You Will Know The Truth And The Truth Will Set You Free."

Taylor smiled and whispered, "Yes indeed . . . yes indeed."

-THE END-

Contact Carroll Ray, Jr.
or order more copies of this book at

TATE PUBLISHING, LLC

127 East Trade Center Terrace
Mustang, Oklahoma 73064

(888) 361 - 9473

Tate Publishing, LLC

www.tatepublishing.com